PRINCESS OF HAWTHORNE PREP

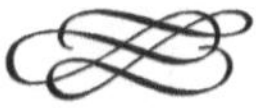

JENNIFER SUCEVIC

The Breakup Plan

The Football Hotties Collection

The Girl Next Door

The Hockey Hotties Collection

AUSTIN

My fingers lock around Delilah's as I tow her through the first floor of Kingsley's mansion. I should have known the place would be packed. It's wall-to-wall people.

People I can't fucking stand.

Classmates slap my back and congratulate me as I navigate the thick crowd that fills the first floor. I give a few chin lifts in acknowledgment and ignore the rest. Do these assholes really think I'm going to forget that they treated me like shit from day one?

Yeah…not gonna happen.

The heavy beat of music reverberates off the walls and inside my head as we make our way to the spacious kitchen.

"Do you want something to drink?" I ask, glancing over my shoulder to meet Delilah's gaze.

From the wary expression on her face, she doesn't want to be here any more than I do. One hour, two tops, and then we'll take off. I just want to get her alone again. I can't stop thinking about what it felt like to sink inside her tight heat. The way her pussy gripped my cock, strangling the fuck out of it. I'm totally obsessed with this girl and don't know how I'll get enough.

Thank fuck I don't have to.

She's mine.

I've never felt this way about another female. None ever mattered. But Delilah is different. There's an attraction that vibrates in the air, charging it, making it impossible to breathe. It was there from day one.

"Just a water," she says, raising her voice to be heard over the laughter and chatter that presses in on us.

People scatter out of my way as we step inside the kitchen where the booze flows freely. I'll say this about Kingsley—the guy knows how to throw a wicked party. A girl I recognize from one of my classes is stretched out on the marble island with her shirt shoved above her lacy bra as a guy slurps a body shot from her bellybutton before sucking the lime from her mouth. There's a game of cups going on at the table. A resounding cheer goes up when one team wins.

I shake my head.

Yeah…this was definitely a bad idea.

I cut a path to the massive fridge and yank the handle, grabbing a chilled bottle of water for Delilah. The guy manning the keg passes me a red Solo cup filled to the brim with golden liquid. I need something to take the edge off and hopefully, this will do the trick.

She twists off the cap and brings the rim to her lips.

As I do the same, my gaze coasts over the sea of classmates all in various stages of drunkenness. It won't take long for clothing to be shed. My lip curls with the need to get the hell away from them.

"Let's go outside and sit by the firepit. It's too damn crowded in here." It's fucking stifling. It's tempting to yank at the collar of my hoodie.

Once we push through the French doors that lead to the stamped cement patio, the cool night breeze hits us. I inhale a lungful of fresh air, finally able to breathe again. The further we get from the suffocating confines of the house, the more my muscles loosen until most of the tension has drained away.

With my gaze locked on the seating arrangement that surrounds the firepit, we navigate the groups of people standing around and shooting the shit. My grip tightens on Delilah as a couple guys attempt to wave me over.

I don't bother with them.

Believe it or not, the girls are even worse.

Most have spent the last month ignoring me, acting as if they're better than my family. Only now have they turned their attention my way. One smiles before tucking a stray lock of dark hair behind her ear.

Aubrey.

I think that's her name.

"Looks like your fan club is trying to get your attention," Delilah jokes, breaking into my thoughts.

"They're not my friends," I say with a snort. "Come Monday, half of them will pretend I don't exist."

It's the truth, and we both know it. There's too much bad blood between my ancestors and this small, tight-knit community. There doesn't seem to be anything I can do to overcome the stigma of being a Hawthorne.

Luckily for us, there's no one occupying the couch. We set our drinks down and I drop onto a plush cushion before pulling Delilah onto my lap. The weight of her soft body feels so damn good. My hands settle on her curvy little hips to lock her in place as she snuggles against my chest.

For the first time in a while, contentment fills me. It's not something I've experienced since moving to this god-forsaken town in the middle of Wisconsin. Especially after Dad unexpectedly died of a heart attack. As I stare at the crackling orange flames that twist in the firepit, my mind reluctantly tumbles back to what life was like three short months ago. I was a starter on my varsity high school football team, and senior year was stretched out ahead of me.

That meant girls and parties.

College applications and continuing the recruitment process.

It was all good.

And I couldn't have been happier.

All that was blown to shit when my father's estranged mother, Rose Hawthorne, keeled over.

What did the old bitch leave us?

A fucking mansion.

Along with a company that had once upon a time been co-owned with the Rothchilds.

And a legacy of hate that is impossible to vanquish.

With Delilah by my side, none of that matters.

If I have to claw my way over Jasper to a starting position on this team, that's precisely what I'll do. It's only when Delilah burrows closer to my chest that the memories fade into nothingness. A shiver works its way through her body as silvery moonlight spills over her long, pale blonde hair.

Fuck, she's beautiful.

I mean *really* beautiful.

The first time I saw this girl, I couldn't take my eyes off her. One way or another, I knew she would be mine.

And now she is.

Even though the music from inside has become muffled, faint wisps along with the low and steady thump of the bass can still be heard. It all but pulsates in the air.

When another shudder slides through her, my brows draw together in concern. "Are you cold?"

Whatever it is this girl needs, I want to be the one who gives it to her.

"A little," she says with a quick shrug and a smile.

"Want to head back inside the house?"

"No, I'd rather stay out here where it's less crowded."

Unable to resist the lure of her mouth, my hand slides into the thickness of her hair before dragging her close enough for my lips to settle over hers. It only takes one stroke for her to open and our tongues to tangle. I have no idea what it is about Delilah that affects me this way. She's like an addiction pumping through my blood, setting it on fire until it blazes through everything in its path. I don't think I'll ever be able to fight my way free of her.

Especially now that she's given herself to me. The idea that her body has been molded specifically to my cock drives me fucking insane. If I have anything to say about it, that's the way it'll stay.

"Get a room," a loudmouth asshole shouts, drawing my attention away from her.

"Or don't," his friend laughs. "I wouldn't mind watching that girl get fucked."

My muscles tense as irritation washes over me. There's no way in hell anyone else will ever catch sight of her being pleasured.

For good measure, I stroke my tongue against the velvety softness of hers one last time before grudgingly drawing away and glancing around. I spot the two dickheads with the big traps loitering near the pool.

"Hey, Garrickson?" I call out, raising my voice in order to be heard over the noise.

The redheaded kid meets my gaze with a stupid grin dancing across his face.

"Shut the fuck up," I growl.

Then, I scowl at his friend. "You, too."

Their smiles dim in wattage as they glance at each other before disappearing into the throng.

"So fucking childish," I grumble, pissed they intruded on the moment we were having.

"Welcome to high school," Delilah says lightly. What I've noticed is that she doesn't like confrontation and avoids it at all costs.

Since their comments don't seem to bother her, I decide to let it go. There's no need to ruin our evening.

My muscles loosen as my lips hitch at the corners. "Yeah, I guess so."

A burst of wind whips over us and another shiver shimmies across her flesh. Even though she's wearing a lightweight sweater, it's not enough to stop the cool breeze from slicing through the garment. When she presses closer, I grab the hem of my sweatshirt and yank it off before dragging it over her blonde head until the thick material settles around her waist.

"Better?"

"Much," she says with a smile that arrows clean through the heart of me. "Thanks."

Once she's wrapped up in my hoodie, she snuggles against my chest before slanting a look upward. "Aren't you cold now?"

"Nope. I've got you to keep me warm."

My hands slip beneath the hem of the sweatshirt before drifting along her ribcage and settling under the gentle swells of her breasts. All I'd have to do is inch my thumb upward and I'd be touching her softness. The sweatshirt is so oversized on her small form that no one would be the wiser.

Her gaze stays fastened to mine as I stroke her bare flesh.

This right here is what heaven must feel like.

Minutes tick by before she lifts her head and glances around the party that rages around us. Her muscles stiffen as she averts her head. Impatient for her attention, I nip at her plump lower lip. That's all it takes for her gaze to slice to mine. It's a surprise to find distress clouding her expression.

I search her wide blue eyes for clues as to why her demeanor changed. It's like a light switch flipped. One moment, she's all warm and pliant in my arms and the next, she's stiff as a board.

"What's wrong?"

She forces a smile. "Nothing."

That's all it takes for my contentment to dim. "Don't lie to me."

With the moonlight slanting over us, I notice the color seep into her cheeks. I glance over her shoulder, knowing exactly who I'll find.

I'm not wrong.

"Looks like we have an audience," I mutter, gazed locked on Jasper.

Unease flickers across her face. "Unfortunately."

The corners of my lips lift as one hand slips from beneath the sweatshirt before sliding into her thick hair and dragging her forward.

"Let him watch," I growl. "You belong to me."

My lips crash onto hers as my tongue delves into the warmth of her mouth.

Fuck that guy.

He'll never have her again.

He'll never touch what's mine.

Just as I sink into the kiss, Delilah's palms settle against my chest to push me away.

The moment I give her an inch of space, she gasps, "I need to use the bathroom." Her expression turns strained as thick tension weaves its way through her voice.

My eyes narrow as I scour her face for the truth.

Is there a reason she doesn't want him watching us?

He's the past.

I'm her future.

Even though I hate myself for asking, the words escape from my lips before I can stop them. "Are you sure that's all it is?" And now I sound like a needy bitch.

I don't want to believe that her ex has anything to do with the abrupt change in her behavior.

She blinks, looking thrown off by the question. "Of course. What else would it be?"

The way her gaze darts away makes me suspect otherwise. I shift as my attention is reluctantly drawn over her shoulder for a second time. The smug smile that tugs at the corners of Jasper's lips has a potent concoction of anger and uncertainty igniting within me.

When my attention resettles on Delilah, I can't help but scrutinize her expression with more care. It's impossible to believe that she could be playing games. Especially after she gave me her virginity.

I had assumed we'd moved past all that.

Was I wrong?

As much as I try to banish my suspicions, I can't shake the strange feeling of foreboding that settles in the pit of my gut like a heavy stone.

"I'm not sure," I say carefully. "Maybe you don't want Jasper to see us together."

"You're right, I don't," she admits quietly. "But not for the reasons you assume."

Hurt flickers in her eyes before she clears her throat and rises to her feet. "I'll be back in a sec."

In the blink of an eye, the atmosphere between us turns oppressive. I have no idea how to smooth over the thick tension that has sprung to life, creating a wedge between us. How is it possible that a few minutes ago, we were kissing and my hand was shoved up her shirt and now...

Now I'm unsure where we stand.

It's on the tip of my tongue to apologize. To clear the air before she walks away.

Instead, I sink further into the cushions and attempt to keep my anger under wraps. "I'll be here waiting."

Her tight smile tells me she's acutely aware of the friction that has sprung up between us.

"Okay."

The edges of my lips sink as my gaze stays fastened on her as she weaves her way through the thick crowd. Once she vanishes from sight, I plow a hand through my hair in frustration and flick a glance at Jasper just in time to see him slink inside the house.

Fuck.

More than anything, I want to believe Delilah is telling the truth.

"Hey."

Knocked from my thoughts, I glance up and find my sister. Kingsley is steadfast at her side as if they're conjoined twins. He's never far. Almost as if he can't bear for her to be out of his sight. I'm used to it just being the two of us. It's weird to have another person constantly dogging her heels and in her business. It's going to take time for me to get used to this situation.

I force my muscles to loosen and shove the thoughts that have been circling to the back of my brain. The last thing I want is to ruin Summer's night with this bullshit. She's just as protective of me as I am of her.

Maybe even more so.

Ever since I was diagnosed with dyslexia in elementary school, she's stood at my side, smacking kids upside the head when they made fun of me. Summer has always breezed through her classes. Academics have never been an issue for her, and she's spent hours tutoring me when I needed help. It would be all too easy to hate her if she wasn't such an amazing sister. There are times when I suspect she's fought wars on my behalf that I'm not even aware of.

My twin scans the area before her gaze resettles on me. "Where's Delilah? I thought you two arrived together."

I jerk my chin toward the house. "She went to use the bathroom. She'll be back any minute."

And then we'll talk, because I won't allow this bullshit with Jasper to linger in the air like a foul stench and ruin our evening.

With a tilt of her head, Summer scrutinizes my expression. Even though I haven't said a word, she realizes something isn't quite right. I feel her silently picking through my brain, searching for the truth. That's the thing about my twin—she's always had the uncanny ability to decipher my private thoughts. I've never been able to keep anything from her.

It's almost a relief when Everly joins our trio along with a few guys from the football team. There are a couple of players that I get along with. Unfortunately, most are loyal to Jasper and follow his lead.

We shoot the shit about the game and the trip to Lake Michigan next weekend. It's a school-sponsored activity for seniors. From all the stories I've heard, there won't be any chaperones in attendance. The annual camping trip is a Hawthorne Prep tradition that dates back to the first graduating class.

Why in the hell these adults would think it's a good idea to send a bunch of unsupervised kids to the beach for three days is beyond me. It'll be mayhem and possibly murder.

I'm not looking forward to it.

All right...maybe that's not a hundred percent true. I'm looking forward to having Delilah to myself.

Conversations swirl around me as I half listen to the plans that are being made. It's only when I glance at my phone that I realize thirty minutes have slipped by and Delilah hasn't returned from the bathroom. My gaze reluctantly arrows to the spot Jasper had been loitering. His friends are still there, talking and laughing, but he's MIA.

How did I not notice that?

Fuck.

When I rise to my feet, Summer asks, "Are you taking off?"

"Nah, I'm gonna head inside and grab another beer." Even though I rarely lie to my sister, I can't bring myself to admit the truth. Summer doesn't trust Delilah after everything that went down, and I get it.

If the situation were flipped, I'd feel the same. Hell, I still feel that way about Kingsley. Trust isn't something that is freely handed over. It needs to be earned, and it's going to take time for my twin to come around.

But she will.

Eventually.

When I say nothing more, her eyes narrow. Before she has the chance to interrogate me, I swing away and head for the door that leads inside. Even though she's no longer in my line of sight, I feel the steeliness of her gaze boring into my back.

The party is even more jam packed than when we arrived over an hour ago. It becomes necessary to push and shove my way through the crush of bodies. Since I stand a few inches over six feet, I'm able to easily scan the raucous group.

Where the hell is she?

What's taking so long?

It's the question that eats away at me the most.

As much as I don't want to believe the worst or that she's duped me for a second time, the suspicions circling in the back of my brain refuse to be silenced. Each second that ticks by only reinforces them. It doesn't escape me that the other person I haven't caught sight of yet is her ex.

Or maybe he's not her ex at all. Maybe this is some kind of twisted game they've unwittingly drawn me into. The idea that they might have snuck off together drives me fucking insane and has me wanting to tear Jasper apart limb by bloody limb.

A mixture of fury and distrust roils through me as I scan the kitchen, forcing my way through the press of bodies toward the hallway where the bathroom is located. Maybe the line is long, and she got stuck in the middle of it.

I ask a few people if they've seen Delilah. The question is met with bleary-eyed stares. After another five minutes, I pull out my phone and give her a call.

It goes straight to voicemail.

That only amps up my feelings of unease. My fingers fly over the miniature keyboard as I tap out a message.

Where are you?

I stare at the cell, willing her to answer as the party continues to rage, becoming rowdier by the minute. A couple of drunken idiots stumble into me. When I swing around and glare, they scurry off with a mumbled apology.

I fire off another message.

You need to answer me, Delilah.

Crickets.

To both texts.

My brows snap together when they go from being delivered to read. My breath gets clogged at the back of my throat as I wait for a response.

But one never comes.

What the actual fuck?

I'm about to crush the phone in my hand when three little bubbles appear.

Fucking finally.

My eyes stay glued to the screen as I wait.

And then wait some more.

What the hell is she doing?

Writing a damn book?

I just want to know if she's all right.

I'm about to send another text when a photo pops up. My heart stutters in my chest before slamming painfully against my ribcage. It's one of Delilah and Jasper. Their heads are bent together and she's smiling at the camera.

Another one rolls in of them kissing. I stare at the screen as an icy wave of shock slams into me, threatening to suck me to the bottom of the ocean.

His tongue is shoved down her throat.

Before I can fully process the last photo, another one appears.

No.

Fucking.

Way.

There's no damn way it's real.

I stare intently, hoping my eyes are playing tricks on me, and the image will morph into something else. Something less damning.

But it doesn't.

The photo is crystal clear.

His fingers are tangled in the long strands of her blonde hair, holding them away from her face as he presses her against his groin. His dick can't be seen, but it's more than obvious what's going on.

When a fourth pic appears, rage floods every cell of my body.

Jasper grins at the camera.

Her BJs are the best, aren't they, bro?

My fingers bite into the smooth plastic of the phone case before squeezing until the small device is on the verge of shattering. It's so tempting to hurl it across the room. Although that won't erase the images that have been seared into my brain.

When a hand settles on my shoulder, I swing around, ready to throw fists. Summer's eyes widen at my expression and the rage vibrating off me in heavy waves.

"Austin," she whispers, searching my face for answers to questions she has yet to pose. "Are you all right?"

Even though her words are barely discernible over the loud beat of music that vibrates off the walls, I hear them loud and clear as they echo in my brain.

Unable to summon my voice, I shake my head.

Her attention drops to my clenched hand and she pries the phone from my curled fingers. Before I can steal it back, she unlocks the home screen and pulls up the messages. I know the exact moment she finds the photos. Her eyes widen, and her jaw drops.

She scrolls for a few seconds before jerking her gaze to mine. "What the fuck?"

Unsure how to respond, I release a steady breath. "I don't know."

"Every time I think about forgiving that bitch, something else happens." With a huff, she presses the slim device into my palm.

Even though there's nothing funny about this situation, a mirthless chuckle escapes from me.

Nailed it.

My thoughts exactly.

"In light of current events, I'm taking off. I can't be here any longer," I say.

Summer's teeth scrape across her lower lip. "You're not going to talk to her?"

"Nah." I hold up the evidence in my hand. "She seems kind of preoccupied at the moment."

Her shoulders collapse as sadness floods her green depths. "Sorry, Aus."

I glance away, not wanting her to catch a glimpse of the hurt that lurks within my eyes. "Yeah, well...guess I was a dumbass for believing her lies in the first place. Looks like she and Jasper made a fool of me again."

Before she can give me a useless load of bullshit, I swing away and stalk to the massive front door. I need to get the hell out of here before I rip this place apart with my bare hands, searching for the pair.

The last thing I want to see is their smirking faces for getting yet another one over on me.

DELILAH

*S*unlight slants across my face, making it impossible to stay submerged in slumber. As much as I try to fight it, I lose the battle and gradually surface. As my eyelids flutter open, I realize that my head pounds an insistent drumbeat with the worst headache I've experienced in my life.

Argh.

And my mouth…it's so cottony.

Like I haven't had a drop to drink in days.

What the hell happened last night?

I carefully pick through my memories but come up empty, which is…strange.

It takes a few minutes to force open my eyelids. They're ridiculously heavy. My brain remains sluggish as if I'm trying to fight my way through mud. When they're finally open, I squint against the harsh sunlight pouring in through the window before staring at my surroundings. It takes my befuddled brain a handful of seconds to realize that nothing in the room looks familiar.

My heart rate explodes as I jackknife up in bed. The hasty movement sends pain slicing through my throbbing brain as a wave of nausea immediately follows. Any second, my head is going to roll right off my shoulders. And then I won't have to worry about this headache.

The sheet and blanket slinks down my body and settles at my waist. My hands drift to my head to keep it in place as a tortured groan escapes from me. The noise would be startling if I didn't know where it originated from. If I were in my own bed, I'd toss the covers over my head and attempt to sleep whatever this is off, but that's not possible.

Not when I don't have any idea where I am.

I don't think I've ever felt more out of sorts or confused.

"Here," a deep voice says, shoving a plastic bottle into my trembling hand. "Drink this. It'll make you feel better."

Grateful for the water, I twist off the cap and bring the bottle to my lips. As liquid dribbles from the corner of my mouth, my gaze settles on the boy who drops onto the desk chair while staring at me with a mixture of concern and curiosity.

"Thank you," I croak after downing half the contents and swiping the back of my hand across my face.

"No problem."

Breaking eye contact, I glance around the tiny space before my gaze resettles on whiskey-colored eyes. "What am I doing here?"

That question has Duke Carmichael leaning forward and resting bare elbows on outstretched knees. "You were pretty fucked up last night when I found you in Kingsley's game room. I didn't think you'd want to be dropped off at home in that condition, so I brought you here instead to sleep it off."

"Fucked up?" I echo stupidly before shaking my head.

As soon as I make the slight movement, I realize it's a mistake and groan as the ache in my brain grows until it feels like my head will explode. I've never been prone to migraines, but I imagine this is what one must feel like.

"How much did you drink last night?"

I search my memories. "I...can't remember."

The thing is, I've never been much of a drinker. It's kind of hard to keep your wits about you if you're shitfaced. And around Jasper and the crowd he runs with, that can be dangerous. Even when I've been stone-cold sober, situations have turned hazardous.

But last night, I was with Austin. Attempting to summon any other specifics makes my head throb harder.

With a frown, his brow furrows. "You must have had something. It was hard to wake you up and when I did, you were barely coherent."

Goosebumps break out across my skin before scampering along my arms.

That doesn't make sense.

I squeeze my eyes tight and rack my brain, trying to dredge up even the tiniest detail, but it all remains blank. It's frightening. I've never experienced anything like it before. I've never had a, for lack of a better word, hole in my memory.

"Did you take something?" he asks, drawing my attention back to him.

Take something?

What does that mean?

One second slowly ticks by and then another before the implication hits me.

My eyes bulge. *"Drugs?"*

"Yeah." He shifts on the chair, all the while steadily holding my gaze. "There were plenty of people passing shit around last night. Did you try something?"

"No," I croak, shocked he would ask. "I barely drink." My tongue darts out to moisten parched lips before I tack on, "You know that." Hurt floods through me.

He shrugs. "People do stupid shit. Especially when they're at parties. It happens all the time."

Maybe so, but I've never done drugs. Not even pot. My mother would kill me.

Shit.

Mom.

I drag a hand over my face.

"What's the last thing you remember?" he prompts.

The game and watching Austin dominate on the field. And then deciding to go to Kingsley's, even though I should have gone straight home afterward. She'll probably ground me for life. The woman has been all over my ass since the breakup with Jasper. All this will do is reinforce her opinion that I can't be trusted to make good decisions.

When I remain silent, his voice softens. "Delilah?"

For a second time, I squeeze my eyes tightly shut and do a quick mental rewind.

I went to school.

Came home.

Watched the game.

Waited for Austin afterward.

We made out in the front seat of his SUV before heading to the party. We were only going to stay for an hour. The place had been packed and we headed outside.

That's where it all goes dark.

There's just…nothing.

Why can't I remember?

My hand drifts upward to my temple as if that will help jar something. "My phone," I mumble. "I need to text Mom. She's probably freaking out by now."

Or worse.

Much worse.

Duke leaps to his feet, eating up the distance that separates us when I spy my cell on the nightstand.

Just as I reach for the silver device, he barks, "Wait!"

My hand stalls midair as my gaze widens, locking on him as he snatches the phone before I can get to it.

An expression I can't quite identify lurks in his eyes. "There's something I need to tell you first."

I search his face, startled by his strange behavior. He's normally so chill. At least with me. Air gets clogged at the back of my throat, and it takes effort to force the word from my lips.

"Okay."

"Are you absolutely positive that you don't remember anything from the party?"

A heavy silence settles over us. I don't understand where these questions are coming from.

Or what they mean.

"No matter what happened, I won't judge you." He studies me as if it's possible for him to discern the answers without me giving voice to them. "You understand that, right?"

A sick knot blooms in the pit of my belly. The growing nausea no longer has anything to do with the pounding in my head.

"Yeah, but I still don't remember anything." There's a part of me that wants to shut down this bizarre conversation so I can stay blissfully ignorant, but the more rational part understands I need to know what's going on.

No matter how terrible it turns out to be.

A steady puff of air escapes from him as he glances away with a frown. "There are photos going around," he mutters, gaze reluctantly settling on mine. "They're...pretty bad."

My mouth dries as I force myself to remain calm. "Okay. I don't understand what that has to do with me."

There's another moment of oppressive silence as tension crackles in the atmosphere. "They're of you, Delilah."

Shock crashes over me, knocking me off balance. Out of all the things I expected him to say, that wasn't it. My hand flutters to my chest in confusion. *"Me?"*

"Yeah." His gaze drops to the slim silver device in his hand before he reluctantly passes it over. "They're of you and..." His voice trails off.

My teeth sink into my lower lip, worrying it as I key in my passcode and stare at the home screen. I wince at the slew of text messages from Mom along with a half dozen missed calls that pop up.

Yup. Definitely grounded for the rest of my life. She's probably checking out convents as we speak.

What I notice next are a bunch of unopened messages from people I don't really talk to.

Like Sloane.

And Aubrey.

And dozens of guys.

More than that, actually.

Why would any of them bother to text me?

Or even talk to me?

Let alone acknowledge my existence?

There's a distant tickle in the far recesses of my brain as I stare at Aubrey's name. As soon as I try to bring forth the memory, it vanishes like a curl of smoke. Dismissing the strange thought, I click on the first message.

Half a dozen photographs pop up.

Of me.

And Jasper.

Ones of us kissing.

Disbelief sets in as I continue to scroll.

The last one is the worst.

It looks like…

Like…

I'm blowing him.

Oh god.

No.

These can't be real.

My brain whirls as I drag the phone closer to my face and scrutinize the girl on the screen. She has the same thick blonde hair and is wearing the same thin sweater I still have on. This girl bears an uncanny resemblance to me because it's…*me*.

There's no mistaking it.

My face is as clear as can be. Almost as if someone went to the trouble to make sure it was captured for posterity. I clap a hand to my mouth as the acidic taste of bile rises in my throat. Any moment it's going to spew all over the place.

"You don't remember any of this?" Duke asks cautiously as if he realizes that I'm teetering on the brink.

As I continue to stare at the images, I force myself to think about the previous twenty-four hours, but like before, everything remains blank. There aren't any memories. It's like staring at a stranger's antics.

"No, nothing," I choke out as my bewildered gaze lifts to his. "I don't understand how I could have done all this but have no recollection."

"Me neither," he says carefully, brows lowered. "I know that you usually don't drink, but maybe you did last night?" There's a pause. "I mean, Austin had a great game yesterday and everyone was celebrating."

I shake my head. "No, I didn't."

Another heavy silence falls over us before he clears his throat and drops another bomb. "The pictures were blasted out to everyone."

I can only stare as those words sink in.

Everyone at Hawthorne Prep is what Duke is alluding to.

Austin is going to—

My eyes widen.

Austin.

He'll assume I betrayed him.

Again.

With shaking fingers, I hit the messaging app on my cell and scroll down the list to find his name. As soon as I pull up our convo, I catch sight of the photos. Air gets knocked from my lungs, making it impossible to breathe.

I sent them to him from my phone.

Why would I do that?

My mind cartwheels, painfully trying to piece everything together so that it will make sense.

But it doesn't. I'm at a total loss.

I scroll upward and find the messages he sent.

Where are you?

You need to answer me, Delilah.

A couple minutes later, I sent the photos.

Horror sets in as I read the last text.

Her BJs are the best, aren't they, bro?

Iciness seeps into my veins before gradually spreading throughout the rest of my body.

Jasper.

He did this.

I don't know how, but he's the one behind the photographs.

Hot tears prick the backs of my eyes. And here I'd foolishly thought that I'd managed to escape him unscathed.

Guess the joke's on me for lowering my guard.

DELILAH

"Call if you need anything," Duke says as my fingers wrap around the handle of his pickup truck as it idles near the curb.

When the door creaks as I open it, I hesitate and meet his concerned gaze. At the moment, he's the only friend I have, and I'm grateful for his support. Thick emotion wells inside me.

"Thank you."

The edges of his lips lift into a rare smile. "There's nothing to thank me for. We go way back. We'll be friends no matter what."

The one lesson I've learned in life is to never take anything for granted, and that includes friendships.

"Still...I appreciate it." My attention is reluctantly drawn to the tiny house that sits in the middle of a postage-stamp sized yard. "I should probably head inside and face the music."

The thought of doing that is enough to make the muscles in my belly contract.

He follows the direction of my gaze. "Yeah, my guess is that Carrie is gonna shit a brick when she sees you." He refocuses his attention on me. "I would have texted her from your phone, but I didn't know your passcode."

I blow out a steady breath, emptying my lungs. If he'd done that, Mom would have demanded that I get my ass home and been irate when I didn't walk through the door ten minutes later. Either way, it was going to be a damned if I do and damned if I don't situation.

"Thanks again for the ride. I'll see you Monday," I say before forcing my feet into movement and exiting the vehicle.

As soon as I settle on the grass near the curb, I suck in a deep breath and then force it out again. This is one conversation I'm dreading. My relationship with Mom has shifted drastically in a short span of time. Barely does it resemble what it once was.

My mind tumbles back over the past couple of weeks. Everything changed when I accidentally walked in on her and the headmaster of Hawthorne Prep locked in a passionate embrace in the copy room. Not only is he her boss, but he's married with kids who attend the elite prep school. Add in Jasper filling her head with lies and her own preconceived notions about the Hawthorne family, and our house has become a warzone. I'm constantly creeping around so as not to set her off.

Me waltzing into the house the morning after I should have come straight home from the game is a powder keg of a situation just waiting to explode.

Each forced footfall along the narrow concrete path that cuts through the lawn feels more like a walk to my death. Nausea continues to grow inside me as I cautiously push open the front door and step inside the tiny living room. As soon as I do, Mom pokes her head around the corner of the kitchen.

Her icy blue eyes skewer mine in place as she snaps into the phone, "She just walked in the door. I'll call you later." Her voice escalates, ratcheting up several notches with each word. "Where the hell have you been all night? I was worried sick!"

I cringe as guilt suffuses me and blurt, "I'm really sorry, Mom."

She straightens to her full height. "*You're sorry?* That's all you have to say for yourself?"

My shoulders collapse under the weight of her fury. She's practically bristling with it. "I, ah...fell asleep."

"Fell asleep?" She stares at me like a horn has just sprouted from my forehead. "Where the hell were you all night?" She flicks a glance at her narrow wristwatch. "It's after nine o'clock in the morning. I could have sworn that I told you to come straight home after the football game."

Unable to hold her gaze, mine darts away as she stalks from the kitchen to the dining room before planting her fists on slender hips.

When I remain silent, she snaps, "Well? I'm waiting for an explanation."

There's no way I can tell her that I attended a party and then blacked out. That would go over like a lead balloon.

I clear my throat and cautiously wrap my lips around the lie. "I was with Duke. We were, um, watching a movie, and I fell asleep."

Her eyes narrow as she studies me. I can't help but shift beneath her relentless scrutiny.

"What the hell were you were doing at Duke's house? Once the game ended, you were supposed to come straight home. That was our agreement, Delilah."

"I know," I whisper. "And I'm sorry for causing you any worry. That was never my intention." I heap another lie onto the growing pile. At this point, does it even matter? "The game ended a little early and he asked if I wanted to watch something. Thirty minutes in, I fell asleep."

With a shake of her head, she presses her lips together. "I don't understand why you decided to disobey me."

"I don't either. It was stupid. Like you said, I should have come right home."

"You're damn right it was!" She folds her arms tightly across her chest and continues to glare. It's the one that makes me feel about two inches tall. "After everything that's happened, I hope you realize there are going to be consequences for your actions." There's a pause before she adds, "You're grounded until further notice. And I'll be thinking long and hard about allowing you to go on the senior camping trip next weekend. Until you earn my trust back, I don't think you'll be doing much of anything."

Relief rushes through me that I'm getting off so easily.

"Okay." With a nod, I bow my head and try to appear disappointed about the punishment. After last night and the pictures that are now spreading like wildfire throughout the student population of HP, I have zero interest in going anywhere with my classmates.

She stabs a finger in my direction. "And don't try to change my mind, either, because it won't work. I'm furious. Do you realize that I sat up all night, worrying?" Unshed tears shine in her blue eyes as she blinks furiously. "I called the hospital a few hours ago just to make sure you hadn't been involved in an accident."

That last statement sends another wave of guilt crashing over me. "I'm really sorry, Mom. I made a mistake. It won't happen again."

"Better not," she grumbles before pressing her lips together and swiping at the lone tear that treks down her ashen cheek. "Just go to your room. I don't want to look at you right now."

Instead of apologizing yet again, I slink through the house to my bedroom with my tail tucked between my legs. My head still throbs a painful beat, but it's nowhere near as bad as when I woke up an hour ago.

Once inside the safety of my room, I close the door and sink to the mattress before pulling out my cell. Nerves spring to life as I stare at the dark screen for several minutes, wondering if it's possible to mend the situation with Austin. After receiving the photographs last night, I imagine he's furious.

My fingers shake as I type out a simple message.

I'm not sure what else to say.

Can we talk?

It takes at least five minutes to work up the courage to hit the send button.

With air wedged in the middle of my throat, I stare at the tiny screen and wait for a response.

AUSTIN

Alt rock blasts in my ears as I curl fifty-pound weights in each hand and stare out the bedroom window that overlooks the backyard. The leaves have turned bright red, orange, and golden yellow as they drop from the tree and carpet the lush lawn. Steps away from the set of French doors in the kitchen is a heated pool that has been winterized until next spring. Farther back from the sprawling mansion is a patch of woods that separates our property from the perfectly manicured eighteen-hole golf course.

It couldn't possibly be a more idyllic setting.

In reality, it's anything but.

Even after my muscles become fatigued and sweat beads my brow, I push myself past both my physical and mental limits. It's only then that my mind clicks off and I can forget about Delilah and what a shit-show the other night turned into.

A huff of breath escapes from me as I set the weights on the floor and swing around to grab my water bottle. Movement catches the corner of my eye and I find my sister perched on the edge of the mattress, staring at me with a pinched brow.

I rip the headphones from my ears and toss them onto the queen-sized bed. "Jesus Christ, Summer. What the hell are you doing here?"

I straighten to my full height and arch my spine before lifting the water to my mouth and guzzling down a third of it.

Her lips quirk reluctantly at the corners. "Waiting for you to finish pumping iron."

The fact that her smile doesn't quite reach her somber eyes tells me everything I need to know about this impromptu visit.

Before she can fire off any questions, I grunt, "I'm fine. You can stop worrying about me, okay?"

She studies me silently as if I'm a bug pinned to a Styrofoam board for a science project. "Are you sure about that?"

Nope.

Not in the least.

But I'd rather slit my own wrists and bleed out in front of her than admit I've been played.

Or hurt.

Again.

I mean, really…

How stupid could I be for letting down my guard and trusting Delilah a second time?

I knew better. The voice was there, chirping at the back of my brain, and I refused to listen. Refused to see her for the conniving bitch she is.

So yeah…I got what I deserved.

It was a tough lesson, but I finally got it through my thick head that Delilah Robinson can't be trusted. She might give off an innocent and sweet vibe, but she's far from it. She and Jasper have been fucking with me the entire time.

And I allowed myself to be manipulated because of pussy. I all but handed over my heart and watched her stomp on it while Jasper sat there laughing. Even the thought of how they must have cracked up at my stupidity has molten lava rushing through my veins.

If that girl thinks this is over, she's dead wrong.

Unwilling to let Summer see how fucking enraged I am, I avert my gaze. "Yup. I'm totally over it." I force my shoulders to loosen before adding carelessly, "It was never that deep. You of all people should realize that."

From the corner of my eye, I watch the emotion play across her face.

Anger.

Uncertainty.

Confusion.

My sister doesn't need to know that I'm being eaten alive with the blinding need for revenge. She'd probably try talking me out of it. But that's not going to happen. The only way I can move on is to bring Delilah to her knees and make her pay the way I should have from the very beginning.

"You don't need to keep it all bottled up inside. We can talk about it." She shifts on the bed and leans forward, her eyes pinning me in place. I get the feeling she's trying to see straight done to my soul and discern the truth for herself. "It would probably help."

I swing away, refusing to allow her in. Summer is sneaky. She knows exactly how to weasel her way inside my brain.

And I love her for it.

I truly do. But there are some things a sister shouldn't have knowledge of, and my plans for Delilah are one of them. She might hate the girl and want to bitch slap her into next week, but she wouldn't want me fucking with her the way I plan to.

"There's nothing to talk about."

"Austin…"

Her voice dips before trailing off.

I huff out an irritated breath before grabbing the small white towel from my dresser and swiping it across my forehead. "Delilah Robinson was just a girl in a long string of them." I jerk my shoulders. "Sure, I was interested in getting to know her, but it was never that deep. As far as I'm concerned, she and Jasper deserve each other." I force out a light chuckle before raising my brow and sneering. "What? Did you think I was heartbroken over some chick from the sticks I just got together with?"

When her face scrunches with uncertainty, I press my advantage, only wanting to end this. "Come on, Sum. You know me better than that."

"Yeah, I guess," she mutters. "It's just that I thought she might be different. You seemed to really like her."

That softly spoken comment is like a knife to the heart, because the truth is that everything felt different with Delilah.

Me included.

I slam the door shut on those thoughts.

It doesn't matter what the hell was going through my fucked-up brain.

None of it was true.

It wasn't real.

She played me like a fiddle.

"Nah. I haven't thought twice about her since the party." Inspiration strikes. "In fact, I talked to that other girl, Aubrey. She seems cool."

Summer grimaces. "Ewww. She's friends with Sloane, and you know exactly what I think about her. Find someone else."

"Don't worry, I'm all about keeping my options open. Kind of like the good old days."

She snorts out a laugh and rolls her eyes. "You mean your manwhore days?"

"Yup, those are the ones."

For the first time since I found her sitting on my bed watching me, it feels like she just might drop this brutal convo and move on. Relief crashes over me and my shoulders incrementally loosen. "Yup. Now that I'm getting more play time on the field, everything is finally falling into place."

That's a bit of a stretch, but we'll just go with it for the sake of this convo.

"I'm glad," she says softly. "It's the way it should have been from the beginning." There's a pause before she tacks on, "It's the way it would have been in Chicago if we'd never been forced to move to Hawthorne."

She's right about that, but it's hard to dwell on. My life would have been totally different back home. Even though Mom briefly considered returning after Dad died, that option was quickly nixed. There's no chance of us picking up and moving back now.

And what would be the point?

The season will be over in less than a month.

Summer rises from the bed before heading to the door. As she crosses the threshold, she turns and meets my gaze with a steady one of her own. "Just remember that my door is always open if you want to talk."

Unwilling to allow this exchange to backslide into dangerous territory, I smirk. "Except when it's locked because Kingsley's in there."

Color seeps into her cheek as her eyes widen. "Shut up. I'm trying to be nice to you, you big jerk."

A grin curls around the corners of my mouth before I eat up the distance between us and tug her into my arms. "I appreciate it." Then, I drop a kiss against the crown of her dark head. Summer is a solid eight inches shorter than I am. "You're the best sister anyone could ask for."

She presses closer. "I just don't want to see you hurt."

My gaze settles on the windowpane again and the scenery that lies beyond it. "I know."

A second ticks by before she sniffs. "No offense, but you stink."

With a snort, I set her free. "None taken."

She retreats a few steps before jerking a thumb over her shoulder. "I'll see you in thirty minutes for dinner."

I nod as she slips into the hallway. The moment she disappears from sight, the smile fades and my earlier thoughts of revenge rush back to fill my brain.

Delilah might think she's won this battle, but I'll be damned if I don't win the war.

DELILAH

My belly churns as we slowly roll through the iron gates of Hawthorne Prep. It won't take much for me to vomit all over the place. Mom slept through her alarm this morning, and now we're running late. The parking lot is already filled with expensive SUVs and sports cars. Heads swivel as Mom slides into the last row. Most schools are set up with staff parking located near the entrance of the building, while kids are in the back if there's enough space.

That's not the way it is here. I suppose that tells you everything you need to know about HP and who really runs this place.

I shrink away from the intense scrutiny before glancing at Mom. She hasn't said much since the blowup Saturday morning. Whenever our gazes collided, a look of disappointment would flash across her expression. There were so many times I wanted to explain the circumstances, but didn't, knowing it wouldn't make the situation better. I have no idea how to repair the damage that's been inflicted on our relationship. Part of me wonders if it's even possible. Or is this the way it will forever remain?

Once the engine has been killed, she gathers up her purse and thermal lunch bag before exiting the vehicle without a word. My gaze reluctantly slices to the clusters of students loitering outside the building. Already, I can feel their speculative gazes aimed in my direction. I didn't think it was possible for my life to jackhammer to a lower point.

I was wrong.

This is so much worse.

Paralysis takes hold as I stare out the windshield. It's so tempting to slide over to the driver's seat, start the engine, and gun it out of the lot. For just a second or two, I squeeze my eyes tightly closed and pray the situation isn't as bad as I assume.

Deep down—

"Delilah," Mom snaps, standing in front of the old Honda Civic, "get a move on or you'll be late for first period."

My eyelids fly open before slicing to hers through the glass. Her lips are smashed together, and irritation shimmers around her in suffocating waves. I grab my backpack from the floorboards and pop open the door before scrambling to the pavement.

"Any day now," Mom mutters, tapping her foot.

"Sorry."

Before I can reach her side, she swings away, stalking to the entrance of the sprawling stone building. We pass pockets of students talking and joking with one another. My face heats as they turn and glance my way. Smirks simmer across their faces as they point and stare at their phones before flashing the screens at their friends and laughing. A couple guys shoot sly looks my way before elbowing the person next to them.

I haven't taken more than a handful of steps on school property and already I know every single student at HP has salivated over the photographs.

If I didn't realize it before, I do now—today will be a total nightmare.

Mom's brows pinch together as she frowns. From the side of her mouth, she mutters, "Is it my imagination, or is everyone staring?" One hand flutters over her skirt to smooth out the nonexistent wrinkles. "Do I have something on me? Is my hair sticking up?"

"No. You look fine."

There's no way I'll make it through the morning without someone bringing the pictures to her attention. And then...

I wince, not wanting to imagine her reaction.

"Hmmm."

It's a relief when she remains silent before hustling up the wide stone stairs to the set of double doors and slipping inside. My steps slow as I reach the entrance. Even though I feel dozens of eyes crawling over me in the parking lot, I'm loath to enter the building. The daunting realization that the entire day is stretched out ahead of me brings a sharp pinch to my belly.

Mom throws a glance over her shoulder as she holds open the door. "I need to get to the office. I'll see you after school. And remember, you're grounded. No staying after and no friends." Her voice turns stern. "And *certainly* no Austin Hawthorne." Her face scrunches as if she's spotted something grotesque.

I almost snort.

There's nothing for her to worry about on that front. I reached out at least half a dozen times over the weekend and he never responded, which is a pretty clear indication of where things stand between us.

It's obvious he believes the worst in me and is unwilling to hear my side of the story.

"Okay."

With one last steely look aimed in my direction, she swings away before getting swallowed up by the crowd in the hallway and disappearing. Now that I've been left to my own devices, I hunch my shoulders and lower my head before moving through the thick press of bodies. A growing wave of whispers and giggles ripples in my wake.

I wish the shiny black and white marble floor would open and swallow me whole.

"Hey, Delilah," Aiden Wendt yells, his voice echoing off the paneled walls, "you look hot on your knees. Any chance I can get in on the action? Is there a rotation or request form I can fill out?"

My gaze collides with his smirking one before I rip it away and stare down at the floor, moving as quickly as I can through the hall-way. More questions and comments are shouted as I pass by.

They're impossible to ignore.

It's a relief when I finally reach my locker. My fingers tremble as I spin the dial. It takes four attempts at the combination before the metal door pops open. I just need to grab my books, and then I can get the hell out of here. The corridor is like shark-infested waters and I'm bleeding out.

For a few brief seconds, I consider ditching school. I could walk right out the front entrance and never return.

I glance longingly toward the exit.

It's so tempting.

Except, it would only exacerbate the situation at home. Tears prick the backs of my eyes as I resign myself to the next eight hours of hell.

When a shadow falls over me, I steel myself for the inevitable. I know who it is without looking.

"What do you want?" I growl, trying to mask the quiver that weaves its way through my voice.

When the question is met with silence, I force myself to meet his gaze head-on.

Deep down, I knew that when we broke up, Jasper would make my life miserable, but I never imagined he would stoop so low.

Maybe I should have.

All the telltale signs were there, and I turned a blind eye and ignored them. Jasper wants to break me. He won't be happy until I crawl back and beg his forgiveness. Then, he'll put a collar around my neck so that everyone knows I'm his pet.

I straighten my shoulders and stand a little straighter.

I'll be damned if that happens.

A slow smile spreads across his lips as he lounges against the locker next to mine and folds his arms across his chest. Once upon a time, such a smile aimed in my direction would have had my belly stirring with butterflies.

Now, it makes me sick to my stomach.

"To see how you're doing."

That's all it takes for my temper to explode. My hands clench uselessly at my sides as I whirl around. "How do you think I'm doing? You took pictures of me in compromising situations and made sure everyone at school saw them." I step closer before stabbing a finger into his hard chest. "I don't even remember talking to you Friday night." My eyes narrow as my mind spins, trying to latch onto a plausible explanation. "What did you do? Drug me?"

With a loud snort, he rolls his eyes. "Please, you were totally trashed. It's not my fault you can't hold your liquor and blacked out. You were hanging all over me, begging for my forgiveness." He throws an arm wide. "Ask anyone who was there and they'll tell you." He leans closer until his warm breath can feather across my lips. "What was I supposed to do when you begged to suck my cock? Turn you down?"

He's lying.

He has to be.

There's no way in hell I'd go anywhere near Jasper after everything he's put me through. After I spent weeks contemplating how to escape our relationship. And he wants me to believe that I begged to give him a blow job?

The thought is enough to have bile rising in my throat.

"No," I whisper, refusing to consider one word that comes out of his mouth.

He shoots me a wounded look. "And here I thought we were back together. How disappointing."

I suppress a shudder. "That's never going to happen."

"I'd be careful about making promises you can't keep," he singsongs.

When he reaches out and trails a finger along the curve of my jaw, I bat his hand away and take a swift step in retreat.

Even though it's dangerous to turn my back on him, I swing toward my locker and grab a stack of books that will get me through my morning classes before slamming the door shut.

Just as I attempt to dart around him, he slides in front of me, blocking my escape and pushing me in the chest. Not expecting the shove, I stumble backward. His hand slices through the air, hits my books, and knocks them to the floor where they scatter at my feet. Papers fly into the flow of traffic before being trampled. My eyes widen when he advances, pressing me into the cold metal until I'm left with no other choice but to flatten against the locker.

A nasty glint lights up his gray eyes as if he's enjoying this interaction.

"You know what I can't figure out?" he rasps.

My heart slams painfully into my ribcage. It doesn't escape me that there are dozens of witnesses, and not one damn person can be bothered to step in and stop Jasper from accosting me.

Instead of responding, my lips stay pressed together in a thin, tight line. We both know it's a rhetorical question.

"Why do you think you're so much better than me? You live in a fucking dump, drive a piece of shit, and don't have two nickels to rub together. You wouldn't be here without your precious scholarship."

His growled-out words turn my blood to ice.

He presses closer until my breasts are smashed against the hard lines of his chest. "You walk around here like you're some kind of princess, when in reality, you're not good enough to lick my shoes."

My tongue darts out to moisten my lips. "That's not true."

It takes effort to tamp down the fear rampaging through my system. The scent of it will incite further violence. It's only now that we're broken up that I realize what Jasper Morgan is fully capable of.

And that's anything.

Consequences mean nothing to him.

His eyes turn stormy as uncontrolled rage flashes in them. "Yeah, you do."

He's close enough for his warm breath to drift across my lips. My muscles tense as I wait for his next move. There's nothing to stop him from inflicting untold amounts of damage.

"You're a whore, just like all these other girls," he growls as one hand snakes out, slithering up the length of my bare leg and disappearing beneath my tartan skirt.

My mouth turns cottony as fear rushes through me. When I press closer to the locker as if it's possible to put more distance between us, an ugly chuckle falls from his lips.

"What's the matter, Delilah?" His fingers bite into my flesh, and I wince as pain radiates through my thigh. "You only like it when trash touches you?"

His face lowers as his lips hover over mine. I press my palms against his chest and push with all my strength, but he doesn't budge an inch. When his lips lower, I twist my head to the side.

And meet the steely-eyed gaze of Austin.

Every single protest dies a quick death on the tip of my tongue as the frigidness of his expression freezes me to the core. There's so much anger filling his green eyes. It couldn't be more different from how he stared at me Friday night.

Jasper nips at my earlobe as I stare in horror. It's like I'm paralyzed. Unable to move or turn my head away. I know exactly what this looks like. That's all it takes for a little piece of me to shrivel and die. Before I can fight my way free, Austin swings away and stalks down the hall, disappearing from sight.

Any hope that he might have cooled off enough to listen to my side of the story has now been snuffed out.

DELILAH

Jasper's dark laughter chases me down the corridor and follows me into my first hour classroom as I slump onto my chair and glance at the digital clock that hangs over the exit.

The bell rings throughout the building at exactly half past seven.

Whispered comments whip around me as Coach Baker settles on his chair before reclining back and kicking his shoes up on his desk. The loudspeaker buzzes as the morning announcements are read.

"All right everyone, settle down and listen up," Coach says. "Then we'll finish the chapter on rational functions. Remember, there's a test next week."

Most of the class groans.

"This coming weekend is the annual senior camping trip," Mrs. Baxter says in a chirpy, grandmotherly voice. "This is a chance for all you seniors to prove just how mature you've become and to bond with your fellow classmates."

A loud cheer goes up in the room, followed by lots of hooting and hollering. Exuberant voices can be heard echoing down the hallway.

The senior camping trip is a three-day excursion to Lake Michigan. There are about a dozen families who own vacation homes along the sandy shores, Kingsley and Jasper being two of them. Students get divided up between the available locations. And a few brave classmates who enjoy the wilderness pitch tents at a nearby recreational area on the beach and rough it. It's supposed to be a bonding opportunity as well as a reward for making it to senior year.

Was it really only last week that I was looking forward to spending time with Austin?

After everything that's happened, there's no way I'm going. Jasper will continue to hunt me, making my life hell. A chill scuddles down my spine at the idea of being at my ex's mercy for the three-day trip without an adult in sight. Mom already threatened to take it away. I'll have to make sure she pulls the plug altogether.

It shouldn't be difficult.

I'd much rather spend the weekend hibernating in my room and licking my wounds in private. If I'm lucky, someone else—or a bunch of someone elses—will blow their lives up, and this photo fiasco will die a quick death.

One can hope, right?

Just as the announcements end, Mrs. Baxter says, "Delilah Robinson, please come to the office."

The muscles in my belly contract as snickers explode from the students seated all around me.

When I remain frozen in place, Coach Baker raises his brow and jerks his head toward the door. "Get moving, Ms. Robinson."

"Maybe Pembroke is looking for a little of what you gave Jasper Friday night," Aiden Wendt says in an obnoxious voice, loud enough for everyone to hear. "Those knees are gonna get chafed from all the time spent on them."

Heat slams into my cheeks as I gather up my books with shaking hands and hug them close to my chest. A few more comments are shouted as I rush from the classroom. Even though their laughter and childishness shouldn't bother me, tears sting the backs of my eyes. I have to blink to prevent the wetness from splashing onto my cheeks.

My brain whirls, wondering why I'm being summoned. I've done my best to avoid our headmaster since I threatened to expose his affair with my mother. Whenever he catches sight of me in the hallway, his eyes narrow and he glares.

It's enough to have me shrinking away.

The soles of my shoes echo against the polished marble tile that stretches throughout the hallways as I reach the office and push through the door. Mrs. Baxter glances at me from her desk. The slight smile that lifts the corners of her lips doesn't quite reach her eyes as she holds my gaze for a moment or two before dropping it.

"Go right in, Delilah. Mr. Pembroke is waiting for you."

The pit that has taken up residence at the bottom of my belly swells in size. Mrs. Baxter is usually so cheery and outgoing, always willing to engage in a little banter.

That's not the case today.

Barely could she meet my eyes.

"Thank you."

As tempting as it is to flee the space, I force my feet into movement. The sooner I talk with Pembroke, the quicker I can get out of here. Once I reach his closed office door, I glance over my shoulder at the older woman. There's a pinch to her brows as her gaze remains focused on the computer screen. I release a steady breath before lifting my hand and rapping my knuckles against the thick wood.

"Come in," the headmaster barks from the other side.

Another burst of nerves dances down the length of my spine as I turn the handle and push open the door, peeking my head inside the inner sanctum.

"Hi, Mr.—"

My voice falls away as I meet my mother's eyes. She's standing near Pembroke with her arms crossed tightly against her chest. Her eyes are red rimmed and puffy, as if she's been crying.

When I remain frozen in place, he snaps, "Come inside and shut the door, Delilah."

The tension radiating off Mom in heavy waves is enough to choke on. My teeth sink into my lower lip as I step over the threshold.

The silence is deafening as Pembroke extends an arm toward the lone chair parked in front of his massive antique desk. "Take a seat."

My gaze darts from him to Mom, who dabs at the corners of her eyes with a tissue, before slicing back to him again, where it reluctantly settles. My fingers tangle in front of me, the curve of my nails sinking into my palms.

The headmaster steeples his fleshy hands on the shiny surface of his desk before leaning forward. Not once does his gaze deviate from mine. It would be impossible to miss the spiteful glint of pleasure that sparks in his pale blue eyes.

"It's come to our attention that some rather unsavory photographs have been circulating throughout the student population."

And just like that, I'm in freefall.

Oh, shit.

My wide gaze flies to Mom in time to see a fresh tear leak from the corner of her eye and roll slowly down her ashen cheek.

"How could you do this?"

I shake my head almost violently. "No, I—"

"Shut up! I don't want to hear any more of your lies."

My mouth drops open as I stare in shock.

"And you can forget about the camping trip this weekend! You're grounded until further notice. It'll be school and then straight back home. That's it. That's your life." With each word, her voice escalates until it reverberates off the plaster walls.

I wince, knowing Mrs. Baxter, and anyone else loitering in the office, is privy to every shrill word. She probably knows all about the photographs. It's the reason she could barely meet my gaze.

"I just can't believe you would engage in this kind of deplorable behavior! And then, to make matters worse, you allow someone to take pictures, as if you're proud of acting like a whore." Disgust vibrates in every syllable as she shakes her head. "I don't understand what's going on with you! It's like you're a totally different girl. One I don't know." Another lone tear crawls down her cheek.

I open my mouth before snapping it shut. There's no point in trying to defend myself. She refuses to believe anything I say.

"Carrie," Mr. Pembroke soothes. "I think you're being a bit hasty with your punishment. If you want my professional opinion on the matter, I think you should allow Delilah to attend the senior trip. Perhaps a little time away, out in nature, would be the perfect opportunity for some much needed self-reflection and growth."

Thrown off by the suggestion, Mom's eyes bulge as she blinks.

I'm just as shocked by this turn of events.

Why does he care if I attend the senior trip?

"Edmond, you can't possibly be serious! There's no way Delilah should be allowed to attend an unsupervised outing." She turns glaring eyes my way. "With my luck, she'll end up pregnant."

Heat scalds my cheeks. "That's not going to happen."

"You know what? I never thought you'd allow someone to take photographs of you either, but apparently, I was wrong."

I wince.

What am I supposed to say in response to that?

"I understand that your daughter broke your trust, but she made an error in judgment. I highly doubt it's something she'll repeat in the future." There's a pause as Pembroke flicks his gaze at me. "Isn't that right, Delilah?"

My teeth scrape across my lower lip in confusion. Why is he trying to smooth over the situation? What's in it for him?

When I remain silent, his voice sharpens and eyes narrow. "Delilah? An answer, if you please."

"No." My shoulders wilt under the intensity of his death stare. "Nothing will happen."

Mom shakes her head. "I'm still against this decision. She shouldn't be allowed to go. Not after pulling this stunt."

"You're absolutely right," he agrees smoothly. "But we all make mistakes. One of the most important lessons a person can learn in life is the self-awareness to recognize when they've deviated too far from their intended path and then course correct." He lifts his fleshy hands. "It's unfortunate that some children need to learn this lesson the hard way." His icy stare lands on me. "Delilah happens to be one of those stubborn individuals. It's better for her to learn it now rather than later when the stakes are much higher. Wouldn't you agree?"

Mom worries her bottom lip with uncertainty.

I scream silently in my head.

No.

No.

No.

Don't let him talk you into this.

Her eyes cloud with indecision. "You honestly think I should allow her to go away for the weekend?"

"I do." He clears his throat, tone turning brisk. "Now that a course of action has been settled upon, you should return to work. If you don't mind, I'd like to spend a few minutes chatting with Delilah." There's a pause. "Perhaps impart some wisdom for her to mull over."

Mom stares at me for a long, silent moment before her gaze returns to Pembroke. "All right." Her shoulders wilt as if the weight of the world rests on them. "Maybe you'll have more luck getting through to her than I have."

Mom doesn't utter a peep before slipping out the door and closing it softly behind her.

And then we're alone.

A prickle of unease blooms in the pit of my belly as I shift awkwardly on my chair and wait for him to impart his so-called wisdom. Instead of launching into a long-winded lecture, he picks up his phone from the polished mahogany desktop and stares at it for about twenty seconds. Every so often, he swipes the screen as if scrolling.

"This is quite the photo collection, Ms. Robinson." He flicks his beady gaze at me. "Certainly not how a student at an elite prep school should behave."

Heat scalds my cheeks as I realize what he's been staring at while I've been sitting in front of him.

"I must say, your mother also enjoys being on her knees. Perhaps you can exchange some tips and tricks."

My heart stutters as my lower jaw falls open.

Did...he really just say that?

By the way his lips curl around the edges, he did.

Even more than that, he's loving this.

Loving my fall from grace after I forced his hand a few weeks ago.

He holds up the phone. "Just so we're clear, if anyone finds out about this affair, I'll kick your ass out of Hawthorne Prep so fast, your head will spin. After I'm done dragging your reputation through the mud, not even the public school will take you. Have I made myself perfectly clear?"

"Yes."

"Excellent." His eyes harden as he bares his teeth. "Now get the hell out of my office before I change my mind and have you physically removed from the premises."

With that, I leap from the chair and scurry from the suffocating space.

DELILAH

Unable to meet the secretary's gaze, I fly through the outer office. I can't bear to see the condemnation that is probably filling her eyes. The door slams shut behind me with a resounding thud as I stumble into the corridor and suck in a lungful of oxygen. The lemony fresh scent of polish fills the air as nausea roils at the bottom of my gut, threatening to escape.

With a quick glance down the long stretch of empty hallway, I race toward the nearest restroom. The soles of my shoes echo off the marble tile as I push into the small space.

It's a relief to find it empty.

Once I reach the sink, my fingers grip the edges of the porcelain as I hang my head and squeeze my eyes tightly shut, focusing on my erratic breathing.

A long, slow breath in before steadily blowing it out.

Everything that's happened since Friday night circles viciously through my head. Waking up in Duke's bed. Discovering the photographs. A hole where my memories should be. Mom's anger. And now this.

Not only do I have to find a way to get through the remainder of my senior year, but I have to survive this three-day trip as well.

The thought is enough to bring a sting of tears to my eyes.

Just as my heart rate settles and the nausea fades to more of a dull ache, the door to the bathroom bursts open. I crack my eyelids just enough to stare at the mirror before meeting icy green depths. A gasp escapes from me as I whirl around to face Austin.

Brilliant anger shimmers around him like a living, breathing entity. It's overpowering in its intensity. My body trembles under the relentless force of his gaze.

"I texted you," I whisper.

With a tilt of his head, he studies me. "What exactly do we have to talk about? You sucking Jasper's cock?"

This is exactly what I was afraid of. That he would jump to conclusions without hearing my side of the story. I'm not sure if there's anything I can say that will make the fury and distrust evaporate from his eyes.

But I have to try.

I can't allow Jasper to destroy my relationship with Austin.

"Please, just give me a chance to explain." When his expression doesn't soften, I stumble over my words in a rush to get them out. "Everything from that night is a blur. There's a lot I can't remember."

His lips lift into a mirthless smile. "I guess it's a good thing Jasper took lots of photos." His voice dips, dropping several octaves until it sounds as if it's been scraped raw. "The two of you must have had a good laugh at my expense."

With a shake of my head, I take a tentative step toward him. All I want in this moment is to feel the comforting strength of his arms wrapped around me, holding me tight and telling me that everything will be all right.

But he doesn't move in my direction.

"I swear—"

"Save it!" he growls, his raised voice echoing off the stark white tile. "You're nothing more than a fucking liar, and I was an idiot for lowering my guard and believing you were different."

His harsh words slice through the very heart of me and send pain radiating throughout my body. It's almost enough to have me doubling over.

Does he really believe I'm capable of playing that kind of game?

"You have to know that's not true. I'm nothing like these people. And I hate Jasper. Probably more than you do."

He snorts. "I didn't think it was possible to despise anyone more than Jasper Morgan, but you know what?" Animosity flares in his eyes as his upper lip curls. "I was wrong."

My heart stutters before pounding a painful staccato beneath my breast as he stalks inside the room. I scramble back a couple of steps, attempting to keep a safe distance between us. The farther he moves into the space, the more it shrinks around us, until the walls are pressing in on me.

His lips lift as his tone turns chiding. "What's wrong, Delilah? Why are you running away? I thought you enjoyed playing games? Isn't that what this has been? One giant mindfuck?"

I shake my head almost frantically. "Of course not. Please, Austin. You have to know that everything between us was real."

A ferocious growl rumbles from deep within his chest and I wince as the sound ricochets off the walls. "Shut the hell up. I don't want to hear any more lies from your mouth."

The closer he gets, the more my body trembles. I have no idea what he'll do when he gets his hands on me. The look simmering in his eyes is murderous.

"They're not lies."

His lips curl into a malicious smile. "Do us both a favor and drop the innocent act."

Icy tendrils of fear wrap around my heart and squeeze until sucking air into my lungs becomes impossible. My hands fly out to hold him back. Although, I think we both realize that the feeble attempt won't do much to keep him at bay.

I've never seen Austin like this.

Not even after the charity function.

When my spine hits the wall, I realize there's nowhere left for me to run.

I'm trapped.

By the hard glint that lights up his eyes, he recognizes it as well and relishes the thought of having me at his mercy.

"What's wrong, sweet girl? Your little game coming back to haunt you? Did you really think you could fuck me over for a second time and I'd just let it go?"

When I open my mouth to deny the accusation, his hand shoots out, the fingers wrapping around my throat as a squeak of shock escapes from me. The firm pressure doesn't cut off my airflow. It's just enough for me to understand who's now in control.

And it's not me.

"What are you going to do now?" he asks in a deceptively calm voice. "Hmmm? Run back to Jasper and cry?"

His grip tightens as he growls out my ex's name.

"No," I whimper.

"That would be the correct answer." With a snarl, he cocks his head. "With all your scheming, you must have forgotten what I know. Maybe it's time for everyone to find out that Pembroke is boning your mother."

The headmaster's earlier threats echo hollowly throughout my head. Mom's concerns about needing to find another job if the board fires her chase after them.

"Please don't."

"Why shouldn't I?" His face looms closer as he bares his teeth. "You made me look like a fool, and I plan to make you pay for it."

"I swear it wasn't me. I didn't do it."

His grip intensifies until I'm gasping for air. "No more lies." There's a moment of silence before he says, "Know what I want most of all?"

One lone tear leaks from the corner of my eye and treks slowly down my cheek.

When I remain silent, he growls, "To punish you."

Fear slices through me as my heart slams painfully against my chest.

I can't stop the question from popping free. "How?"

His eyes narrow as his expression turns contemplative. "I'm not sure yet. I'll have to think about it. I guess since you enjoy being on your knees so much, we'll start there."

I can only blink as his fingers loosen from around the slender column of my throat and rise to settle on the top of my head. Before I can wrap my brain around what's happening, the pressure increases and my legs buckle as I sink to the tile floor at his feet. Unable to help myself, I glance up and meet his eyes. A potent concoction of liquid fire and rage swirls through them.

It's enough to singe me alive.

"That's exactly where you belong. On your knees, sucking my cock."

No. Not like this.

Not when he's so filled with vengeance.

"Austin, please…"

"You know what's better than hearing that word slide off your lips? Watching tears pool in your eyes while you say it. Nothing gets me harder."

Wetness hovers on my lashes and rolls down my cheek. As it does, he reaches out and thumbs it away with a surprisingly gentle touch before bringing it to his lips and licking it off.

"Remember how we discussed exploring your sucking abilities? That's exactly what we're going to do." His voice dips, becoming lower. "Open my fly and take out my dick."

Nerves explode inside me as I gulp. It feels like there's a lump of wet sawdust sitting in the middle of my throat, making it impossible to swallow. My gaze drops to the bulge at his crotch.

"Better hurry, sweet girl. We don't have all day. Any minute, the bell is going to ring, and someone could walk in and see you."

Fear spikes through me at the thought of that happening. It would only add more fuel to the gossip mill that's already churning. There's no way I could show my face around here again.

My fingers tremble as I reach out and flick open the button of his pressed khakis before lowering the fly. The slow grind of metal teeth fills the silence of the room. I release a steady breath and grip the elastic band of his boxer briefs before pulling the material down until his erection can spring free.

My gaze fastens on it with reluctant curiosity.

Already, he's thick and swollen. The vein that runs from the root to the bulbous head swells with blood flow.

When a deep chuckle rumbles up from his chest, my attention jerks to his face, only to find a smirk tipping the corners of his lips.

"I've caught sight of Jasper in the locker room. He's nowhere near this size. I bet you couldn't even feel him at the back of your throat. Don't worry, sweet girl. That's not going to be a problem for me. You'll feel every thrust when I fuck your face."

My mouth dries at the thought.

His words should disgust me.

What does it mean that they don't?

I'm much too afraid to dig deeper for an answer.

He wraps one hand around his boner before bringing the tip to the seam of my lips.

When I open without further prodding, another laugh slides from him and fills the space between us. It's a deep and low sound that claws at the bottom of my belly and ignites arousal in my core.

His forcefulness shouldn't turn me on.

But there's no denying the truth.

Maybe I can hide it from him but not myself.

"Eager for my dick, are we?"

His other hand drifts across my cheek before the fingers tunnel through my hair, wrapping around the side of my skull before tightening so that I'm held firmly in place. There's no way for me to move a muscle unless he grants permission.

Instead of pressing the thick length between my lips, he lazily circles the tip around them. A trail of moisture is left behind in his wake. His eyelids lower to half-mast as his stare intensifies. I couldn't rip my attention away from the hunger in his eyes even if I tried. There's something so compelling about the expression on his face.

It's a potent concoction of need and anger. It's difficult to tell where one emotion ends and the other begins. They're thickly entwined. No matter how much Austin hates me, he still wants me.

His touch is surprisingly gentle as he glides the head over my parted lips before trailing it over one cheek and then the other. When he drags the soft tip along my temple, I squeeze my eyes tightly closed as it drifts across my lids.

First one.

And then the other.

He strokes my cheek again before arriving at my mouth.

"Open your eyes. I want them locked on me the entire time. Do you understand?"

His command has them flying open and colliding with his.

"Good girl."

As much as I try to stymie the reluctant pleasure that floods through me, it's an impossible task. My thoughts are a tangled, thorny mess. I don't understand how I can want this when what he's forcing me to do should be humiliating.

I'm not on my knees because I want to be.

I'm here because Austin shoved me to them.

There's a difference.

And yet, it doesn't matter.

"Kiss the tip, sweet girl. Show me who owns you."

There's not the slightest hesitation on my part as my lips pucker before making contact with the velvety skin of his crown. Without thinking, my tongue darts out to lick the drop of moisture that beads the slit. A slight saltiness hits my taste buds as my tongue slips out for a second time.

Before I can make contact, his fingers tighten in my hair, dragging me back and tilting my head upward to meet his hard stare.

"Did I give you permission to lick me?" he growls.

The question vibrates throughout my body before settling deep in my core.

"No," I whisper, gaze obediently locked on his.

In that moment, as I tilt my head and gaze up at him from my knees, the world shrinks down until it only encompasses the two of us.

There is just him.

And me.

He's all I'm cognizant of.

The words that fall from his lips.

The way his gaze singes mine.

The feel of his firm grip stinging my scalp and holding me firmly in place.

"That's right," he agrees smoothly. "I didn't." Pleasure ignites in his eyes as he smirks. "So fucking greedy even when I'm forcing you to suck my dick. You can't help yourself."

There's little point denying the accusation.

He won't believe me.

I won't believe me.

When I remain quiet, thunderclouds erupt across his expression as he jerks me forward, feeding me the thick length until it does exactly as he promised and nudges the back of my throat. My eyes widen as I adjust to his girthy size. Only half his cock fills my mouth. I can't imagine what it'll feel like to take the entire thing.

The slight smile tugging at the corners of his lips tells me he's able to read my thoughts.

"That's a lot more than you're used to, isn't it? No one is choking on Jasper's pinkie-sized dick, now are they?"

I moan when he presses forward, sliding deeper inside my throat until almost the entire length has disappeared between my lips. Any moment, I'm going to gag. My mouth has never felt this full. I unlock my jaw and breathe through my nostrils as my pleading gaze stays pinned to his. I'm seconds away from freaking out. The vise grip he has on me doesn't allow for movement.

"That feels so damn good," he groans, thick dark lashes fluttering as a look of pure bliss flickers across his face. The anger recedes as euphoria floods his expression.

His happiness is addicting.

And I want more of it.

I want to be the only one capable of giving him this kind of intense pleasure.

More than that, I don't want to see the rage and distrust return when he stares at me. Once this is over, it will. It only makes me want to draw out this moment for as long as possible even though I know it won't—*can't*—last.

The longer he stays motionless, the more tears sting my eyes.

Just when I'm about to choke on his thick length, he withdraws. Relief floods through me as I fill my lungs with fresh air, but my respite is short lived. Before my racing heart can settle, he nudges my lips again. His grip tightens on my scalp, and I open so that he can slide inside, surging farther than last time. When the muscles of my throat constrict, a growl rumbles up from deep within his chest.

"Fuck."

With one flex of his hips, his length slides in and then out. When he nudges the back of my throat, I swallow and another groan escapes from him. His movements become rhythmic as his fingers tighten in my hair. More wetness gathers in my eyes as he glides so far down my throat that the nest of dark hair at his groin tickles the tip of my nose.

"Unbutton your shirt," he says with a grunt.

I blink and stare at him as he fucks my mouth, just like he promised.

"Open your shirt," he growls for a second time. "I don't like repeating myself."

With my mouth stuffed full of his cock, my fingers shake as they rise to the first pearly button. I slip it through the fabric loop before they drift to the second and third until the perfectly pressed material gapes, revealing my simple white undergarment and the swath of sun-kissed skin beneath.

"Now take your tits out of the bra."

This time, there is no hesitancy. My fingers delve inside the cups before shoving down the material. My nipples tighten as the cool air of the room wafts over them.

"You have the most perfect breasts."

His cock swells in my mouth as his hips piston, picking up speed.

Just when I think he's going to come, he pulls away. A choking sound escapes from me and spittle dribbles from the corners of my mouth as he retreats a step. With his hand strangling his cock, he continues to pump his erection, all the while watching me through hooded eyes.

"Press your titties together."

A groan rumbles up from deep within his chest as I push the swells of my breasts until they're practically touching. When his fisted hand picks up even more speed, I can't help but stare in fascination as he jerks his dick. The rough way he handles it looks almost painful. Another deep, guttural sound escapes from him as thick ropes of cum erupt from the tip and land on my chest.

I gasp as he paints my naked flesh with his warm release.

"Fuck," he growls, continuing to throttle his thick erection with a hard grip until his knuckles turn bone white. It's only when he softens that his fingers loosen.

In the silence of the room, his harsh breath echoes off the tile walls and my heartbeat jackhammers a mad rhythm until the dull roar of the ocean fills my ears.

Austin's gaze never relinquishes mine as he tucks himself away and zips up his pants. "Now smear my cum all over your tits."

I blink away the thick haze that threatens to swallow me whole. "What?"

When he steps closer, it becomes necessary to crane my neck to hold his icy stare as he hunkers down until we're eyelevel. The silence that stretches between us only ratchets up the growing tension that fills the space.

"What don't you understand?" His deceptively soft voice sends chills scampering across my skin. "I want you to spread my jizz all over those sweet little titties."

It takes effort to shake off the shock that paralyzes me before my hands slowly rise until my fingers are able to find the sticky wetness and rub it in tentative circles. My gaze stays fastened to his even though his stare has dropped to my breasts. Darkness and arousal smolder in his vibrant green depths.

"Who would've thought coming all over your tits would be hotter than ejaculating down your throat?" he muses, more to himself than to me.

As I massage the pearly fluid into my skin, he reaches out and tweaks one nipple before scooping up a tiny dollop of his ejaculation and rubbing it over the stiffened little bud. He turns his attention to the other breast before repeating the movement.

Arousal explodes deep in my core, and I try to stomp it out, not wanting it to blaze out of control. When he pinches the other tight peak, it roars back to life again, stronger than before. Any moment, my body will go up in flames.

When my fingers still, he growls, "Massage all of it in and don't you dare wash any of it off."

He dips his finger into another glistening drop before bringing it to my lips and spreading it around. My breath catches as he slowly presses the thick digit deep inside my mouth.

"Suck in clean."

Instead of questioning the directive, my tongue curls around his finger. A burst of saltiness explodes in my mouth. When a moan escapes from me, a look of intense satisfaction settles over his expression and he pulls free.

I don't understand the strange sense of loss that fills me. Everything he's done in this bathroom has been to humiliate and degrade me.

And yet…

I would be lying if I didn't admit that, on some level, I enjoyed it.

Or maybe it's simply being near Austin again. That he gazed at me for a few fleeting moments with something other than anger and distrust.

No matter what he believes, I never lied or betrayed him. I wish there were a way to make him understand the truth.

Jasper set me up.

And let me fall.

What other explanation is there?

Even if I could trick Jasper into admitting the truth, Austin wouldn't believe one word that comes out of his mouth. He'd assume it was more fuckery. I'm frustrated that my ex continues to screw with me and there's nothing that can be done to stop him.

When Austin presses a freshly coated finger to my lips, I obediently open and lick off his cum.

When every drop has been kneaded into my skin, I slide the cups of my bra over my naked breasts. My fingers shake as I fasten the shirt until the last button has been secured. With each shift of my body, I'm intensely aware of the stickiness against the cotton fabric. I won't be able to go for more than a handful of minutes before what happened in this bathroom rushes back to haunt me.

Once I straighten, I step toward the long row of shiny white porcelain sinks.

"What are you doing?" he barks, deep voice resonating off the walls.

My feet stutter as I glance at him. "Washing my hands."

"Leave them." Two strides are all it takes for him to eat up the space between us until his chest presses against the tips of my breasts and it becomes necessary to crane my neck in order to hold the steeliness of his gaze. "I want you to feel me all over your body for the rest of the day. You might have fucked me over, but nothing has changed. You still belong to me. And if I find out that you've been anywhere near Jasper, I'll broadcast to the school and anyone else who will listen that your mom and Pembroke are fucking."

My teeth scrape across my swollen lower lip as my eyes plead with his. "Can't we sit down and talk? Let me explain."

Humor flickers across his expression. "Hell no. I told you payback is going to be a bitch, and I meant it."

"I don't understand." My gaze flickers away as pain radiates throughout my being. "You hate me."

His fingers slip beneath my chin and he turns it so that there's no other choice but to meet his eyes.

"You're right, I do. But that doesn't mean I'm not going to use your body every chance I get. Once I tire of it, you can run back to Jasper." His other hand snakes under the hem of my skirt and settles over my pussy before giving it a possessive squeeze. "For the time being, this cunt belongs to me. Do you understand?"

I gasp when his grip tightens, the fingers sinking into the soft skin. "Yes."

He cocks his head. "Tell me why."

"I..."

He shoves the flimsy cotton to the side and slides one finger deep inside until it's buried to the hilt.

Sharp shafts of need explode in my core as he presses deeper, grinding his palm against my clit. "Tell me why I get to use and abuse this pussy any damn time I want. No matter where we are, you'll allow me to do it."

My mouth turns bone dry. As much as I want to glance away, that's impossible. Heat gathers in my cheeks as my inner muscles unconsciously clench around his finger.

"So fucking needy, aren't you?" he says with a laugh that borders on a growl. "Tell me you understand the situation and maybe I'll let you come."

A whimper slips from my lips as I flex my hips, trying to find a little friction.

His fingers bite into my chin. "I can't hear you."

My movements still as he holds me firmly in place. This time, when tears pool in my eyes, it's for entirely different reasons. My pussy throbs around the thick digit buried deep inside my body.

As much as I want to tell him to go to hell, I can't. The words refuse to budge from the tip of my tongue. Instead, I hear myself say, "Because you own me."

"What do I own, sweet girl?"

Oh god.

"My pussy."

"What else?"

I stare blankly until he taps my lips with his finger.

"My mouth."

"That's right. I own it all. Your titties and all your holes. They belong to me until I'm tired of them. Do you understand?"

"Yes."

"And why am I doing this?"

"To make me pay."

His face looms so close that I can feel his warm breath feather across my lips.

"And that's exactly what I'm going to do—bring you to your knees and make you pay."

The chill of his words sends a shiver skating down my flesh before settling in my core like a heavy stone. The most damning part is that I don't know if I'm terrified or turned on.

Or maybe it's a potent concoction of both.

And that's more disturbing than anything else.

"Austin—"

He draws his finger almost all the way out before thrusting it back inside again. "Everything that happens from here on out will be for my enjoyment, not yours."

I gasp as a dizzying amount of pleasure spirals through me. Shame floods me that I'm so damn close to coming. My eyelids feather shut. It wouldn't take much, and he knows it, which is exactly why his movements still.

"Any guesses as to how Pembroke found out about the photos?"

The casually thrown out question is like a bucket of frigid water dumped over my head, and my eyes spring open.

"*What?*" I'd assumed our headmaster caught wind of the scandal because it had spread through the hallowed halls of HP like wildfire.

When my eyes widen, he smirks. "That's right. I paid him a little visit this morning."

My lips part as the air hisses from my lungs.

"We had a nice chat about his ongoing relationship with your mother and the pictures. Needless to say, I no longer have to worry about getting kicked out of this hell hole." He tilts his head before clicking his tongue. "You, on the other hand, are in a far more precarious position."

"You...*told him?*" The words come out sounding more like a croak.

He smirks. "Did you really think you could fuck me over without paying a price?" His eyes harden into frigid green chips of ice as his finger stays buried deep inside me. "Not very clever of you."

My brain somersaults as the conversation with Pembroke plays through my brain on repeat. Suddenly, it all clicks into place. "That's why he insisted I attend the camping trip."

His lips lift into a malicious smile. "Yup."

Hot tears prick the backs of my eyes before one falls, sliding down my cheek. I hate myself for not being strong enough to keep it trapped inside where he can't delight in my misery.

He continues to pump his finger in my pussy. "Still want to come?"

"No," I choke out.

The smile grows wider as a wicked gleam fills his eyes. "We'll see about that."

Before I can ask what that means, he grinds his palm against my clit and sensation reluctantly sparks to life inside my core. I hate him for being able to manipulate my body with such ease. I'm so slick that his finger glides in and out of me effortlessly. The pressure of his hand makes it impossible to ignore the orgasm steadily building within.

As much as I want to deny him, I can't.

"All you have to do is say the word and I'll stop, sweet girl."

My lips part, but I can't bring myself to force it out.

Stop!

Stop!

Stop!

When I remain silent, satisfaction kindles in his eyes as his tempo increases and everything within me becomes whipcord tight. "What's the matter? Thought you didn't want me to make you come?"

A tortured moan escapes from me as the bell rings throughout the school. Instead of dampening my arousal, it only sends it skyrocketing, and my limbs tremble with the harsh need coiled tightly in my core.

"Since we're running out of time and your pussy is sobbing for release, let's switch up the rules. Either beg me to come or I'll stop."

Our gazes remain locked.

When he attempts to yank his hand away, I gasp. "Please don't." He stills as my fingers settle on his broad shoulders, sinking into the wool of his navy blazer to keep him locked in place.

"You know what I want to hear."

"Please make me come," I blurt, unable to stop the words from tumbling out. Shame rushes through every fiber of my being even as my inner muscles clench, locking around him.

A tortured whimper escapes from me when he jerks free. Just when I think he'll leave me high and dry, he shoves me backward until my spine hits the wall before closing the distance between us. He drops to his knees and hikes up my skirt, hooking a finger in the soaked fabric of my panties and dragging it to the side until my pussy is exposed.

His mouth fastens onto me, licking at my clit before stabbing inside my heat. His fingers pull my lips apart as he attacks my sensitive flesh. That's all it takes for me to explode. It's only when my knees weaken from the intensity of my orgasm that he straightens to his full height. His tongue darts out to lick the shiny arousal from his lips as his heated eyes stay locked on mine.

The bathroom door flies open, and a few chattering girls spill into the silent room. Their steps slow when they catch sight of Austin. Their eyes pop wide before sliding to me. My hand flutters, smoothing over the wrinkled fabric of my skirt to make sure I'm completely covered.

By the smirks they shoot at each other, they know exactly what we've been up to.

Without another word, Austin turns on his heel and stalks from the space. Only when he shoves out through the door and disappears into the noisy corridor do my muscles weaken. My reluctant gaze shifts to the three girls. The way they stare in disdain has heat scalding my cheeks. All I want is for the tile floor to open up and swallow me whole.

Gaze locked straight ahead, I force my feet into movement and rush past them.

As I do, one of the girls murmurs, "Slut."

And with that, my shame is complete.

DELILAH

By the time fourth hour is over, I want to crawl in a hole and die. Not only are people gossiping about the pictures, but the three loudmouths have spread it all over school that I was fucked by Austin in the girls' bathroom during first period. Snickers and ugly comments ripple like a wave as I hurry past with my head down and shoulders hunched. If it were possible to draw even more into myself, I would.

I caught a glimpse of Mom in the hallway before fourth hour. She met my gaze before quickly averting her eyes. It would have been impossible not to see all the disappointment swimming within them.

Even though I have no appetite, I open my locker. Before I can reach inside for my lunch, two of Jasper's friends sidle over.

Aiden Wendt leans his bulk against the metal as his friend settles on the other side, hemming me in. "Hey, Delilah."

Fear spikes in my blood. Even though we're in the middle of the corridor and there are plenty of people walking past, I know better than to expect any of my classmates to jump in and help.

I learned that lesson the hard way while dating Jasper.

"What do you want?" It takes effort to keep the quiver from weaving its way through my voice.

He shrugs like we're good friends just standing around shooting the shit.

Nothing could be further from the truth.

My gaze stays pinned to Aiden. Out of the two boys, he's far more dangerous. The other one is a follower.

"Just wondering if you'd be interested in giving us a two-for-one special?" the other one asks. Barely contained laughter simmers in his voice. "We heard you enjoy a little swordplay in your mouth."

Aiden presses closer. "You've been a busy girl today. What happened in the bathroom during first hour sounds seriously hot. We just want in on the action. That's all."

I straighten my shoulders. "Fuck off and leave me alone."

"I'd much rather have you get me off instead."

With a growl, I shove my palms against Aiden's chest until he stumbles back a step. The amusement slides off his face as a nasty glint fills his eyes. When I rush forward to hit him again, his friend grabs me from behind and hauls me against his chest. His arms lock around me, holding me in place so that I can't get away.

Fear floods my system, mixing with the adrenaline spiking through my veins.

"You really think you're hot shit, don't you?" Aiden growls. "Maybe what you need is for someone to show you your place in this world. Especially here at Hawthorne Prep."

"Let me go," I yell, wriggling in his arms.

When they tighten around my ribs, I wince. Aiden takes a step toward me, and I brace for the pain he's sure to inflict.

"You touch one damn hair on her head, and I'll fucking wipe this floor with your ass."

Aiden falters, his gaze slicing from me to the newcomer. I don't think I've ever been so relieved to hear Austin's deep voice. My body wilts as my knees buckle.

When the guy behind me doesn't move, Austin growls, "Let her go or you'll deal with my fists."

He sets me free with a small shove that sends me pitching forward into the bank of lockers. Air rushes from my lungs as my cheek presses against the cool metal.

From the corner of my eye, I watch as Austin closes the distance between the two boys. Aiden straightens to his full height, which is still a handful of inches shorter than Austin. Neither is a match for him.

"Until further notice, Delilah is off limits. She belongs to me."

"But Jasper—"

"I don't give a fuck what Jasper says. He can take it up with me if he has a problem. Delilah is mine. No one touches her. Or talks to her. Don't even look in her direction. As far as you're concerned, she doesn't exist. If I find out that people are gossiping about her and spreading more rumors, they'll fucking answer to me. Do I make myself clear?"

He cracks his knuckles. The loud popping sound leaves me wincing.

"Now get the fuck out of here."

Aiden hesitates as his friend scurries out of Austin's sight.

"She's just a stupid whore," Aiden grumbles, clearly not happy to have his fun spoiled.

Austin steps closer, invading his personal space before murmuring fiercely, "Call her that again and you'll be picking up your teeth off the floor. Got it?"

Instead of answering, Aiden turns and glares at me before stalking down the hallway.

It's only when he disappears around the corner that I close my eyes and suck in a harsh breath to calm everything that rampages wildly within. Once my heart rate settles, I force them open again, prepared to have yet another run-in with Austin.

Except...I'm alone.

The hall is vacant.

I blink and wonder if him riding to the rescue was nothing more than a figment of my imagination.

Why would he care if someone else hurts me?

Especially when he wants to do the same.

Another handful of seconds pass before I shove myself away from the metal and grab my lunch from the locker, slamming the thin door closed. Before this incident, I was going to brave the cafeteria and hopefully find Duke.

Now…there's no way I can deal with everyone turning and staring at me. It's doubtful I could withstand the thirty minutes of torture without falling to pieces.

Swinging in the opposite direction, I hustle toward the photography studio on the other side of the school. As I step inside the spacious room filled with sunlight, I search the area for Mrs. Chambers, the head art teacher. The tension roiling around in the pit of my belly gradually dissolves when she sails out of her office near the back of the room in a long, flowing dress. The necklaces she wears around her neck clink together with every step. There's something calming about her presence.

Even though I'm self-conscious about the gossip buzzing around school, I beeline in her direction. "Hi, Mrs. Chambers."

She glances at me in surprise before a warm smile overtakes her features. "Hello, Delilah. I wasn't expecting to see you again so soon."

I shift from one foot to the other and blurt, "I was wondering if you'd be around during the lunch period?"

My mind reluctantly tumbles back to Jasper finding me alone in the studio and then cornering me. I don't want that to happen again.

"That was the plan." Her brow furrows as she tilts her head in question. "Is there something I can help you with?"

"I, um, thought I'd use this time to look over my portfolio for the spring show."

She nods in approval before tucking a stray lock of hair behind her ear. "That sounds like an excellent idea. If you'd like another opinion about some of the pieces, just ask."

"Thank you, I will." Relief floods through me.

As bold as Jasper's behavior has grown, he wouldn't dare lay a hand on me in front of an adult in a position of authority.

At least, I hope he wouldn't.

Except for the run-in before school this morning, I've been successful in avoiding my ex. I know his schedule by heart and have steered clear of the areas he usually lurks. The problem is that I won't be able to escape him forever.

Despite Austin's warning, Jasper does what he wants.

Takes what he wants.

And that includes me.

I set my lunch on one of the tables and then head over to my thick folder where my photographs are kept. Once settled on a stool, I carefully spread them out in front of me. Everything that happened this morning gradually drains away as I study the images.

This right here is my happy place.

If only it were possible to spend all of my time in this studio.

Or outside, searching for the perfect shot. I glance out the window with longing. It's such a beautiful day. The need to escape this prison floods through me. But I can't do that. It would only cause more problems with Mom.

Just as I refocus my attention, Everly and Summer step inside the studio. The dark-haired girl laughs at something her friend says before her green eyes land on me. That's all it takes for any lightheartedness simmering in her expression to vanish as her lips wilt at the corners. Even from here, the frostiness of her gaze freezes me to the core.

Much like Jasper, I've gone out of my way to avoid Austin's twin. I send up a little prayer, hoping she'll ignore me rather than engage in a confrontation. I don't think I can take much more before splintering apart into a million jagged pieces.

What's become obvious is that I'm public enemy number one at Hawthorne Prep. And the ones who don't consider me an adversary think I'm an easy target.

Instead of leaving, Summer pivots and stalks toward me. It would be impossible not to notice the way her hands clench and unclench at her sides. I've tangled with her enough these past few weeks to know that I'm about to get an earful.

Hopefully, that's all I'll get.

I tense, bracing for impact.

Three.

Two.

One.

"Seriously, what the hell is wrong with you?" she seethes, practically foaming at the mouth. "Why are you so intent on hurting my brother?"

Embarrassment heats my cheeks as I glance to where Mrs. Chambers was quietly working and realize that her desk is empty. She must have disappeared inside her office.

I shake my head. "No, that's not—"

Summer whips up a hand. I'm almost surprised when she doesn't eat up the distance between us and slap me across the cheek.

"I don't want to hear it. I saw the pics." She lowers her face to mine and growls, "I was there when you sent them to Austin."

The image of that scenario actually playing out leaves me squirming. It's not difficult to understand why he's so angry and desperate to lash out and inflict damage.

After everything we went through and all the promises that were made, it would cut to the bone.

"I never sent them to Austin."

Her expression turns incredulous as she arches a slim brow. "Is that supposed to make it better?"

I squeeze my eyes tightly closed for a moment and attempt to organize my thoughts. "What I meant to say is that I wasn't with Jasper at the party and I never cheated on Austin. I...I don't know what happened Friday night."

Her brows slam together as her upper lip curls in disgust. "What do you mean? Were you seriously that drunk? Because guess what? It's not an excuse for hooking up with your ex."

"No," I blurt desperately. "I don't remember having any drinks. We arrived at the party and were outside for a while." I scour my brain, trying to figure out where everything went so wrong. Where the memories should be, it's blank. I jerk my shoulders in frustration. "I don't remember much after that. All I know is that I woke up in Duke's bed the next morning."

"Duke's bed?" Everly's gaze sharpens. "You slept with him?"

"Of course not."

Summer snorts.

"Then how did you end up spending the night with Duke?" the auburn-haired girl asks.

I drag a hand over my face. "I don't know. He found me passed out in Kingsley's game room and took me back to his house to sleep it off."

"But you just said that you can't remember what happened. So, for all you know, you were with both of them." Disgust flashes across Summer's expression.

My mouth turns cottony. "Duke and I are friends. That's it."

"Sure." Her tone is riddled with disbelief as she draws out the word. "From what I hear, you're," she lifts her hands and makes air quotes with her fingers, "*friends* with a lot of guys around here."

"That's not true."

Ironically, all I've done the entire time I've been at HP is keep to myself. Instead of opening her eyes and considering for a moment that Jasper has been pulling strings like a puppet master, everyone wants to believe the worst in me. My shoulders slump under the heavy weight of the realization that arguing with Summer, or anyone else, is futile.

"Sure seems like it." Dismissing me with a cold look, Summer swivels toward her friend. "I know we came here so you could talk with Mrs. Chambers, but I can't be in the same room with this girl or I'm going to lose it."

Barely do the words escape from her mouth before she spins on her heel and storms from the art studio.

With a sigh, Everly watches her friend disappear before turning her attention to me. After a handful of silent seconds, her expression softens. "I'm sorry. I didn't mean to imply anything about you and Duke. I know you're friends."

"That's all we are," I reiterate before popping a brow. "Although, why would it matter if I slept with him? I was under the impression that you didn't like the guy."

"I don't," she shoots back quickly.

Too quickly.

"But you care if I spent the night in his bed?"

A splash of color hits her cheeks as she averts her eyes. Ignoring the question, she mutters, "Like Summer, I don't want to see Austin get hurt. He's my friend too."

Instead of pursuing the topic, I release a steady breath. "I know."

Her gaze flickers to the last place we saw Summer. "After everything that happened at the fundraiser and then those pics...you can understand why she's pissed, right?"

Of course I do.

It looks bad.

Really bad.

"I promise I'm not with Jasper. I broke off our relationship before the charity event. He pretended to accept it and said we could still be friends and then he..." My voice trails off. "Humiliated Austin in front of everyone." I shake my head and force myself to continue. "He refuses to let me go. Everything he's done...it's to make my life miserable so I crawl back to him. And Friday night was just another twist in the game he's playing. Whatever happened to me, there's no doubt in my mind that Jasper is somehow behind it."

Shock fills her eyes. "What a douchebag. I never understood why the two of you were together in the first place."

"I don't know," I mutter. It feels as if that decision will haunt me for the rest of my life.

He's never going to stop.

Not while we're attending Hawthorne Prep.

After a few silent moments, Everly clears her throat. "You really don't remember those pictures being taken?"

As much as I hate the doubt that flickers across her expression, I can't blame her for being skeptical. If this were happening to someone else, I'm not sure I would believe them either. It all seems farfetched.

"No, I don't. I look at them and it's like I'm staring at a stranger."

My fingers rise to massage my temples where a headache brews. "Honestly, it would be so much easier if I did. Then I could take responsibility for making a crappy decision and fucking up."

Instead, my memories are a blank canvas.

And that's the scariest part of all.

DELILAH

$\mathcal{J}$f I'd been holding out hope that Mom would change her mind at the very last minute and refuse to let me attend the camping trip, that's no longer a possibility. Since Duke is supposed to pick me up in ten minutes, my guess is that I'm stuck with my classmates for three grueling days. I can only liken it to being trapped in a room with feral animals, all the while praying I make it out alive.

Am I being a tad bit dramatic?

Maybe.

Then again, maybe not.

I've been assigned to Kingsley's house with Summer, Austin, and a bunch of other people. Even though it's not a good situation by any stretch of the imagination, it's better than getting stuck at Jasper's vacation house. Dread snakes its way down my spine. I can only guess at the diabolical plans he'd have in store for me if that were the case.

"I swear to god, Delilah Rose, you'd better behave on this trip," Mom grumbles as I reluctantly drop my duffle bag near the front door. "If I catch even a whiff of impropriety, you can kiss the rest of senior year goodbye." She glares before planting her fists on slender hips. "You've really pushed me to my limit this week. I can't take much more of your out-of-control behavior. I'm not sure why you're trying to force me over the edge, but trust me, I'm already there." Her voice wobbles on the last syllable.

Even though it's tempting to argue, I find myself saying, "I'm sorry, Mom." The last thing I want to do is cause her any more grief or heartache. She's been through more than enough.

Instead of accepting my apology and softening her stance, she swings around and stalks to her bedroom without another word. Just as I'm about to turn away, resigning myself to the thick tension that's now a part of our relationship, she wheels out a small red suitcase.

My brows pinch together, thrown off by this new development. She never mentioned a word about taking off for the weekend. "Are you going somewhere?"

She stops in her tracks as a scowl settles over her pinched features. "That's none of your business. It's high time you start remembering that *you're* the child and *I'm* the parent. Unlike you, I don't need to ask for permission."

Every conversation with her feels like a battle and I hate it. I have enough to contend with at school. Instead of home being a safe refuge, it's the furthest thing from it.

"I know," I say with a sigh. "It's just that you didn't mention anything about going away for the weekend."

Her shoulders loosen incrementally as a painful silence stretches between us. Just when I think she won't bother with a response, she grudgingly admits, "Edmund booked us a room at a quaint little bed and breakfast in the country. I thought it might be nice to get away and relax. I haven't been on a trip since…"

Her voice trails off and I realize that we're both remembering Dad.

She clears her throat and glances away. "Anyway, I thought we could both benefit from getting out of Hawthorne for a couple of days. Maybe when you get back, we can sit down and talk about everything that's been going on." There's a pause. "We can't keep going like this."

"I know."

Her lips quirk slightly at the corners. Just when I think her expression will soften and she might even pull me in for a hug, she grumbles,

"I'm serious about what I said, Delilah. You need to be on your best behavior."

"I will, promise. You don't have anything to worry about."

Doubt flickers across her expression as there's a blare of a horn from the driveway. For a moment, I hesitate before rushing forward and throwing my arms around her slender shoulders. We've always been so close. Especially after Dad died. I don't want this tension to continue tainting our relationship.

Mom holds me close before whispering, "I love you, Delilah."

For the first time in almost a week, everything inside me loosens as my grip tightens. "I love you, too."

"Please spend some time thinking about the decisions you've been making and the path you're on."

"I will." It's on the tip of my tongue to tell her to enjoy her impromptu vacay except...I just can't force myself to say the words. She's spending the weekend with a married man. At some point, it's going to end and she'll be devastated. I don't believe for a single moment that Pembroke has any intention of leaving his wife.

My arms loosen before I gradually retreat. With a wave, I pick up my bag and open the door before stepping onto the tiny front stoop. As soon as I do, I realize that the vehicle idling in the driveway isn't Duke's pickup truck.

It's Austin's black G-wagon.

That's all it takes for a trapdoor to spring open, and then I'm in freefall. Our gazes collide through the windshield as I remain frozen in place.

It's only when the driver's side door opens and Austin steps out of the expensive SUV that I come alive. He's wearing dark wash jeans that hug his muscular thighs and a black hoodie with the name of his previous high school in Chicago stamped across the front in big bold letters.

My heart trips and my mouth turns cottony as the space between us disappears.

"Duke was supposed to pick me up," I whisper as a thin waver weaves its way through my voice. Images from Monday in the girls' bathroom flash through my brain like a slow-motion picture show.

Me on my knees.

Him pumping his thick cock.

Ropes of pearly cum decorating my chest.

Heat scalds my cheeks as I push those thoughts away.

Thankfully, I was able to avoid him for the rest of the week. I took alternative routes in an attempt to avoid both him and Jasper. I spent my lunch break in the photography studio, working on my art exhibit portfolio.

"There's been a change in plans," he says, leaning down to pick up my bag before stalking to the Mercedes. With one click of the key fob, the hatch opens and he tosses my duffle inside before walking back to the driver's side door and staring at me.

My mind somersaults, trying to come up with a reason as to why this arrangement won't work. Seconds tick by and my brain remains frustratingly blank. It's bad enough that we'll be forced to spend the next seventy-two hours under the same roof, but being trapped in the stifling confines of his vehicle with him?

It will be nothing short of torture.

When I don't make a move toward the SUV, he jerks a brow. "You gonna get in or what?"

The way his green depths burn into mine has my skin prickling with awareness. Even though I try to resist the urge, I shift under his penetrating gaze. My eyes flicker away before being reluctantly drawn back again. "I'd rather ride with Duke."

Anger cracks in his eyes like lightning. The force of it is enough to have me taking a hasty step in retreat. "Luckily for you, he's in the backseat. His truck wouldn't turn over this morning."

Oh.

My shoulders slump with the realization that my fate has been sealed and I force my feet into movement. Every step feels like a slow march to my death. As I pull up along the passenger side door, I catch sight of someone already sitting there.

A girl.

She flashes me a bright smile as our gazes lock through the tinted window.

Aubrey.

My attention jerks to Austin in silent question.

"You'll have to sit in the back," he says with a grunt.

I should be relieved not to be up front with him.

So…why aren't I?

I scrape my teeth across my lower lip before grabbing the handle and yanking it open. A burst of air escapes from my lungs as I find Duke and Everly sitting in the second row. Out of all my classmates, these are the only two I can count as friends.

Duke scowls at Everly for a long, silent moment as if they were just in the middle of an argument. It's only when he drags his gaze from her and meets mine that his expression softens.

Marginally.

"Hey," he says.

"Hi. I heard your truck wouldn't start this morning."

He jerks his shoulders and mutters, "It's a piece of shit. Hopefully, my brother will take a look at it this weekend and it'll be a quick fix."

I nod before peeking around him to find the auburn-haired girl. She gives me a tight smile before glaring at the muscular boy taking up space next to her.

"Hey, Everly."

"Hi. I'm glad you're riding up with us."

"Me, too." It would be so much worse if I were alone with Austin.

I slide onto the plush seat and slam the door shut, locking the five of us in together. As soon as I fasten the seatbelt, Austin reverses the G-wagon from the driveway. Music fills the luxurious cabin, vibrating through the speakers as we roll through the tiny town. It doesn't take long for the brick buildings to give way to the wide openness of the countryside. Another ten minutes and we're pulling onto the highway and making our way to the eastern side of the state. Aubrey keeps up a steady stream of chatter as Austin focuses on the ribbon of road beyond the windshield. It would be difficult not to notice the way her hand constantly flutters to his thigh.

Or bicep.

I can't stop staring.

Each time I make a concerted effort to drag my gaze away, it eventually meanders back to him. The most ridiculous part of this situation is that it shouldn't bother me one bit what Austin does or who he does it with.

We're not in a relationship.

We're…

I don't even know what we are.

Nothing.

We're nothing.

He's blackmailing me.

Punishing me for something I had no control over.

That's the extent of our relationship.

My gaze flickers to the rearview mirror and collides with Austin's. The steely look in his eyes is enough to have my belly hollowing out. I force my attention to the window and try not to think about the long, three-hour ride stretched out in front of us.

It's going to be hell.

Duke gently bumps my shoulder with his larger one.

When I glance at him, he raises his brows and asks in a low tone that only I can hear, "Are you doing all right? You've been awfully quiet."

My attention reluctantly slides to the rearview mirror and electricity sizzles through my veins when our gazes lock. I jerk mine away before I can get sucked into Austin's green depths and focus on the boy beside me.

I force a smile. "I'm fine."

This trip would be unbearable if he weren't here, and for that, I'm grateful. My plan is to spend most of my time hanging out with Duke and avoiding everyone else. Maybe walk the beach and take a bunch of pictures. If there's a bright spot to be found in all this, it's the plentiful photo opportunities the sandy shoreline will present.

"Seems like the gossip has died down." There's a pause. "At least a little bit."

I shrug. Even though I try not to pay attention, people were still salivating over the pics yesterday. Maybe not as much as Monday morning, but I was still getting sly looks aimed in my direction when I walked through the halls.

What I will say is that Aiden and his douchebag cronies have gone stereo silent. They turn their backs when they catch sight of me. And a few of Jasper's friends who continued to shout out lewd comments in the corridors showed up later during the week with blackened eyes.

Has Austin made good on his threat?

I don't know.

It's just a relief to be left alone.

Everly gives us a bit of side eye as we talk before turning away and staring out the window at the passing farmland. She doesn't seem any happier about being stuck here than I am. Now that I think about it, I would have expected her to ride up with Summer and Kingsley.

After two hours on the road, Austin pulls off the highway and into a gas station. Once he kills the engine, he exits the vehicle and everyone else does the same, stretching their legs and heading inside to either use the restroom or buy snacks.

Aubrey and Everly use the single stall room first. When it's my turn, I lock the door and take care of business before washing my hands. So far, the ride has been tolerable. Instead of watching Aubrey attempt to draw Austin into conversation, I've found myself staring out the window at the pretty scenery that flies by.

Maybe I jumped the gun, and this weekend won't be so bad after all.

As I unlock the door and pull it open, a squeak of surprise escapes from me when I find the very person I was just thinking about looming on the other side of the threshold. My eyes widen and my pulse picks up its tempo when he steps toward me, invading my personal space. I retreat with the need to keep a safe amount of distance between us.

Except...is that even possible?

By the harsh look marring his expression, I don't think so.

"What are you doing?" It takes every bit of self-control to keep the quaver from invading my voice and revealing my inner turmoil.

"Giving you a friendly reminder as to who owns you."

My mouth turns cottony as I swallow down my nerves. "That's not necessary."

"Oh, but I think it is, and that's all that matters."

His fingers lock around my bicep before forcing me inside the cramped space. He releases one arm long enough to slam the door shut, making escape impossible. Once the lock clicks into place, he steers me backward until I'm pressed against the wall.

It's only when I've been caged by his bigger body that his hands slide from my upper arms to my wrists. A shiver of arousal dances down my spine as he drags them above my head and pins them in place. My back arches and my breasts thrust outward until the tips are pressed against the sinewy strength of his chest.

My nipples tighten into hard little points. By the darkening of his eyes, my body's response doesn't escape him. Heat scalds my cheeks as I fight the humiliation and keep my chin lifted.

My reaction to him is always the same.

Instantaneous.

Like a punch to the gut.

It doesn't give me much hope for the future.

Air escapes from my lungs in harsh pants. The sound of it echoes in my ears, drowning out everything else.

He smirks. "Already turned on, aren't you?"

Dark desire ignites in his eyes. The various shades of gold and green are almost mesmerizing in their intensity. It wouldn't take much to fall and drown within the fathomless pools. There are times when I wonder if it might be easier that way. To simply lose myself and never surface again. It takes effort to force those disconcerting thoughts from my brain.

He abruptly kicks my feet apart before shoving his thigh between my legs until it's wedged against my core. A whimper of need escapes from me at the firm contact as my clit throbs an insistent beat.

"You didn't answer the question."

No…I didn't.

And I don't plan to. He knows exactly how he affects me. My admittance would only give him more ammunition.

When I remain silent, he nips my lower lip between his teeth, tugging on it until pain flares to life. With our gazes locked, we remain motionless. It's almost a surprise when pleasure blooms in its place, smothering the momentary discomfort.

With one last pull, he releases the soft flesh and I sag against his thigh. I have no idea if it's relief or disappointment that courses through me, and that's the problem. It shouldn't be necessary to fight my feelings for Austin. They should have been snuffed out by his reprehensible treatment this previous week.

What does it mean that they're not?

Unwilling to dwell on those disturbing thoughts, I quickly shove them to the back of my mind. What I need to do is find a way to untangle myself from him once and for all. I can't afford to get wrapped up in someone who only wants to inflict as much damage as possible.

Austin might not realize it, but he has the power to destroy me. My feelings for him run so much deeper than they did for Jasper. The connection between us is undeniable.

Unbreakable.

It's as if we're bound together by an invisible thread. What scares me most is that I'll never be able to fight my way free of this unwanted bond.

"Know what you're gonna do?" There's a beat of silence before he continues. "Ride my thigh until you come."

My eyes flare wide. "What?"

"You heard me," he growls. "I want you to come right here and now while everyone sits in the SUV and wonders where we are."

I shake my head almost frantically. "Please, no."

He presses more insistently against my core, moving it just enough to cause friction. The unwanted sensation reverberates throughout my being.

"Austin…"

"We're not leaving until you *come*. I don't care how long it takes."

Oh god.

Unable to hold myself still, I flex my hips against the thickness of his thigh. The slide of him beneath me is all it takes to have another burst of arousal exploding inside me.

"That's it, sweet girl. Hump my leg."

The husky comment should embarrass me. And on some level, it does. It's mortifying to be reduced to a quivering mass of hormones and commanded to orgasm. But that's not nearly enough to stop me from seeking out my release, and I find myself grinding against him as instinct takes over.

My arms are still locked above my head and his thigh is pressed against me as I hump his leg, just like he demanded. It doesn't take long for my muscles to tighten. And then I'm exploding, moaning out my orgasm. My hips continue to buck until the last shudder has been wrung from me and I wilt against him.

"Tell me, Delilah," he whispers harshly in my ear.

No further explanation is necessary.

"I belong to you."

"That's right. And just like I told you before, I'll you use you any damn time I want. Understand?"

"Yes."

"Good."

He crushes his body against mine until I feel the thick length of his erection pressing insistently against me. Our gazes cling for a long heartbeat before he steps away and slips from the cramped space. As I attempt to find my bearings, my attention lands on Aubrey, who loiters outside the restroom.

The moment our gazes catch, she frowns and swings around, taking off after Austin. My hands shake as I tuck an errant lock of hair behind my ear and draw in an unsteady breath.

I can't help but wonder how I'll make it through this weekend intact.

Perhaps the real question is *if* I'll make it through this weekend.

DELILAH

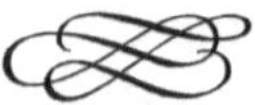

By the time we pull up in front of the massive, two-story beach house, I'm more than ready to escape the suffocating confines of the SUV. I need a little breathing room to find my equilibrium. The intensity of Austin's dark gaze watching my every move through the rearview mirror the past couple hours has set my nerves on edge.

The five of us exit the vehicle as Austin pops the hatch and pulls out the suitcases. No surprise, Aubrey has the most luggage with three oversized Louis Vuitton bags. Everyone else has one. When I lean over to pick up mine, Duke grabs the thick strap along with his own.

"I've got it," he tells me, gently knocking my hand away.

"Are you sure?"

He flashes a rare smile. "Yup. No problem."

From the corner of my eye, I watch the muscle in the other boy's jaw tic.

"Would you mind helping with my bags, Austin?" Aubrey flutters her mascara-laden lashes in his direction. "They're so heavy."

He rips his narrowed gaze from me before focusing on the girl at his side. "Yeah, sure."

With an overly bright smile beamed in his direction, she steps closer and lays a hand on his bicep. "You're just so big and strong. It must be from all the working out you do. I'd love to start weightlifting. Maybe when we return to Hawthorne, we could do it together and you can show me some of your moves."

Her double meaning isn't lost on me.

Or, apparently, Duke.

With a roll of his whiskey-colored eyes, he heads up the front porch stairs. I ignore the couple and trail after him, wanting to put as much distance as I can between myself and Austin.

I'm sure Aubrey will continue vying for his attention throughout the long weekend. Maybe it would be better for everyone involved if he turned his interest elsewhere. That thought has an unwanted prick of jealousy blooming to life inside me and I quickly stomp it out, not wanting to dwell on it.

"Guess that leaves me to grab my own bag," Everly mutters, picking up her suitcase and dragging it to the porch.

"I'll take your bag," I say with a small smile.

She snorts. "Nah, I'm good."

As soon as Duke throws open the heavy front door, raised voices and laughter greet our ears. By the number of cars parked in the drive, we're probably the last ones to arrive.

My belly trembles at the thought of who might be waiting inside. Especially since Aubrey is staying at Kingsley's and not with Sloane and the rest of the crew at Jasper's, which means there's a good chance I'll run into them this weekend.

No matter where I go, Jasper will find a way to wreak havoc. It's what he does best. The thought of having to be constantly on guard or fighting him off is exhausting.

There's only one thing I'm looking forward to, and that's walking the beach and snapping photographs. This is my first time visiting Lake Michigan, and I can't wait to get out and explore the area. I've done a little research online, and from what I can tell, the sandy dunes are beautiful and there's a lighthouse within walking distance.

The point of this retreat might be to bond with my classmates, but that's the last thing on my mind. All I need to do is make it through this weekend without any further incidents. With any luck, life will once again return to normal. It's the only hope I have to cling to at this point.

As I step inside the double story foyer, my gaze bounces around the spacious interior, attempting to take everything in at once. The walls are painted in muted tones of sea glass, and there's a sparkling crystal chandelier hanging from the ceiling. Plush runners cover both the curving staircase that leads to the second floor and the ocean of hardwood that stretches throughout the hallway. I've only taken a few steps inside his home, but it's obvious that Kingsley's beach house is just as luxurious as his mansion in Hawthorne.

It's only when Duke grinds to a halt and drops our bags in the living room that I find a dozen or so people sitting around, drinking and smoking weed.

Aubrey squeals when she spots a few friends. I hold my breath and scan the sea of familiar faces, relieved that Sloane and Jasper are conspicuously absent. Austin sets her bags down before heading outside to grab his own. His gaze flickers to mine before he disappears down the hallway. I release a pent-up breath as my shoulders loosen.

"Since everyone's here, we can talk about the room arrangements," Kingsley says, raising his voice to be heard over the music and chatter.

Other than Everly, there aren't any other girls I'd want to bunk with. I'm praying that we'll end up together. My gaze flickers to Austin's twin, only to find her watching me with narrowed eyes. Our conversation from the photography studio pops into my brain, along with the loathing that had flashed in her green depths.

It's almost difficult to believe that a few short weeks ago, we were friends. Maybe we weren't hanging out, but she's someone I would have liked to get to know better. With everything that's occurred, there's no chance of that happening.

I rip my gaze away from hers as the room assignments are handed out. The beach house has six bedrooms and an array of couches.

Kingsley and Summer take his suite.

Aubrey is given a guest room.

"Delilah and I can share one," Duke pipes up.

I nod, grateful that he's looking out for me. If I can't share with Everly, then Duke is the next best option.

Kingsley shrugs. "Sure—"

"That's not happening. Delilah stays with me."

My head whips toward Austin in shock as he returns from retrieving the last of the bags and drops his duffle to the floor. Nausea explodes in the pit of my belly as our gazes collide. I don't realize I'm shaking my head until his eyes narrow as if daring me to voice the protests that have gathered on the tip of my tongue.

Kingsley flicks a look in my direction. "Does that work for you?"

Tell him no.

Say it.

But if I do that…he'll divulge Mom's secret. If these people find out about her and Pembroke, it'll only exacerbate the situation. The affair between the married headmaster and widowed secretary will make the pictures look like nothing.

I can't deal with anything else falling apart.

Do I have any other choice but to jerk my head into a nod?

Summer shoots me a scowl before stomping over to her brother. Her displeasure echoes throughout the room with each footfall.

"We need to talk in private."

Before he can respond, she shackles her fingers around his wrist and drags him into the kitchen. If I didn't feel so sick inside, the image of Summer forcing her six-foot tall brother into the other room would bring a smile to my lips.

Even with twenty feet of space to separate us, I'm still able to hear the low hum of their conversation. I might not be able to pick up on specific words, but it's obvious Summer is pissed.

With any luck, she'll talk her brother out of going through with this arrangement and forcing me to share space with him. The thought of sleeping in the same bed given the way he feels about me, the way he's laid his hands on my body, is enough to have my belly hollowing out.

"You should have told him to fuck off," Duke growls.

If only that were possible.

It's tempting to pull the muscular lacrosse player aside and confess the truth, but I know it'll only piss him off more, and I don't want to cause further problems between these two. There's already enough tension swirling through the atmosphere to choke on. The last thing I want is for them to get into a fight.

"It's not a big deal," I say in a hushed tone.

"The hell it is. It'll be easier if we just share a room."

Of course it would be, but that's not an option.

I recognize it even if Duke doesn't.

Before I can figure out a way to alleviate his concern, firm hands settle on my shoulders and I'm yanked against a hard chest. I don't have to turn around to know who holds me captive.

"You need to mind your own fucking business, Carmichael."

Duke straightens to his full height as his eyes harden. "Delilah *is* my business."

Austin stiffens, his muscles tensing as if preparing for battle. "Oh yeah, and why's that?"

I press my back against Austin as if it's possible for me to keep him and Duke from coming to blows.

"Because we're friends," he growls, taking a step in our direction.

My eyes widen, silently pleading with Duke to back off.

"Maybe the problem is that you wish it were more. Seems like you're always there, waiting for a chance to ride to the rescue."

Duke's upper lip curls as his eyes stay locked on Austin's. "Fuck off."

"Stay out of my shit and I will. Delilah and I are sharing a room. If she doesn't have a problem with it, then neither should you."

Duke glares at him for a long, silent moment before his gaze resettles on mine and his voice softens. "Are you sure about this? I'm telling you right now that you don't have to stay with him."

I'm hyperaware of Austin's fingers biting into the tops of my shoulders and the firmness of his chest pressed against my spine. "It's fine, promise."

Suspicion flickers in his whiskey-colored eyes. I force a smile, only wanting to deescalate the suffocating tension that hangs heavy in the air. Even the people sitting around and toking up have taken notice of the drama.

He presses his lips together as if he wants to continue arguing. It's a relief when he says, "If you change your mind, let me know."

"She won't," Austin growls in response.

"Looks like there's just one room left," Kingsley says, drawing everyone's attention to him.

Everly pales and sends a pleading look to Summer.

"Can't we reshuffle the arrangements or something?" Summer's gaze flickers toward Aubrey. "Maybe you could switch with Duke and share with Everly."

The other girl wrinkles her nose as if she just walked past a port-o-potty that's been baking under the hot August sun. "No, thanks. I'll keep my single bed. Plus, I might want to have a guest spend the night." She smirks at Everly. "Sorry."

"No, you're not," Everly grumbles.

Aubrey flashes a grin. "You caught me, I'm not."

"All right, I guess we should get settled in and then we'll meet on the beach in a couple of hours for a bonfire and a little bonding," Kingsley cuts in.

Just when I think Austin will release me, his grip tightens and he drags me closer. His warm breath drifts across the outer shell of my ear, sending a shiver dancing down the length of my spine.

"Did you seriously think I'd allow you to sleep in the same bed with him?"

Air gets wedged in the middle of my throat.

"Whether I fuck you or not, no one touches my property. Got it?"

"Yes."

My body wilts when he finally sets me free, and it takes a second to steady myself. After the room clears out, I pick up my bag and make my way to the second floor. As I step into the spacious bedroom decorated in blue tones with cream colored furniture, I glance around and find the bathroom door closed.

I set my duffle near the end of the king-sized bed and rummage through it to find my father's old Nikon. Once it's in hand, I fly out the door and into the hallway.

Even though I realize there's no way to avoid Austin for the duration of our stay, especially with us sharing not only a room, but a bed, I'll take any opportunity to put off another confrontation until later.

As I race down the staircase, I pass by a small group of classmates mixing drinks in the kitchen. I don't say a word as I beeline for the backdoor. It's only when I step outside into the fresh air that I release the breath held hostage in my lungs.

The cool breeze wafts against my cheeks as it whips through my hair. A prick of excitement blooms in my belly as my attention fastens on the horizon and the deep blue waves that roll toward the sandy shoreline.

It's a breathtaking sight.

That's all it takes for my tangled thoughts of Austin to gradually fade. I peel back the soft cover of the bag and carefully pull the camera free from its case before adjusting the lens and snapping a few shots. Everything inside me loosens as I kick off my shoes and allow my toes to sink into the damp sand.

The beauty of the landscape, painted in various shades of tan and blue, does the impossible and lifts my mood. For a few precious hours, I cling to the feeling, knowing there's no way it will last.

DELILAH

$\mathcal{B}$y the time I return to the house, dusk has fallen, and everyone is gathered in the kitchen, eating dinner. Pizza has been delivered and there are at least half a dozen open boxes. The delectable aroma of mozzarella, sauce, and pepperoni hits me, tantalizing my senses. When my belly rumbles, I realize it's been a while since I ate.

After walking the beach for hours, I'm famished. My gaze lifts, immediately settling on Austin at the far end of the table. The way his eyes stay pinned to mine is enough to have my appetite pulling a disappearing act. Instead of grabbing a plate and helping myself to the food spread out on the marble island, I comb my fingers through my windswept hair and duck upstairs.

When I'd jogged across the dunes to the house, a handful of guys were already gathering driftwood to use for the bonfire. It won't be long before everyone heads outside for the evening. I'm sure other classmates staying at nearby houses will venture over.

Ever since I started at Hawthorne Prep, hushed rumors have swirled about how rowdy and out of control the annual senior camping trip can get. Since I want nothing to do with it, sticking close to Duke in order to avoid Austin and Jasper will be my best bet. As much as I hate the idea of dragging him further into my problems, he's the only one I trust.

By the time I wash up and throw on a sweatshirt, the sun has dipped beneath the horizon. The house is oddly quiet instead of bursting with voices and noise. It would seem as if everyone has abandoned the structure in favor of the beach.

As soon as I step foot out the backdoor, music and laughter drift to me on the wind. The closer I get, the louder it becomes. Once I've crested the dune, my feet stutter to a gradual halt as I scan the area. While there are only about a dozen classmates staying at Kingsley's, there have to be at least fifty people gathered around the orange flames. The scent of weed hangs heavy in the air. Everyone is dancing and drinking, living their best lives with abandon.

For just a moment, I consider retreating inside to the relative safety of my bedroom, unsure if I want to join the fray. My mind tumbles back to what happened the last time I was around these people in a party atmosphere. And that's possibly drugged with hours of blank space that I'm unable to remember.

It's a relief when I spot Duke in a sea of faces and make my way toward him. He's talking with a couple of lacrosse teammates. Once I'm within striking distance, he slips an arm around my body and tugs me close.

Every so often, I notice him glance across the fire at Everly. I really don't understand the issue between them. What I've noticed is that Duke deliberately goes out of his way to poke and prod at her. During the drive this afternoon, he was antagonistic and rude. She alternated between ignoring him and hissing like a pissed-off cat.

When his eyes narrow and muscles tense, I follow his line of sight and find Jacob Littleton talking with Everly. She flashes a smile as they flirt.

With a tilt of my head, I ask, "What's your problem with her?"

His attention slides to me for a heartbeat before bouncing back to the auburn-haired girl. "There's no problem. I just don't like her."

I roll my eyes.

Exactly who does he think he's fooling?

"Yeah, you've made that completely clear. What I don't understand is the reason for it. She's super nice." One of the few people who have been kind to me, and the fact that she's friends with Summer makes her position more tenuous. It would've been so easy for her to jump on the other girl's side.

But she hasn't done that. She's remained impartial, walking a fine line between the two of us.

Duke presses his lips into a tight line as he glares across the flickering fire. Rather than respond to my question, he mutters, "I don't know what Littleton thinks he's doing over there."

Through the orange flames that twist toward the sky, I catch glimpses of their smiles. "My guess is that he's hoping to get lucky."

Duke's upper lip curls as a crack of anger flashes in his eyes. "That's not going to happen."

"Oh?" My brows rise. "And why is that?"

"Because we're shacking up for the weekend, and situations that include two dicks and one chick have never been my scene."

I shake my head and suppress the smile that twitches around the corners of my lips. It feels so good to joke around and loosen up with someone. When was the last time I did that?

I can't remember. It feels like forever.

"Do you want my opinion?" I ask tentatively.

"Not really." Moonlight dances over his blond hair as he lifts a bottle of beer to his mouth and takes a swig.

With a shrug, I say, "Well, I'm going to give it to you anyway."

He jerks a brow as his gaze lands on me. One side of his mouth hitches with a smile. I'm struck again by how good-looking Duke is. Especially when he loosens up, which doesn't happen often.

It's too bad. He would be so much more approachable if he'd stop scowling all the time.

"Then why did you ask?"

I roll my eyes and continue. "I think if you gave Everly a chance, you'd discover that she's not the girl you think she is."

All of his humor falls away as his jaw tightens and the muscle in his cheek tics a mad rhythm. "That's doubtful. She's *exactly* who I think she is."

I'm about to say more when a chill zips down my spine and goosebumps break out along my arms. My hands rise, running over the length in an attempt to ward off the cool night air before glancing around. I don't realize who I'm searching for until our gazes collide. Air gets clogged in my chest, making it impossible to breathe as my gaze is ensnared by his. It only takes a moment or two for the bonfire and all the revelers surrounding it to melt away.

The temptation to close the distance that separates us pounds through me like a steady drumbeat. It fills my ears and rushes through my body until it's the only thing I'm cognizant of. Life would be so much easier if he didn't have this effect on me.

That, unfortunately, is not the case. All I can do is hope that these feelings gradually wither and die over time. If not, senior year will be even more miserable than it currently is.

It's only when he averts his eyes, releasing me from his penetrating stare, that I realize he isn't alone. Aubrey is curled up against his side and one muscular arm is slung around her shoulders.

Was it really only a week ago that he held me the same way?

That silent question cuts to the bone and has a dull ache flaring to life in my chest.

Maybe venturing out here wasn't such a good idea after all. I would have been better off locked in my bedroom and reading a book. Instead of turning away, I force myself to watch as her palms stroke up and down his chest before she presses closer. The orange flames flicker and dance, giving me a clear view before hiding the couple.

I hate myself for the hot licks of jealousy that rush through every fiber of my being.

Stop staring.

Look away.

But I can't.

"Instead of trying to punish you for the pictures, he needs to get over it and move the fuck on. He's taking his dickishness to a whole new level," Duke mutters, deep voice breaking into the turmoil of my thoughts and yanking me back to the present.

That's not going to happen.

"At some point, he will," I say softly, hoping it's the truth.

His gaze burns into mine. "He's a fucking idiot for thinking you'd do anything with Jasper after all the rumors he's been spreading."

My shoulders fall as a reluctant sigh escapes from me. "Too much has happened for him to believe the truth."

Duke tugs me close and presses a brief kiss against the crown of my head. "He's missing out, and by the time he realizes it, it'll be too late."

The indisputable truth is that there will never be a time for us. My heart clenches at the realization that Austin and I were over before we ever had a chance to start.

"Thanks," I say with a small smile. "You're a good friend."

Even though I try to avert my gaze, it reluctantly meanders back to Austin. His eyes are narrowed, and his lips are smashed together in a thin line as he glares through the flames. Aubrey reaches up on the tips of her toes and whispers something in his ear. He rips his gaze from mine before staring down at her.

With a grin, she wraps her fingers around his wrist and takes a step before tugging his hand. With one final glare in my direction, he turns away, disappearing into the velvety darkness that presses in at the edges.

Before I have a chance to think about what I'm doing, I untangle myself from Duke's arms and take off after them.

"Hey," he calls after me. "Where are you going?"

I pause, throwing a glance over my shoulder. "To grab a drink. I'll be back in a sec."

Even though there's only firelight for illumination, it would be impossible to miss the concern that flashes across his face, and I know he's thinking about what happened at the party in Hawthorne. "Want me to come with you?"

I shake my head and force a smile. "No, I'll be back in a sec."

Before Duke can take matters into his own hands, I swing away and weave through the throng of writhing bodies, searching each face for one in particular. Every step has my heartbeat ratcheting up, becoming more of a painful tattoo against my chest, until it feels as if it's thudding in my ears.

Part of me wonders what the hell I'm doing.

Am I really chasing after Austin?

Clearly, he's taken off with another girl. If I were smart, I'd put a stop to this madness and make my way back to Duke. Better yet, I'd return to the safety of the house before more damage can be inflicted. Maybe if Austin and Aubrey get together, he'll forget about me and his plans for revenge.

I pause as that thought ricochets through my brain.

That's what I want, right?

It's what I *should* want.

But do I?

No.

I almost wince at the tiny voice at the back of my head.

Before I can talk myself out of this madness, I search the beach, looking for the couple. After ten minutes, it's obvious that they're no longer here. For all I know, they returned to the house and are getting it on. As I continue to scan the area, I notice a small patch of woods on the side of the mansion. There are a few couples sitting in the sand and making out.

All right…maybe they're doing a little more than just kissing.

A heated groan fills the air before getting whisked away by the breeze. Heat scalds my cheeks as I look away. Instead of scampering back to safety, I jog past them until I reach the tree line. Now that I'm away from the beach, the music and voices become muted. It's more of a murmur that mingles with the waves washing up against the shore and the wind that whips through the treetops. The darkness appears thick and velvety enough to touch without the bright glow of the fire to soften it.

Stepping farther into the small patch of woods, I reach out and shove a slim branch to the side before ducking beneath it. I hesitate and squint, examining the area for the slightest movement. It's impossible to see more than twenty feet in front of me.

I take another step and pause, cocking my head.

There's no way they came here. It's way too creepy. They're probably back at the house and Austin is screwing her in the bed we're supposed to share this weekend.

The thought makes me gut sick.

A chill scampers down my spine as I take a hasty step in retreat. I need to get out of here. Instead of returning to the party, I'm heading straight to my room and going to bed. Whether it's the one I'm supposed to sleep in or not remains to be seen.

As I take a step toward the beach, a twig snaps and there's the scurry of tiny paws against the dried leaves that carpet the forest floor. It's followed by a husky laugh and then a moan. I falter and swing around in the direction the sound came from. Whoever is here isn't far.

My teeth rake across my lower lip as indecision wars inside me.

Walk away with unanswered questions or…

Figure out if Austin and Aubrey are hooking up.

If they are, I can only hope that seeing them firsthand will be enough to kill my feelings for him so that I can move on. It's not a conscious decision to move deeper into the woods. My heartbeat picks up speed, thudding harshly against my ribcage as I duck beneath another branch and stutter to a stop when I spot a tall figure leaning against the thick trunk of a tree. As I squint, the shape comes into focus.

"Mmm, that feels so damn good, baby," a deep voice growls.

Realization slams into me that I've stumbled across Kingsley and Summer.

She presses kisses against his neck as her hands slip beneath the hem of his sweatshirt and shove it up his body until the sun-kissed flesh of his belly and chest is exposed under the sliver of moonlight that filters down through the tree branches. Kingsley tips his head back, exposing the thickly corded muscles of his throat as she slides downward.

I really need to get out of here before they figure out they're no longer alone.

Turn away now!

But my feet refuse to obey the commands of my brain. I'm unable to take my eyes off the couple.

God…this is so wrong.

And yet…

Air gets clogged at the back of my throat as her fingers hover over the button of his jeans. Once it's flicked open, she drags down the zipper and sinks to her knees. Arousal ignites in my core as I continue watching from the shadows.

Another deep groan rumbles from his chest before being swept away by the wind. "Are you going to kiss the crown, baby girl?"

The husky question is enough to knock me from the strange paralysis that has taken hold as I carefully back away. Relief floods through me that the couple will remain blissfully unaware of my presence.

I would have died if they'd caught sight of me.

As I clear the small patch of woods, an arm snakes around my waist from behind and yanks me against a hard chest. A hand wraps around my throat so that I'm rendered immobile.

"Look who I caught all by her lonesome," a deep voice growls in my ear.

Jasper.

My heart rate spikes, thundering painfully against my chest. "Let me go."

I try to keep the quiver from my voice, knowing that my fear will only incite further violence.

"Oh, I don't think so. At least, not yet." He strokes the long column of my throat with a startling amount of gentleness.

That's the thing about Jasper. His touch can turn from tender to punishing in the blink of an eye and without explanation.

Actually, there is a reason.

He enjoys it.

Enjoys inflicting pain.

Enjoys the terror he's capable of rousing in someone weaker.

"What were you doing out here in the woods, Delilah? Looking for someone to fuck?" His voice fills with faux sympathy. "Has Austin already lost interest? That was fast."

When I twist in his arms, his grip turns punishing. His fingers tighten around my throat until it's a challenge to draw air into my lungs.

"Stay still. I don't want you passing out on me. Where would be the fun in that? When I finally fuck you, I want you struggling, fighting me with every breath you take."

Panic floods through my system because it's the truth. That's *exactly* the way he would want it.

He doesn't want anything that is given to him.

He wants to fight for it.

Fight me.

"You're a total psycho," I grunt, chest heaving as my brain whirls, looking for a way to escape.

A chuckle slides from his lips. "Just for you, baby. Don't ever forget it."

Tears of frustration prick the backs of my eyes as the question slips free before I can stop it. "Why won't you leave me alone? I don't want anything to do with you."

"That will never happen," he growls, voice vibrating with anger. "You were always meant to be mine."

"No."

He presses his lips to the side of my neck. "Oh, yes. Did you really think for one damn second that I'd let Austin Hawthorne stand in the way of what I want?"

A whimper escapes from me as I squeeze my eyes tightly shut and try to block out his words.

"Looks like we have an audience," Jasper whispers gleefully. "I couldn't have planned it better myself."

Everything inside me sinks. By the excitement bursting from his tone, I know exactly who I'll find. But I can't stop myself from opening my eyes and praying that I'm wrong. My lashes cautiously lift until my gaze can lock on the muscular boy watching us from the top of a dune.

"Aus—"

When I attempt to call out, Jasper's fingers tighten around my throat, cutting off my airway as his other hand rises to my breast before squeezing it cruelly.

"Should we put on a show?"

"No," I wheeze.

He pinches my nipple and I gasp, trying to escape from his punishing touch.

"Mmm, that's right. Grind against me, baby. Show me how much you want my dick," he says loudly enough for Austin to hear.

Even from this distance, it would be impossible not to see the cold rage that flashes across his expression before he swings away, disappearing toward the beach and leaving me to battle my ex on my own.

As soon as his fingers loosen from around my throat, I gulp a deep breath of cool night air into my lungs, holding it captive for a handful of seconds before releasing it back into the atmosphere. My body sags against Jasper's as he holds me firmly in place.

His fingers sink into the soft flesh of my breast and pain explodes within me. Unlike Austin's touch, there is no hint of pleasure to chase after it.

"Here's what you need to get through your thick head—you belong to me, and there will never be a time when that's not true."

Tears spring to my eyes.

No.

No.

No.

I don't realize that I'm chanting the words out loud until someone says, "Let her go, Morgan!"

For a heartbeat, his hands tighten before disappearing. It takes every ounce of strength I have to stay upright and not collapse at his feet. I stagger away on shaky legs before turning to meet Duke's gaze. Concern floods his eyes as they slide from me to my ex.

"Stay away from Delilah."

Jasper straightens to his full height. "What's your problem, Carmichael?"

"You. You're my fucking problem. Now get the hell out of here before I beat your ass."

I stumble backward, only wanting to distance myself from him. I could be on the other side of the world, and it wouldn't be far enough.

With narrowed eyes, he grits his teeth. "You really think you can tell me what to do?"

Duke's hands tighten as he steps toward the other boy. "Delilah has made it perfectly clear that she wants nothing to do with you. That isn't going to change anytime soon."

Jasper smashes his lips together and glares at Duke before his narrowed gaze settles on mine.

"This isn't over," he snarls. "Not by a long shot."

I straighten my shoulders and lift my chin. "It's been over for a while. You just refuse to accept it."

When he takes a quick step in my direction, Duke barks, "Touch her and I'll break your damn arm. Your QB days will be long gone."

Jasper bares his teeth like a rabid animal before stalking away. It's only when the blond boy vanishes into the velvety darkness that swirls around us that I realize I'm trembling from the encounter.

"Thank you," I whisper, barely able to keep my voice from wavering.

What would have happened if Duke hadn't stumbled upon us?

A shiver slithers down my spine.

Unfortunately, I know exactly what would have occurred. He would have made good on every single promise.

Duke's brows pinch together as he glares in the direction Jasper stalked off. It's almost like he expects him to make a reappearance. Truthfully, so do I. Jasper is nothing if not persistent.

His gaze resettles on mine. "I got worried when you didn't return."

"Sorry. I..." My voice trails off. I don't want to admit that I went looking for Austin.

Duke's expression softens. "I'll talk to Kingsley about it in the morning. He can let Jasper know that he's no longer welcome."

Relief courses through me at that knowledge. Now I need to figure out what I'm going to do once we return to Hawthorne.

What Jasper's actions have slammed home tonight is that he will never leave me alone.

DELILAH

My eyes fly open as I'm ripped from sleep and my wrists are shackled before being forcibly dragged above my head. A dark face looms above mine as a scream gathers in my throat.

Any second, it'll burst free.

I'm so afraid Jasper has ignored Duke's warning and found me. And this time, there won't be anyone around to stop him. I blink away the sleep as moonlight spills in through the open window, casting both light and shadow across the brawny figure.

After the encounter with my ex, I scrambled back to the house and retreated to my assigned bedroom before stripping off my clothing and sliding between the sheets. Even through the closed window, I could hear the faint wisps of music and the occasional drunken shout.

"Did you enjoy yourself with him tonight?" comes a deep growl that sounds like it was dredged from the bottom of the ocean. Pent-up fury vibrates through every syllable.

Austin.

Relief sweeps through my body, weakening my limbs. No matter how angry he is, he won't hurt me.

Not in the same way Jasper would.

"You have to know that I wasn't with him willingly."

He snorts. "How fucking stupid do you think I am?" His grip tightens around my wrists as he presses them further into the mattress. "Every time I turn around, you're at his side, allowing him to touch what belongs to me."

"You're wrong. You didn't see everything that happened. Only what you wanted."

He bares his teeth. "Stop fucking with me. I've already told you that I'm done playing games, and that's exactly what you and Jasper are intent on doing. Just admit it."

I shake my head, wishing he would stop and listen for one damn minute. "I had no idea he would be there."

He cocks his head and sneers. "If that's the case, what were you doing alone in the woods if not looking for a hookup?"

I gulp. As loath as I am to admit the truth, there's no point in lying. "I was trying to find you."

He studies me silently in the darkness before lowering his face and ghosting his lips over mine. The caress is far gentler than his expression or tone. "What for? Were you afraid that I was with someone else?"

I lift my chin. "Yes."

"What would you have done if you'd found me with another girl, Delilah?"

Good question.

It's one I asked myself while searching the little forest. Thankfully, I didn't have to answer it.

"I'm not sure."

He nips at my ear. "Want to know the truth? I hate myself for wanting you so damn much. Especially when all you've done is lie and make a fool out of me." He pauses. "Maybe if I screwed another girl, I'd be able to get you out of my system, but here's the problem—I don't want anyone else," he finishes with a snarl. "I only want *you*."

His words both chill my skin and set fire to my blood. It doesn't make sense.

"Austin, please." My tongue darts out to moisten my parched lips. "If you would—"

He pulls away enough to stare into my eyes before shaking his head. "I don't want to hear any more lies. I'm done with them the way I wish I could be done with you."

As soon as the words leave his lips, he releases my wrists. My breath comes fast and heavy as he rolls to the side of the bed. Before I can question his intentions, he yanks off the covers and grips the elastic band of my panties before ripping them from my body and tossing them to the floor. Much like he shackled one wrist, he does the same to my ankle, dragging it wide until he can settle between my outstretched legs.

Tell him no.

Not like this.

But the words refuse to budge from the tip of my tongue.

The truth of the matter is that I've missed Austin this past week and I want him desperately.

Even if it means him taking me in anger.

That first kiss when his lips settle over my core has me arching with an instinctive need to get closer.

"So fucking greedy, aren't you?"

"Only for you," I whisper, knowing he won't believe me.

There will never be anyone else.

Only Austin.

Instead of responding, he attacks my delicate flesh. The velvety softness of his tongue spears deep inside my body before licking me from the top of my slit to the bottom and then back again. He circles my clit until I'm dizzy with the sensation.

When my lashes feather closed, he snaps, "Eyes on me the entire time I'm between your legs. I want you to watch me lick your pussy until you're screaming my name and flooding my mouth with your cream. I'm the only one who will be able to make you fall apart like this."

He doesn't need to remind me.

I feel the truth of his words deep in my bones.

And it scares the hell out of me.

When I shift restlessly, impatient for more, his strong fingers wrap around the softness of my inner thighs to hold me firmly in place. It gives him unrestricted access to every delicate inch of me.

And I wouldn't have it any other way.

His touch gentles as he nibbles at my clit. The muscles in my lower belly contract with need as my fingertips sink into his scalp. Just when I'm on the verge of splintering apart, he backs off, leaving me hanging as the cool air of the room wafts over my soaked flesh.

His sharp teeth sink into the plumpness of my mound and a whimper of need escapes from me. My core throbs a painful tempo that echoes harshly to the tips of my fingers and toes. I'm so damn needy for what only he can give.

If he demanded that I beg for it…

For him.

I would do it without question. I'm a slave to the feelings he rouses deep inside.

"Your pussy is so fucking perfect. And it's mine." There's a pause as he lifts his head to spear me with the intensity of his heated stare. "Do you hear me? *Mine.*"

The last word comes out sounding more like a feral growl that vibrates through my very soul. His possessiveness has a burst of arousal flooding my core with more heat.

"Please," I whimper, writhing beneath him.

He takes a long lap of my soaked flesh. "Please what?"

A groan slips from my lips. "Please make me come."

He drags his tongue over my clit. "Am I the only one capable of making you feel this way?"

How is that even a question in his mind?

"Yes," I whimper, trying to hold myself together.

His voice turns harsh. "Has anyone else ever touched you like this?"

I shake my head as the ache within continues to grow, becoming unbearable. Any moment, it'll swallow me whole. "No. Never."

His warm breath ghosts over me, nudging me closer to the precipice. There's only so much of this torment I can withstand.

And if he stops or walks away…

I'll likely die.

"What did you do with Jasper in the woods?"

"Nothing," I cry as he takes a long lap of my pussy. "I hate Jasper for everything he's done to us."

"I don't know, Delilah. I can't tell if you're the villain of this story or just an innocent victim. But rest assured, I'll get to the truth."

I scream when he spears his tongue deep inside my body.

"One way or the other."

"I promise that I'm not lying. I wish you'd believe me."

"I wish I could, too. I wish it were that easy."

"Austin, please…"

Before I can wrap my lips around the words, he draws my clit into his mouth and sucks it gently. My back bows off the mattress as my core explodes with sensation before ricocheting throughout my entire being.

Even though I press a hand to my mouth to keep the sound trapped inside, it's not possible. It bursts from me in a long, keening wail that echoes in my ears. Austin continues to lick and suck at my flesh until every last drop of pleasure has been wrung from my oversensitive body and I'm a limp mess, staring sightlessly at the ceiling.

As I float back to earth, my gaze finds his again. He's sitting up, staring at me. What I expect is for him to crawl up my body and bury his thick length deep inside my heat, giving us both what we so desperately need.

That flicker of hope is snuffed out when he rises to his feet. All the heat swirling through his dark eyes is now locked behind a mask of indifference.

Even though I'm afraid of the rejection, I can't stop the word from tumbling free. *"Please."*

He shakes his head.

My eyes silently plead with his in the darkness as he takes a step in retreat before swinging away and slipping through the door into the hallway. I stare at the empty space in disbelief before curling up into a tight ball. There doesn't seem to be anything I can say that will alter his opinion of me.

The sooner I come to terms with that reality, the better off I'll be.

DELILAH

It's the harsh sunlight against my eyelids that has me reluctantly surfacing from a restless sleep. I spent most of the night tossing and turning, hoping Austin would slip into the room.

Back to the bed we're sharing.

He never did.

With a blink, I roll over and stare at the other side of the mattress.

It looks the same as it did last night.

Empty.

Untouched.

Where did he end up?

In someone else's bed?

God knows there are enough girls clamoring for a piece of him. The thought of Austin touching someone else after giving me an orgasm makes me sick to my stomach. With a huff, I collapse against the pillows and stare at the ceiling, trying to figure out if there's a way to repair the damage that has been inflicted. That continues to be inflicted at every turn.

Unwilling to dwell on the tangle of emotions, I toss off the covers and gravitate to the window before pressing my face against the cool glass. Even though it's early, the sun is shining as it climbs higher in the cornflower blue sky, glinting over the water that rolls toward the sandy shoreline. There's something mesmerizing about the white-capped waves as they lap at the beach. It must be magical, because it manages to settle everything that riots dangerously inside me.

I glance up and down the long stretch of coastline. There's not a soul in sight. Could there be a more perfect time to grab my camera and head outside?

With any luck, I'll snap a few photos that can be used for the art exhibition at the end of the year. Other than graduating and getting the hell out of Hawthorne, it's the only thing I have to look forward to.

Dressing quickly, I throw on a hoodie and jeans before gathering my hair into a high ponytail. Even though the weather looks picture perfect, it'll probably be windy. I pull Dad's old Nikon from the bag and sling the strap across my chest so it hangs loosely in front of me. Once my shoes and socks are on, I slip from the room and tiptoe down the long stretch of hallway. All the other doors are closed, making the space dark and shadowy in spite of the sunshine. My guess is that everyone partied until the wee hours of the morning before passing out. They probably won't show their faces until early afternoon.

As I bounce from the last tread in the entryway, I swing a left and make my way to the back of the house. Not expecting to see anyone else, I skid to a halt in the sun-splashed kitchen when I find Summer leaning against the marble countertop with a cup of coffee in her hand. It's midway to her lips when our gazes collide.

For a second, we both freeze. If it were possible to slowly back out of the room and erase this moment from our minds, I'd do it in a heartbeat.

But that, unfortunately, is not possible.

Her green eyes turn hooded.

Unsure what to say, I clear my throat. An image of her last night in the woods flashes through my head and my cheeks heat as I hastily shove it away. Thank god she doesn't know I saw them. It would only give her more ammunition to hate me with.

"Morning," I say.

When she grunts out an answer, I inch toward the backdoor, only wanting to escape her suffocating presence.

"Where are you off to so bright and early?"

I lift the camera that hangs across my chest. "To snap a few pictures. It's beautiful out."

She arches a well-sculpted brow. "Or maybe you're meeting up with someone?"

Tired of her accusations, I straighten to my full height. "No, I'm not."

"I'm sure Jasper mentioned that he's only a couple houses up the beach."

A burst of anger rushes through my veins at the insinuation. Unable to stop myself, I take a step toward her. "I'm not going to have this conversation with you again. I broke up with Jasper and don't want anything to do with him. If you choose not to believe me, there's nothing I can do about that."

Her eyes narrow as if she wasn't expecting me to clap back. "After the way the last couple of weeks have played out, it's hard to believe anything that comes out of your mouth."

My shoulders wilt.

It's so tiring.

Tiring to constantly be proving your innocence.

"I know, but I'm telling you the truth."

She sets the mug down on the gleaming counter with enough force to have coffee sloshing over the rim. "Do you seriously think I'm just going to stand by and allow you to hurt Austin?"

My heart clenches at the fierce expression that settles over her pretty features. There's no denying the love she feels for her brother.

"What Jasper did…" I shake my head and try to find the right words that will convey everything I feel inside. "My heart broke for Austin, but I had nothing to do with it."

Indecision flickers across her face. It's the first break in her stoicism that I've seen. "Honestly, I don't know what to believe."

I press my lips together and glance away as our conversation stalls and an uncomfortable silence blankets the atmosphere. Instead of continuing this useless exchange, I turn toward the exit, only wanting to flee.

Just as I reach the door and lock my fingers around the brushed nickel handle, I hesitate. Even though I should walk away, something won't allow me to do it.

I swing around and meet her gaze. "I get why you're angry. You think I purposefully set out to mess with your brother, but that's not what happened. If anyone's inflicted pain and damage, it's him." When she opens her mouth to argue, I hold up a hand. "It's the truth. Whether you want to believe it or not. Regardless, what's going on between us isn't any of your business. It's between Austin and myself. You need to let us work it out on our own."

If that's even possible.

She jerks a brow. "Is that so?"

I straighten to my full height and hold her penetrating stare. "Yes."

Her eyes stay locked on mine as she brings the mug to her lips and takes a sip. It's as if she's silently assessing me above the rim.

My guess is that I've surprised her.

I've always been quiet, more comfortable lurking in the background, watching life unfold from a safe distance. That's no longer possible. If I've learned anything over the past couple weeks, it's that I need to stand up for myself, otherwise these people will chew me up and spit me out.

Honestly…it feels good to give voice to the thoughts swirling through my brain and not keep everything bottled up inside where it can silently fester.

When she remains quiet, I take that as my cue to leave. Nothing between us has been solved, but it feels like a small victory on my part. I could have allowed Summer to voice her opinion without saying a word, and I didn't.

It's a relief when the glass sliding door slams shut behind me. For just a moment, I squeeze my eyes tightly closed and inhale a breath of fresh air, holding it captive before gradually releasing it. As I stand motionless, allowing the chilly breeze to slide over my cheeks, I realize my body is shaking.

My fingers wrap around the banister as I jog down the wooden steps before making my way across the dunes to the shoreline. As I reach the water, my conversation with Summer gets shoved to the back of my mind as excitement grows inside me and I raise the camera to my face, snapping a few photos of the water along with the stretch of empty beach. I lift my face to the sky as the warmth of the sun pours over me and spot a few seagulls circling lazily overhead.

Contentment like I haven't experienced in a long time suffuses every cell of my being as I walk along the hard-packed sand, careful to avoid the waves that lap at the shore. After passing a few sprawling mansions, I drop into a squat and pick up a small clam shell before wiping off the tiny grains of sand that cling to the smooth exterior and slip it into my pocket for safekeeping.

This moment has made the entire weekend worth it.

Everything loosens within me as I take about a hundred different shots of the lake, houses, trees, the dunes with their tall tan and green grasses that wave gently in the breeze.

This place is pure magic.

There's something about the sand, water, and sun that soothes everything raw and chafed inside until it's almost possible to forget about all the hurt that's been inflicted. I want to bottle up this feeling and keep it with me long after I leave the beach.

As I stare through the viewfinder, a shape takes form in the distance, and I realize that it's a person. I press the shutter trigger a few times in quick succession as the guy continues to jog toward me. My heart stutters a painful beat when I realize it's Austin. Even though the temperature hovers in the mid-sixties, he's wearing a black tank that shows off the bulging muscles of his biceps. It's enough to make my mouth turn cottony and my pulse hitch.

I stand rooted in place and continue snapping shots. Already, I know that when I return home, I'll pour over the photographs. Physically speaking, Austin Hawthorne is a perfect specimen. More god than man. The closer he gets, the harder my heart slams against my ribcage as memories from last night circle through my head.

The pleasure at his touch along with the hurt that sliced through me when he pulled away, walking out of the room without so much as a backward glance. His gaze stays locked on mine as his pace slows before he eventually comes to a halt a few feet away.

His cheeks are pinkened from his exertions and his breath is labored. "You're up early."

I squint and shield my eyes from the rising sun that pours down on him. "You, too."

With a shrug, he glances over the water. "Couldn't sleep."

I press my lips together, refusing to ask where he spent the night and if it was alone.

"I wanted to take some pictures before the sun got too high." I sweep my hand toward the lake. "It's gorgeous."

Instead of following the gesture, his eyes stay locked on mine. "It is."

Our conversation stalls and I shift beneath his penetrating gaze. Even though the answer is obvious, I hear myself ask, "You're out for a run?"

"Yeah. I needed to clear my head and it always helps."

"How far did you go?"

He glances at the black sports watch wrapped around his wrist. "About three miles. I made it to the lighthouse before deciding to turn back."

"I was thinking about checking it out and taking some pictures. I've never seen one up close."

"It's pretty cool."

After last night, it's obvious that we're both tap dancing around each other. It's as if there's a magnetic force pulling us together. Does he feel it too or is it all one sided?

I wish I knew.

Almost desperately, I want to clear the air so we can put the past behind us and move forward. I want him to hear me out and realize once and for all that his accusations are unfounded. My tongue darts out to moisten my wind-chapped lips as I gather my courage.

It's now or never.

Before I can get the words out, he asks, "Did you want to head back with me?"

I blink as everything sitting on the tip of my tongue melts away. I'm loath to ruin this moment between us. One where he isn't glaring or laying his hands on me in anger.

Even though my plan had been to stay away from the mansion as much as possible, I hear myself say, "Yes."

Spending time with him, being close, outweighs my decision to keep my distance from my classmates. I have no idea if that need will ever dissipate.

It's a depressing thought.

Silently, we fall into line and set out down the beach. Instead of focusing on the beauty of the scenery, I'm hyperaware of his bigger, muscular body dwarfing mine. The shift and play of his muscles as we walk.

Even though there's a breeze, the scent of his woodsy cologne mingled with sweat from his workout overpowers my senses, cocooning me in familiarity. Images from last night fill my head before exploding in my core, making it throb to life. There is nothing like the feel of his dark head buried between my thighs, licking me, tormenting me until there's no other choice but to splinter apart.

"Did I mention we vacationed here this summer?" he asks, knocking me from the whirl of my thoughts.

I glance at him in surprise. "Before you moved to Hawthorne?"

He nods as we walk at a leisurely pace as if neither of us is in a hurry. "Yeah, we rented a house from a family friend in Chicago." His green depths ensnare mine, holding them captive. "I didn't realize it at the time, but that's when Summer met Kingsley."

My mind tumbles back to the beginning of the school year and my brows draw together. "Really?"

"Yeah, it was a pretty messed-up situation when we first arrived. I can't get into the specifics, but the issue has been resolved."

When the twins first started at Hawthorne Prep, Kingsley made Summer's life a living hell. There didn't seem to be a way for them to set aside their differences and get along, much less date. And yet, that's exactly what happened. They've become inseparable.

A little pang fills my heart that I'll never experience that with Austin. We'll never make it to the other side. Whatever took place between Kingsley and Summer, it can't be as bad as what's happened to us.

"I'm glad for them," I say quietly.

Maybe even a little jealous that they've found their happily ever after.

But I keep that comment to myself.

"He's an okay dude," he says with a shrug. "As long as he continues to treat her right, I don't have a problem with them together."

A companionable silence falls over us as we make our way back to Kingsley's sprawling house. It reminds me of how it was before Jasper destroyed it with the photographs. I'd do anything to recapture those few precious moments.

"Austin?" His name is out of my mouth before I can reel it back in.

He flicks a glance at me. When my feet grind to a halt, his do the same.

"Can we talk?" It takes effort to keep the tremor from invading my voice. "Please?"

His unguarded expression vanishes as his eyes turn into hard chips of green ice that cut me to the bone. Even before he has a chance to open his mouth, I realize this conversation was a mistake.

"There's nothing for us to talk about."

Desperation floods through me. "That's not true. If you'd just hear me out. Give me a chance to explain everything that happened…"

He swallows the distance between us before winding his hand around my ponytail and hauling me close. His grip tightens until I have to tip my head back to relieve the sting of my scalp.

Our gazes cling.

"I don't want to hear any more lies."

"They're not lies."

His eyes darken, turning stormy. It's a strange contrast to the chilled sunshine slanting down on us. My heart thuds a painful rhythm against my chest as we stare. When his grip intensifies, I lift my chin. A whimper escapes before being snatched away by the wind as his gaze drops to my parted lips.

"You tried to prove your innocence once by giving me yours, but that didn't mean jack shit, did it?"

"It meant more than you'll ever know. And I'd do it all over again, if it changed anything between us."

There's a play of emotion across his face.

Lust.

Longing.

Anger.

Suspicion.

It's all there, each one vying for precedence.

"I wish it were possible to go back in time and wipe the slate clean. I don't want it to be like this," I whisper.

His mouth hovers over mine as we hang in suspension. Energy stirs around us, electrifying the atmosphere.

When he remains silent, I blurt, "I swear this isn't a game."

He nips my lower lip, tugging it between his teeth before sucking the fullness into his mouth and releasing it with a soft pop.

"That's not what Jasper says, now is it?"

"We both know he's a liar. He's been messing with you since you first stepped foot on the campus of Hawthorne Prep."

"And you would know that better than most because you were right there at his side, weren't you?"

I hate the answer more than he'll ever know. "Yes."

Surprise flickers in his eyes.

When he remains silent, I add, "Only because I didn't know how to leave. I was afraid of his reaction. That he would lash out and try to hurt me, which is exactly what he's done. He won't stop until he destroys everything between us and forces me to return to him."

His grip tightens around my hair as he drags my head back further until my throat is completely bared. I tense and wait for his next move. I could put up a struggle, but what would be the point?

There's a tiny part of me that expects him to inflict pain. Instead, the velvety softness of his tongue licks at the delicate column. Everything in me loosens at the gentle onslaught. Even when his teeth scrape across the hollow of my sensitive skin, I remain still.

Barely am I breathing.

He draws the flesh into his mouth and sucks it mercilessly. There's no way it won't leave a mark. When my muscles become weak, his arms tighten, crushing me against his broad chest. It feels as if he'll never let go, and I don't want him to.

"*If* you're actually broken up."

"We are. I swear it."

"And is that what you'll do? Crawl back to him?"

"No," I whisper. "Never."

Austin rains sweet, featherlight kisses down upon my face. A million of them. They're as delicate as a butterfly wing. There and gone before I can fully sink into the caress.

"What about me?" There's a pause as air gets trapped in my throat. "Will you crawl to me, if that's what I demand?"

My eyes widen and my heart stills for one painful second before exploding into motion until it feels like it might burst from my chest. When I remain silent, he nips at my flesh, and I can't stop the moan from escaping.

"Answer me," he growls before repeating the question. "Will you crawl to me if that's what I demand?"

"Yes." As soon as the word breaks free, I know it's the truth.

If it meant that he'd take a leap of faith and shut out Jasper and his lies one final time, not allowing him to destroy the fragile relationship we've discovered, then yes...I'd do it.

"On your hands and knees?" he presses.

The thickly murmured words swirl darkly through my head before settling deep within my core and throbbing an insistent beat.

His teeth scrape against my abraded flesh. "Answer me, sweet girl. Would you crawl on your hands and knees to prove your innocence?"

The response escapes from me when he nips at my throat. "Yes."

"Does the thought of doing that turn you on as much as it does me?"

It shouldn't. There's a place deep within my brain that knows I should loathe what he's saying. What he's asking.

What does it mean that I don't?

"All I would have to do is slip my hand beneath the waistband of your jeans, slide past your panties and discover the answer for myself."

If he did, he'd find the cotton completely drenched.

One hand firmly grips my ponytail while the other slides from around my back, along my ribcage before drifting down my belly. My breath catches when his fingers hover over the silver button before dropping to the apex of my thighs and pressing against my center. My teeth sink into my lower lip to keep the moan trapped inside where it belongs.

His pupils dilate, swallowing up the green and gold flecks that swim in his eyes as he rubs me through the thick denim. Even though two layers separate his fingers from my pussy, arousal explodes, and my body tightens with need. As much as I want to remain still, I can't stop writhing, seeking out more pressure so that he can push me over the edge and into oblivion.

Just when orgasm feels imminent, his hand falls away and he releases his hold on my hair before retreating a step. Now that he's no longer propping me up, my knees buckle, and I sink to the sand. It takes effort to blink away the thick haze cocooned around me.

Seconds tick by. When I finally lift my head and crane my neck, my gaze fastens onto the tented material of his athletic shorts that is just inches away from my face. I can't help but stare at the thickness of his erection. When I finally rip my attention away and meet his eyes, the heat filling his stare nearly sets me to flames.

For a long, silent moment, our eyes stay locked before he drops down so that we're eye level. He reaches out and strokes the curve of my cheek with gentle fingers. His deep voice is barely audible and slides over my skin like a whisper.

"Just remember what you promised, sweet girl. Don't be surprised when I hold you to it."

Before I can respond, he pops up and takes off running down the beach. I can only sit and stare, my heart thundering painfully beneath my breast, as a kernel of apprehension fills me.

DELILAH

*K*ingsley extends a hand as I step onto the deck of his boat. Much like his beach house, it's massive. I can't help but stare at the luxurious surroundings in awe. I've never been on a vessel of any kind and couldn't begin to dream of one this size.

About a dozen classmates laugh and chatter as they make themselves at home on the plush leather seating arrangements that wrap around the front of the boat and near the controls. Someone brought a cooler filled with alcohol and is already cracking open bottles.

The muscles in my belly contract when Sloane steps onboard with a squeal and hugs Aubrey before squeezing in next to Austin. My brows pinch as I glance at the dock with unease, hoping Jasper won't show up.

Austin's gaze stays pinned to me as I glance around, looking for a place to settle. I don't have to meet his eyes to know his attention is locked on me. I feel it. My skin comes alive whenever his gaze rakes over my body. Never in my life have I been so finely attuned to another human being as I am with Austin Hawthorne. It's enough to set my nerves on edge, making it impossible to focus on anything other than him. My world narrows until he's all that fills it.

Duke catches my eyes and pats the empty space on the couch.

Thankful for his kindness, I gravitate toward him before gingerly settling on the curved cushion. Kingsley starts the engine and tosses off the lines from the pier before hopping back onto the deck and settling at the controls. It's obvious from the easy way he maneuvers the boat that he's done this many times before. Within five minutes, we're pulling out of the marina and heading for open water. It doesn't take long for the waves to turn a deeper and darker blue.

As we pick up speed, the breeze whips across my face and through my hair. The babble of voices that surround me get drowned out by the motor as the boat slaps against the water. Even though the sun is shining brightly, the wind cuts through my sweatshirt. I draw my knees to my chest and hug them tight, wishing I'd brought a jacket or blanket to wrap. The scenery is beautiful, but it's freezing.

Duke leans toward me before asking, "Are you cold?"

With a slight smile, I nod. "Just a little."

He wraps a brawny arm around my shoulders and tugs me close. The only thing that stops me from burrowing against his comforting warmth is the knowledge that Austin is watching with narrowed eyes. That's the moment I realize my mistake. When Duke asked if I was cold, I should have lied and said I was fine.

When I attempt to put a bit of distance between us so I'm not pinned against his side, Duke tugs me even closer before dropping a kiss against the top of my head.

I squeeze my eyelids tight, afraid to glance in Austin's direction. Thick tension ratchets up in the air until it becomes unbearable. Unable to stop myself, I flick a look at Austin. There's a steeliness filling his eyes and I'm reminded of the way he stared down at me on the beach this morning when I sunk to my knees. A shiver slides through me that has nothing to do with the wind.

Just remember what you promised, sweet girl. I'm going to hold you to it.

As the memory echoes throughout my brain, a pit blooms at the bottom of my belly. I realize what's going to happen before the words are out of his mouth. Barely is there time to brace myself.

"What's wrong?" Duke whispers, his warm breath ghosting over my ear.

My tongue darts out to moisten my lips as I twist in his arms to meet his searching gaze. "I, ah—"

Before I can blurt the rest, Austin's deep voice slices through the noise.

"Come here, Delilah."

Too late.

Much too late.

My muscles turn rigid. I'm like a rabbit caught in the crosshairs of a hunter's rifle.

Duke twists his head and scowls at the other boy before glancing at me again. His expression softens as our eyes lock. "Just ignore him."

If only that were possible.

When I made that promise earlier this morning, I meant it. I just didn't expect…

Maybe I should have.

I press my lips together before taking a peek. Sloane and Aubrey are curled up against each side of his stretched-out body. His muscular arms rest along the back of the plush cushions. They're not wrapped around the girls or encouraging their intimacy.

When I give my head a barely perceptible shake, silently pleading with him not to do this in front of everyone, his eyes turn hard, their penetrating green gaze skewering me in place, making it difficult to draw in breath.

"Come here." His low voice vibrates throughout the atmosphere before settling in my core like a heavy stone. From the way Aubrey's eyes dilate, she feels it as well and cuddles closer to his chest before pawing at him.

All conversations abruptly grind to a halt. It's obvious that our classmates have gone quiet and are watching the scene unfold with growing interest.

"What do you want with her, Hawthorne?" Duke snaps. "Just leave Delilah alone."

Austin's gaze never falters from mine. "Now."

The command is like a punch to the gut.

Or maybe the punch is lower.

"Ignore him," Duke repeats, only louder this time. "He's just as much of an asshole as Jasper."

That's where he's wrong. Austin is *nothing* like my ex. Duke might not understand what's going on, but I do.

This is a test.

And the only way to pass is to keep my promise.

With at least a dozen curious eyes watching, I gather my strength before rising unsteadily to my feet. I keep my attention focused on Austin the entire time. It would be impossible to miss the satisfaction that flickers in his green depths.

When I take a tentative step, he says softly, "Hands and knees."

Oh god.

My mouth turns cottony as heat scalds my cheeks, making them feel as if they're on fire.

"Delilah," Duke snaps. "Don't do it."

I can't bring myself to glance at the muscular lacrosse player. I'm afraid of what I'll find in his expression.

The boat sways beneath my feet as I lower myself to the smooth wood of the deck. Even over the noise of the motor, the silence that surrounds us is deafening. Another wave of humiliation crashes over me as I hang my head and inhale a deep breath before forcing myself to meet Austin's penetrating gaze.

At the first movement forward, I hear, "OMG, what is she doing?"

"Is she actually...*crawling* to him?"

Unable to focus on the burst of chatter, I stare at Austin, silently begging and pleading with him to end this before it goes any further. Instead, he watches me as I carefully move toward him.

The time it takes to reach him seems to stretch forever, almost as if I'm a million miles away when in reality, there are only ten or twelve feet separating us.

"Damn," some guy says.

I refuse to look.

When I'm directly in front of Austin, I have to tilt my head to hold his gaze as he stares down at me. Aubrey is still curled up on one side of him and Sloane is on the other. Unless he wants me to sit on his lap, I have no idea where I'm supposed to go.

It's as if he can read my mind.

His expression remains impassive as he spreads his thighs farther apart. "You can sit at my feet."

My eyes widen as his words circle viciously through my head. It takes effort to swallow down my protests as I force myself to settle between his outstretched thighs. The low hum of voices explodes around me, but I keep my gaze pinned to the teak. Any moment, I'm going to self-combust from the mortification that eats me alive.

I remind myself that this was my choice.

Austin didn't force me to do anything.

"What is she? Your pet?" Aubrey grumbles, none too pleased to have me near Austin.

"No."

He doesn't bother to explain the situation.

Even though my back is turned, I feel the burn of his gaze licking over me, heating me up from the inside out. It's almost laughable that I'd been looking forward to the boat ride so I could snap some photos. Now, I just want to get it over with. My life has turned into one humiliating moment after another, and there doesn't seem to be an end in sight.

Austin's palm settles on the top of my head before stroking down the length of my ponytail.

"See? She's exactly like a dog," Aubrey says with a nasty laugh.

"Well, I'm not cleaning up after her if she takes a shit on the deck," Sloane snickers.

Austin remains silent, continuing to stroke his hand over my hair. If we weren't in front of all these people, I might actually find the touch soothing, but I can't shake off all the prying eyes.

Minutes tick by and the conversations pick up around us. The tension in my muscles gradually loosens. Each time his fingers drag across my scalp, the sensation echoes throughout my being. He repeats the gesture until I'm lulled into a strange state of relaxation.

Or maybe it's the gentle rocking of the boat as it moves over the waves.

Just when my eyelids begin to droop, he wraps my hair around his hand until the length is taut and pulls against my scalp. I gulp when he carefully tugs until I'm left with no choice but to tip my head back against his thigh and meet the dark depths staring down at me. Once my attention is locked on him, it's impossible to look away. The longer our gazes stay fastened, the more everything around us fades until Austin is all I'm cognizant of. He leans forward until he can place his other hand against the delicate column of my throat.

"Your pulse feels like a hummingbird beating its wings against a cage."

When I swallow, the light pressure against my flesh grows in intensity. His grip remains loose.

"I didn't think you would go through with it," he murmurs.

"I promised that I would."

Our gazes continue to cling, and in that moment of intense connection, nothing else matters. Not the way these people are watching us or the mortification I'd felt as I crawled to him.

Just Austin.

A potent concoction of heat and tenderness swirls through his eyes.

It's intoxicating.

And I want more of it.

I want him to always look at me that way.

Is it possible that I've finally broken through the wall that separates us?

"I'm bored," Aubrey whines now that Austin's attention is riveted elsewhere before rising to her feet. "I need a drink."

"Girl, same. I'm entirely too sober for this," Sloane agrees.

Once they take off, the world shrinks down even more. There are still people sitting around us and talking, but I'm no longer cognizant of them. My focus is centered on Austin and the way his eyes are locked on mine. He continues to stroke my throat with gentle touches that lull me into a strange state of contentment.

"Did you bring your camera?"

"Yes."

"Then go take your pictures."

Those five words should have me jumping up and racing away.

I certainly shouldn't need to be told twice.

Instead, I stay rooted in place, eyes locked on him. "Are you sure?"

"As much as I'd like to keep you here for the rest of the trip, I won't. You've proven yourself."

Relief rushes through me.

For a long moment, his grip stays locked around my hair as his other hand strokes the delicate column of my throat. My body loosens as I close my eyes, enjoying his touch. It no longer matters who is watching or what they're saying.

It's almost a surprise when a whimper escapes from me.

"So fucking perfect," he whispers before both hands disappear.

When I crack my eyes open, our gazes lock and arousal explodes in the air around us.

"Go. Before I change my mind." His voice drops several octaves, sounding as if it's been scraped raw.

As I straighten, using his knees to balance, his hands wrap around my waist, helping me to rise. On shaky legs, I stumble to where my camera bag sits on the couch next to Duke. My gaze hesitantly flickers to him and I steel myself for the condemnation I'll find in his expression.

I'm not wrong. There's a mixture of confusion and anger swirling through his eyes.

"I'm going to take a few photos," I force myself to say.

He shoots a look at Austin before his attention resettles on me. I can tell he's trying to figure out what's going on between us.

"Want me to come with?"

"No, but thank you."

I open up the soft black bag and slip the old Nikon free. Kingsley cuts the engine, making it easier to move around the boat. With my camera in hand, I cautiously make my way to the front where it's less crowded. It's windier and there's less seating available. Brilliant sunlight beats down on me and I can't resist the urge to tip my face toward the sky and enjoy the warmth as it strokes over my bare skin. I draw a deep breath of fresh air into my lungs before slowly releasing it.

Then, I lift the camera to my face and adjust the lens until the water and the land is just visible on the horizon and press the shutter button. When a few seagulls soar overhead, I tip the camera upward and lock on them in the viewfinder. The water is such an intense blue. As it laps at the side of the boat, I can't help but wonder how deep it is.

It's beautiful but fathomless.

Goosebumps prickle along my arms and I retreat a cautious step, not wanting to get too close to the edge. Ridiculous as it sounds, I never learned how to swim. Even standing near the deep end of the pool at school makes me uneasy.

As I stare out over the endless stretch of waves, my head grows dizzy and nausea blooms in the pit of my belly. I press a hand to my lower abdomen to stifle the growing sickness.

It doesn't work.

Maybe it would be best to sit down again. When I was settled at Austin's feet, I didn't feel any of this. Probably because I was too focused on him and the way he was touching me.

I release a slow breath and head back to where I left the camera bag. As I pass Aubrey, she lifts the container of water to her lips and takes a swig.

"You're such a loser," Sloane says. "Don't you want something a little stronger than that?"

The blonde tips a bottle of beer to her lips and takes a long drink, draining nearly a third of it.

"You know I need to focus on my grades."

"Community college, here you come," Sloane snickers.

Aubrey glares at her so-called bestie.

A strange sense of déjà vu hits me as I pause and frown, the words circling madly in my head. Aubrey and I are barely friends. I can't remember the last time we actually engaged in a conversation and yet, I could swear she told me this. With narrowed eyes, I rack my brain, trying to figure it out. The answer is there, just within reach, but I can't quite seem to grasp it.

"You partied too much and now you have to get your grades up or you won't get into college," I whisper. It's a little freaky to hear the words echo in my head and yet be unable to recall where and when I heard them.

Fear flashes across Aubrey's pretty face before it's quickly masked behind a scowl.

Sloane tilts her head and eyes me as if I'm a circus oddity. "You're so weird. What? Are you spying on her now?"

I blink and concentrate on the memory, trying to tease it free. "No, she told me," I mutter, annoyed with myself for not being able to recall exactly when it happened.

The strange thing is that I can almost see the words coming out of her mouth. An image of Aubrey in her cheerleading uniform flickers in my brain. The last time she wore that was...

I straighten to my full height. "The night of Kingsley's party."

I remember.

Well...a snippet at least.

"I don't know what the hell you're talking about. We never even saw each other." She smirks. "I heard you were blackout drunk and got it on with Jasper. Maybe you're delusional." Her expression fills with faux sympathy. "That's so sad. You should probably get some help."

No.

She's wrong.

I shake my head and take a tentative step in her direction. "That's not true. I barely drink, and we did have a conversation." I squeeze my eyes tightly shut and try to conjure up the image again, searching my memories for more details. "We talked inside the house."

It was...in the kitchen. The music had been pumping, reverberating in my ears. I'd just wanted to return to Austin. During the past week, no matter how much I thought about it, the only thing I could remember was sitting outside by the firepit.

We'd kissed.

Jasper had been lurking in the shadows.

And then…

It all fades to black. As if the memories have been wiped clean.

Only now do I realize I spoke with Aubrey. At least for a few minutes in the house. What took place afterward is anyone's guess. I focus on our conversation from that night. Most of it is still a blur. What sticks out in my brain is that she needed to lay off the drinking and get her grades up.

With a shake of her head, she glances away. There's a tightness to her jaw as her voice turns snappish. "Sorry, that never happened. I would remember if we talked."

My brow furrows. "Are you sure?" It seems like such an insignificant thing. And yet, I need her to acknowledge it.

I'm so damn sure about it.

"Maybe Aubrey's right and you need some serious help," Sloane says with a laugh before swinging away and bailing on the conversation.

Disappointment floods through me.

Is she right?

Am I losing it?

No.

I straighten my shoulders. I'm going to get Aubrey to admit the truth no matter what it takes. When she attempts to follow her friend, I lock my fingers around her forearm to stop her.

"Why are you lying to me?" I ask.

"I'm not. We never spoke that night. Now let me go, loser."

With that, she jerks her arm away before shoving me in the chest. The boat bounces over a wave and I lose my balance, tripping over my own feet. As the backs of my thighs hit the railing, my eyes widen, locking on Aubrey's as I tumble overboard. Panic fills me before attempting to swallow me whole. The camera drops from my hand as I try to grab the railing, but it doesn't do any good. The metal slips through my fingers and a scream escapes from my lips as I hit the frigid water and slide beneath.

AUSTIN

*I*t all happens in slow motion.

One second, Delilah is talking with Sloane and Aubrey, and the next, she's stumbling into the railing and falling over it. My heart lodges somewhere in the middle of my throat as she disappears from sight.

The high-pitched scream that fills the air has the hair at the base of my neck prickling as I leap from the couch and race across the deck before diving headfirst over the side and plunging into the chilly depths of Lake Michigan.

As I arrow into the water, I scan the murkiness that surrounds me but don't immediately spot her blonde head.

Fuck!

I surface before sucking in a lungful of air and diving back down, using my arms and legs to propel me forward. It's almost impossible to see more than a foot in front of my face. Panic and fear engulf me, spreading through my veins like ice and weighing me down. My lungs burn from lack of oxygen as spots dance in front of my vision. With a kick of my legs, I force myself deeper.

There's no way I can give up, but I won't be able to stay under much longer.

Just as I'm about to shoot to the top, I spot her long blonde hair fanned out around her. A golden halo shining in the darkness like a beacon. Relief explodes through me as I cut through the water and grab her arms, dragging her forward.

Her eyes blink open and our gazes lock for a heartbeat before drifting shut again. With her lifeless body secured against me, I propel us upward. The moment we break the surface, I gasp for breath as Delilah remains motionless. Her skin has been leached of all color and her lips are an unnatural shade of blue. Panic spirals through me and I can't help but wonder if I'm too late.

I didn't react quickly enough.

I didn't find her fast enough.

What the hell will I do if that turns out to be the case?

Her eyelids fly open and it's like a switch has been flipped as she claws at the surface of the water and then me.

"I have you, baby. Just relax. You're safe now."

Even though my words are gentle and we're no more than a couple yards from the boat, it does nothing to quell her panic. It only seems to incite it. Her large blue eyes go wide, nearly rolling in her head as she flails, coughing up water.

She continues to struggle as I maneuver her in my arms until her back is pressed against my chest. Once she's turned away, one arm slides around her ribcage to keep her anchored to me as I use my other to propel us toward the boat. Barely am I cognizant of our classmates hanging over the edge and watching us. Summer throws a striped life ring into the water about two feet away. As it drifts into reach, I pull it toward us until Delilah is able to wrap her arms around it. She clutches it to her chest and continues to cough and splutter.

I need to get us out of the water before she goes into full panic mode. As we reach the boat, Duke drops a swim ladder over the side. Unwilling to release the flotation device, she flails about with one arm.

"You need to let go of the ring. I won't let anything happen to you, I promise."

Her wide, frightened eyes flicker to mine. Pure terror lights them up.

Just as I'm about to wrestle it from her, she shoves it away and throws herself at the ladder, clinging to it as if for dear life. A choked cry escapes from her as she grasps it, attempting to hoist herself up the rungs. My hands settle on her bottom, forcing her upward as Duke leans down to grab hold of her wrist.

"You're safe," I grunt, only wanting to put her at ease. "Everything's going to be all right."

When the sole of her Converse slips on the slender tread, a startled cry escapes from her. Duke grits his teeth as he lifts her from the water. Her feet dangle for a couple of seconds before Kingsley snatches her from the air, wrapping his hands around her waist and dragging her over the railing and onto the deck.

It's only when Delilah is safely onboard does the adrenaline leak from my body and I realize my limbs are shaking. The waves lick at the side of the vessel as my heartbeat thunders in my ears until it's the only thing I'm cognizant of.

I've always been physically strong, but right now, after the terror of almost losing her, I feel weak as a kitten. It takes every bit of strength and energy to haul myself from the water. The moment I crest the railing, my gaze scans the dozen or so faces watching us. People have their hands pressed to their mouths as they stare in shock. The party atmosphere is long gone.

Voices drone in the background as someone scrambles to find a towel or blanket to wrap around Delilah as she sits huddled on the floor. It's only when my attention locks on her that everything settles and I can once again breathe. I hadn't realized how anxious I'd become when she'd been out of my sight until this very moment.

Her teeth chatter as her frightened gaze fastens on mine. With her arms banded tightly around her middle, she looks small and lost. That's all it takes for instinct to pound through my body, propelling me forward.

Water drips from my hair and soaked clothing. People scatter out of my way as I swallow up the distance between us until I'm close enough to pull her into my arms. A sob escapes from her as she rises to her feet and lands against my chest. Her body shivers almost violently.

Or maybe that's me.

"You need to get out of these wet clothes," I tell her.

When she fails to respond, I pull back just enough to search her eyes for comprehension. They swim with tears and there's a glassy, faraway look filling them as if she's not really here with me.

Shock.

She's in shock.

It's more important than ever to get her out of these drenched clothes and warm her up. The whimper that escapes from her when I untangle my arms and pull away breaks my heart.

"Shhh," I say. "I need to strip off my clothes and then we'll get you out of yours."

She remains unresponsive, continuing to tremble as I grip the hem of my sweatshirt and tug it over my head before peeling away the wet T-shirt. The cotton clings to my chest, feeling colder than when I was submerged in the lake.

I kick off my shoes and yank off the sopping socks before flicking open the button of my jeans and shoving the thick denim down my legs until I'm standing in nothing more than black boxer briefs.

It takes a moment to realize that the boat has become quiet enough to hear a pin drop.

"Well, damn," Sloane mutters.

I don't bother glancing at the circle of people gathered around us as I strip off Delilah's sweatshirt and the sodden shirt beneath. My gaze falls to her breasts and my mouth dries. Her bra has turned almost translucent and her pink-tipped nipples are puckered, poking insistently through the thin fabric. Goosebumps ripple across her flesh.

Someone clears their throat and it's tempting to swing around and bare my teeth. Instead, I drop to my haunches and loosen the laces of her shoes. Like everything else, they're waterlogged.

I glance up and say softly, "Lift your foot."

Her skin has turned almost ghostly as the teeth chattering grows louder.

When she continues to zone out, I lower my voice, attempting to break through the thick mental fog that has descended. "Pick up your foot, Delilah. I need to take off your shoe."

She blinks before slowly following the command.

Once her Converse have been removed, I straighten to my full height and go to work on her jeans. The button gets flicked open and the zipper dragged down before the material is peeled over the curve of her hips and thighs. Her trembling fingers settle on my shoulders as she lifts one foot and then the other. It's only when I've tossed the soaked material to the side that I stare at her panty-covered pussy. She's wearing pale pink underwear and the outline of her lips is clearly visible through the thin cotton.

"I need a blanket," I shout.

The last thing I want is any of these assholes ogling her while she's in such a vulnerable state.

A few seconds later, Summer shoves her way through the press of bodies and carefully drapes a thick blanket around her shoulders. My sister's concerned gaze remains locked on Delilah as I gather her up like she weighs nothing at all and stalk to the curved couch near the back of the boat. I settle on a plush cushion with her held securely in my arms before gently arranging her on my lap until we're both covered by the thick blanket. Her body trembles as she burrows against my chest. Her chilled skin presses to mine as I stroke my hands over her arms and back, trying to warm her.

Another blanket is thrown over us as I hold her tight. After a few minutes, the group pressing in on us gradually disperses, giving us a bit of breathing room as Kingsley starts up the engine and heads back to the marina.

Just as my muscles loosen, my gaze collides with Summer's. Her brows are tightly knit as she studies us silently. There's a pensive expression etched across her face. Almost as if she's trying to work out a complicated arithmetic formula in her head.

Once we return to shore and she gets me alone, she'll bombard me with questions.

Ones I need time to sort through.

When she raises a brow in silent inquiry, I jerk my shoulders. That's as much as I'm willing to share. A frustrated puff of air escapes from her. We've always had that strange twin thing between us. We're able to communicate with a single look or lift of the lips.

And right now, I hear her loud and clear.

Summer thinks I'm crazy for getting closer to this girl when all she's done is betray me at every fucking turn, making me look like a lovesick loser. But here's the thing—I can't explain the deep need I have for Delilah. It's one that rampages through my veins. I've always been able to walk away from a girl without so much as a backward glance. There's always been too many choices to get caught up on just one.

But that's not how it is with her.

Even though I shouldn't trust one damn word that comes out of her mouth, there's something that keeps me from turning my back and walking away. I don't fully understand it myself.

And crawling to me?

Fuck, that was hot.

Even when Duke tried to stop her, she went through with it. With her gaze fastened to mine as if I was her entire world, she inched across the deck and sat at my feet while I wrapped one hand around her hair and the other around her throat. Even though she was humiliated in front of our classmates, she gave herself over to me just like she promised on the beach.

Almost desperately, I want to believe her actions hold meaning.

But that's the thing…I have no idea if they do.

It could all be a game.

What I do know is that I can't focus on that right now.

Not when she's shivering in my arms.

Not when I almost lost her.

DELILAH

Once we reach Kingsley's beach house, Austin scoops me out of the SUV and tucks me against his chest. I would be lying if I didn't admit how comforting it is to be pressed against all that chiseled strength. I don't care if he stripped me practically bare in front of everyone before pulling me against the warmth of his nearly naked body.

For the first time in a week, everything felt right in the world. Considering that I almost drowned, that's really saying something. I don't want to relinquish the closeness we've found. I'm terrified that once we step inside Kingsley's beach house, it'll vanish into thin air, and he'll be back to staring at me with eyes full of distrust.

As he strides from the driveway to the mansion with me tucked safely in his arms, I force myself to say, "You can put me down now. I'm more than capable of walking by myself."

He doesn't respond as we reach the stairs to the front porch and move into the entryway. There's no hesitation in his step as he swings to the left and carries me up the staircase. It's only when we reach the bedroom that he carefully lowers me to the floor.

Our gazes lock and hold as I slide down his practically naked body. Once my feet touch the plush carpet, he straightens, and the blanket wrapped around my shoulders slips and puddles at my feet. The cool air of the room licks over my bare flesh and my teeth once again begin to chatter. Now that I don't have Austin's body heat to warm me, I'm freezing.

I blink when he swings away, leaving me to shiver in the middle of the room, arms wrapped around myself, as he walks into the attached bathroom. From where I stand, I watch as he leans over the massive clawfoot tub and turns on the faucet. The sound of running water fills the space.

He fiddles with the handles, testing the temperature before straightening and swinging back around. His eyes never relinquish mine as he returns to the bedroom before gripping the elastic band of his boxers and shoving them down his thick thighs until the material lands at his feet.

Even though I tell myself to keep my eyes locked on his, the urge to take in his magnificent body is too much to resist. All those sinewy muscles on display weaken my knees and make me go a little stupid.

My gaze drops to his chest, slowly licking over his pectorals before drifting down six-pack abdominals to the chiseled V that arrows to the part of him that now stands thick and erect. My mouth turns cottony as need blooms in my core. The fact that he licked me to orgasm less than twelve hours ago has done absolutely nothing to dampen the arousal that now rushes through my veins.

It doesn't matter if I've just lived through a traumatic experience and am physically drained.

I want him.

And I can't imagine a time when that won't be true.

A growl vibrates from deep within his chest as I stare my fill. After a handful of silent seconds, he grows impatient and swallows up the distance between us with three long-legged strides. Once he's close enough, both hands settle on my shoulders and he spins me around until my spine is to him. Before I can ask what he's doing, his fingers settle at the clasp of my bra and fiddle with the latch.

The elastic band that stretches around my ribcage springs apart and the thin straps slither down my arms. His fingertips glide across my skin, knocking the undergarment away until it falls to the carpet. My gaze gravitates to the mirror across the room and I watch as his face lowers to the gentle slope of my shoulder. His lips ghost across my shivering skin. Even though I'm freezing, the warmth of his breath and mouth do the impossible and heat me from the inside out.

That's all it takes for the world to go dark.

He gently pulls the rubber band from my hair before carefully fanning the wet strands out around my shoulders. His fingertips trail down my arms and sensation ricochets within me. I love the way his touch gentles when that's what I need and turns demanding when that's what I want. Somehow, he understands my desires without me verbalizing them.

The longer he hovers at my back, the more tension crackles in the air that surrounds us. Just when I can't take another second of this exquisite torture, his fingers slip into the waistband of my drenched panties, slowly sliding them down my hips, over the curve of my ass, and finally thighs. The thin cotton drops to my ankles where it settles.

And then I'm as naked as he is.

A guttural groan escapes from him as his large hands encircle my waist and he drops to his knees. His mouth presses against my chilled flesh as his teeth scrape against one tightly-clenched cheek before giving the same attention to the other. His hands glide from my waist to my backside before cupping the roundness and squeezing it in his palms.

"Such a perfect, heart-shaped ass," he murmurs thickly, sinking his teeth into me.

That's all it takes for my self-control to snap and a moan to erupt, filling the charged atmosphere that crackles around us. Any moment, it'll burst into flames, and we'll go up in smoke.

He peppers more sweet kisses against me, kneading the muscles, banishing the thick tension until it becomes a challenge to remain upright. Only then does he press his lips to each rounded curve before straightening.

His hands settle on my shoulders and turn me until our gazes can lock. The hunger that glows in his heated green gaze is enough to steal my breath away. One arm slips around my waist as the other slides beneath my knees. In one swift motion, I'm hoisted off the floor. It takes less than a dozen steps for us to reach the clawfoot tub, which is filled with steaming water, making the bathroom feel warm and toasty.

Austin sets me down on the mat before leaning over the edge and testing the water. Once it's an acceptable temperature, he steps into the massive porcelain tub and extends a hand.

My body trembles, but I'm unsure if it's from the impromptu swim in Lake Michigan or how tender Austin's touch has turned. As I gingerly step into the water, a hiss escapes from my lips as my foot is submerged in the translucent liquid.

"Is it too hot?" he asks quickly.

When I shake my head, his grip tightens around me and his other hand settles at my elbow to help steady me as I step fully into the water. The faucet continues to run and steam billows around us as he carefully eases himself against the curved porcelain.

A groan escapes from him as his legs widen to make room. "You need to warm up, and this will help."

I swallow past the thick lump that has wedged itself in the middle of my throat, making it impossible to breathe, as I turn and slowly sink to the smooth bottom. His large hands wrap around my waist as he shifts me, arranging my body until we're both submerged and the water can lap at my nipples. His thick erection presses insistently against my backside as his hands slip around my ribcage until both palms are able to cup my breasts. My muscles loosen as I recline until my head rests against the comforting strength of his chest.

"Why does this feel so fucking perfect?" he growls near the outer shell of my ear. The vibration of his words sends tingles scampering down my spine.

I don't know, but it's the same sentiment that's fluttering around in my brain as well.

Before I can come up with a response, his fingers wrap around my nipples, pulling and tugging at them in tandem. They were already stiff from the cool air of the room, but the way he plays with me has them growing painfully erect.

All rational thought vanishes as I writhe against him, seeking out more of his touch. More of the sensations only he is capable of igniting within me. It's impossible to imagine anyone else arousing my body to this kind of fever pitch.

Only Austin.

That thought is as terrifying as it is exhilarating.

"Do you have any idea how scared I was when you fell overboard?" he asks quietly, voiced filled with pent-up emotion.

A shudder slides through me as the memory crashes through my brain. The handful of seconds it took to hit the water and plunge beneath the frigid surface felt like an eternity that was over in the blink of an eye.

"I would have drowned if you hadn't jumped in," I admit softly. "I never learned how to swim."

That confession has his arms tightening, the muscles bulging as he pulls me closer before pressing his lips against the side of my face.

"I wouldn't have let anything happen to you." His mouth drifts along my cheek, peppering sweet kisses along the way. "You understand that, right?"

I twist in his arms just enough for our gazes to collide before nodding. As furious as he's been, I know deep down that Austin will always protect me. Even when he's intent on bringing me to my knees.

The words burst from my lips before I can rein them back in. "I don't want to fight with you anymore. I can't do it."

Guilt flickers across his expression. "We won't. It's over."

A kernel of hope rises within me, blotting out all other emotion. "Do you really mean that?" It's almost impossible to believe that he'll let his anger go.

Just like that.

"Yeah. We both need a fresh start."

Tears prick my eyes.

His hand rises to carefully wipe away the wetness that splashes across my cheek. "Please don't cry." His voice dips, becoming unsteady. "I'm sorry for all the hurt I caused."

"There's nothing for you to apologize for. I know how it appeared. And Jasper was there every step of the way, wanting you to believe that I was messing around. I should have broken up with him after he showed his true colors. Instead, I took the easy way out and stayed."

He strokes my cheek with gentle fingers. "Shhh. It's all right. We don't have to talk about it or him ever again, okay?"

I squeeze my eyes tight and lean into his touch. It's what I've been waiting to hear but never thought would actually happen. "You mean everything to me, and I hate that you were hurt. That you thought I was toying with you."

"I know, Delilah. And I believe you. It's just that the thought of you with him drives me fucking insane. It clouded my better judgment. I see that now."

I force my eyes open and twist to meet his gaze. "You do?"

"Yeah." His eyes cloud as remorse flickers across his face. "I'm sorry for humiliating you in front of everyone."

Thick emotion swells in my throat. "All I wanted was for you to believe me. And if that's what it took to convince you, then I can live with it."

His lips brush across my cheek. "It shouldn't have been necessary. All I could focus on was punishing you. It won't happen again."

I didn't think this moment could become more perfect, but as we continue talking, that's exactly what happens. Everything is finally out in the open. For the first time since Kingsley's party, we're both on the same page.

"You're the only one I want to belong to," I tell him, heart thumping at the prospect.

"That's good, because you will *always* belong to me," he growls before pinching my nipples hard enough to elicit a gasp. Somehow, his touch is both forceful and adoring at the same time. I don't know how he's able to walk that fine line so perfectly. More than that, I don't understand how I can love it.

Crave it.

Need it.

As one hand toys with the erect buds, the other drifts down the center of my ribcage, across my belly before arriving at my mound where his fingers hesitate. So badly do I want them to slip inside my heat and stroke me to orgasm. Instead, they hover, dancing across the plump flesh and lazily circling over my clit. A whimper of frustration escapes from me as I widen my legs, granting him more access.

"Is there something you want, sweet girl?" he growls against my ear as he caresses me until I'm shifting restlessly against him.

When I fail to respond, his voice dips lower. "That's not an answer."

His fingers skate in never-ending loops that drive me insane. The near drowning experience is no longer front and center in my brain. The only thing I'm cognizant of is Austin and the way he's able to ignite a firestorm of need and emotion inside me.

He plays with my nipples while simultaneously stroking my heated flesh. After a few minutes, the hand at my breast glides upward until his fingers can loosely wrap around my throat.

That's all it takes for my pulse to pick up its tempo, fluttering madly against his fingertips. His other hand cups my pussy before flexing possessively, the fingers sinking into my soft flesh and marking me in the most primal way possible.

"This belongs to me. It doesn't matter what happens between us, it will always be mine."

"Yes," I moan, agreeing with the sentiment.

His middle finger slips inside my soaked entrance as the heel of his palm grinds against my clit. My breath catches as I widen my legs a few more inches and arch. The grip around my throat tightens before loosening as he strokes his fingers along the delicate column.

"Do you know how much I enjoy you like this? Draped naked across my body, open and hungry for my touch. Your pussy sobbing for every little caress while my fingers wrap around your throat."

As the words fall roughly from his lips, I bow my spine and tip my head farther back, baring even more of the fragile column.

"I fucking love how much you enjoy surrendering to me. How you trust me enough to hand this power over for safekeeping." Again, his fingers tighten, squeezing ever so gently, making me gasp for breath. My lungs shudder with the deprivation.

What he's doing should frighten me.

It doesn't. Instead…I love it.

Love that he can give me something I never realized I wanted.

Or needed.

Somehow, he was able to recognize it.

"I won't ever abuse this gift." He presses another tender kiss against the side of my face before his grip loosens and I gulp in a lungful of fresh air. "You're so fucking perfect." There's a pause before he adds, "*For me*. You're fucking perfect for me."

Just as my muscles relax, his fingers tighten again, cutting off precious oxygen. "The thought of anyone touching you like this, giving you pleasure, drives me fucking insane."

Even though a whimper escapes as my lungs plead for air, I don't struggle or claw at him. My core floods with arousal as I press into his hand, loving the feel of all that strength wrapped around me, holding me tight, giving me what I so desperately long for.

"Please," I gasp.

"Please what, sweet girl? Press harder or let go?"

That shouldn't even be a question.

When his fingers loosen, I whisper, "I don't know."

The groan that escapes from him is rough and low. It only turns me on more.

"How did I get so lucky?"

I don't know, but I feel the same.

We're two halves of the same whole.

When his grip intensifies, I realize it's exactly what I wanted. My eyes widen as my airflow once again becomes restricted. My hands rise, locking around his forearm as I press into him. Another deep groan rumbles up from his chest and vibrates through my stretched-out body. I arch, forcing my legs even wider, practically coming out of the water as the heel of his palm grinds against my throbbing clit and he slips a second finger inside me to stroke my inner walls.

I don't know how much more of this I can take. It feels like I'm on the verge of passing out and yet, I want it to last forever. There's so much pleasure flooding through every cell of my being as my brain turns hazy. Whether it's from the lack of oxygen or the way he commands my body, I have no idea.

What I do know is that I trust him implicitly to keep me safe. Austin will push me to my limits and then past them until I shatter into a million broken fragments at his clever fingertips. And then he'll carefully piece me back together again.

Just as my muscles turn taut, orgasm imminent, his grip tightens and I gasp. A silent scream echoes in my head as his fingers curl inside me, the palm grinding against my clit.

"Come for me right now," he demands harshly.

And I do.

It's like the floodgates open as I fall apart on command at his fingertips. All of the pleasure culminates into a single crystalline moment that explodes like fireworks behind my eyelids.

My lips part as my inner muscles convulse and an orgasm like I've never experienced before streaks through my body. When his grip loosens, I drag fresh air into my deprived lungs. The scream building within me bursts free as he continues to stroke my pussy, teasing out every last shudder.

Every last cry.

Before I can drag in another fresh breath, his hand rises so that his thumb and forefinger can squeeze my jawbones. The new position forces me to tip my chin higher until I'm thrusting out my breasts.

"That's it, sweet girl. Scream until there's nothing left inside. I want everyone in this fucking house to hear you come. I don't want anyone to ever question the way I make you feel."

Even though his words should embarrass me, rendering me silent, it has the opposite effect. In this moment of utter ecstasy, I don't give a damn who hears me. All I can focus on is the pleasure rampaging through my body, lighting me up from the inside out. After my muscles slacken, he curves his hand over my pussy in a possessive way that makes my heart flip flop dangerously in my chest.

"I fucking love when you come."

It's only when I force my heavy eyelids open that I realize the water is still running and is about two inches away from cresting over the edge of the tub.

When he relinquishes his hold on both my pussy and throat, a strange sense of loss fills me.

His hands wrap around my waist and he twists me around until I have to fold my legs to sit astride him. The tips of my breasts get smashed against the hard lines of his chest as he draws me closer before reaching to turn off the faucet.

With our faces scant inches apart, the warmth of his breath feathers against my parted lips.

"Do you remember what I said to you the first time I was inside your tight little cunt?"

I blink, thrown off by the question.

Even though he said lots of things, one growled-out comment in particular stands out in my brain. "That the next time you have me, you'd turn me over and mount me from behind, taking me like an animal."

A slow smile spreads across his face as his eyes sharpen, turning almost feral. "That's right."

My belly hollows out. I've dwelled on that dark promise more times than I care to admit.

"I never did it, did I?"

I shake my head as my heart thunders painfully beneath my breast.

"I think it's time we rectify that situation, don't you?"

DELILAH

His grip tightens around my waist as he removes me from his lap before rising to his feet. Water sluices down his perfectly chiseled body in rivulets as I stare up at him from where I sit. My face is inches from his cock. It's long and hard. From this position, I'm able to see the pronounced vein that runs the length, throbbing against the skin.

I glance from his thick erection to his eyes, which burn with intensity. Unable to resist, I lean forward, closing the distance between us and flicking my tongue across the tip. His muscles tighten as he cants his hips toward me. That's all the incentive I need to wrap my lips around his crown and draw him into my mouth. A guttural sounding groan vibrates in his chest as his fingers tunnel through the wet strands of my hair, dragging me closer.

"Fuck, that feels good."

My gaze stays pinned to his as his eyelids fall, pleasure overtaking his expression. The tension normally written in the lines of his face softens, making him look more like his eighteen years.

This is when I like Austin best. When he pushes everything that eats away at him to the back of his brain and allows himself to simply live in the moment. Pleasure suffuses me that after everything that's transpired between us, he can lower his guard enough to be vulnerable with me.

When his dick swells, my suction becomes more voracious. I want to stare up at him from my knees and watch as he splinters apart. I want to give him a tiny shred of what he's shared with me. With a grunt, his fingers tighten around my scalp, and he pushes me away until his cock pops free.

His hands are still fisted in my hair when he drops down until his face is level with mine. "Are you trying to cheat me out of taking what's mine?"

"No."

"Good." He nips at my lower lip, drawing the plumpness into his mouth and sucking it greedily. "Because I won't be denied."

With that, he untangles his fingers from my wet strands and slips his hands under my arms before stepping out of the tub. We stand on the bathmat as warm water drips from our bodies and puddles at our feet.

He yanks a fluffy towel from the silver rack hanging on the wall before turning to me. His intentions are written clearly in his eyes. With a surprisingly gentle touch, he swipes the thick fabric over my shoulders and along my arms.

Is he thinking about the time I dried him off after a shower? Memories of what it felt like to explore his muscular body have my core throbbing to life.

Again.

His hot gaze follows the path of his hands as he strokes the plush material across the tips of my breasts. They're already hard and achy from the way he caressed me in the tub. The mere brush of cotton against the stiff little buds has arousal rocketing through my entire body. Air stalls in my lungs.

How can I be so turned on when I came only minutes ago?

But there's no denying the truth.

He knows exactly how to touch me to elicit a response.

My teeth sink into my lower lip as he continues to pat and rub my breasts before tweaking each nipple. The chain reaction from those innocuous touches sets off an explosion deep within my center and a whimper bursts from my lips.

There is no point in trying to stave it off and remain unaffected.

He unravels me in the best way possible.

All I know is that I want more of this.

Of him.

I'm so greedy for all he's willing to give.

He doesn't say a word as he hunkers down to reach my midsection and then thighs. As I stare at the top of his dark head, I marvel at the tightly harnessed power kneeling before me. Any moment, it's going to break free.

He's meticulous in his task, making sure to wipe my belly and hips before stroking the towel against my pussy. My lower lips are sensitive and swollen from the way he played with me in the tub.

Unable to remain still, I shift beneath his hands as he takes his sweet damn time drying me.

When I continue wriggling, he slants a look at me before swatting my clit. "Stop it."

I yelp in surprise. Pain slices through me before it's quickly followed by a heady rush of pleasure. Arousal gathers inside my lower belly, swirling like an impending storm. It wouldn't take much to shove me over the precipice and into oblivion.

For a second time.

"Spread your legs so I can dry that pretty little pussy."

When I widen my stance, hungry for his touch, he drags the towel against my sensitive flesh. A moan wells in my throat as my teeth sink into my lower lip.

"You're fucking soaked," he murmurs. "I don't think it's from the bath, do you?"

Heat rushes to my cheeks at his need to point this out.

We both know it's not.

When I remain silent, he tips his head until his hooded gaze can lock on mine and arches a brow as if impatiently awaiting my response.

"No," I force myself to whisper.

"No," he agrees, voice growing deeper until it sounds like it's been roughed up by sandpaper. "It's not." He carefully caresses me with the thick material, sliding it against my lips.

Over and over again until I want to come undone.

A moan slips free and fills the silence of the room.

"I'm the one who did this to you. Such a soaked little pussy. I just can't seem to get you dry. The more I rub you, the wetter you become." He glances at me again. "Are you crying for me, Delilah?"

My mouth is so dry that swallowing past the thick lump lodged in the middle of my throat is impossible. Barely am I able to concentrate on the words tumbling out of his mouth. I'm only cognizant of the pleasure rushing through me.

I gasp when he gives my clit another swat with the tips of his fingers.

"Yes!"

"Do you understand that I'm the only one who will ever be able to make you feel this way?"

"Yes. Just you," I repeat, voice rising with each syllable. It's becoming more difficult to keep everything contained. I'm caught between wanting him to smack my clit and pleasing him with the correct answer.

"Good girl."

Satisfied with my response, he presses his lips to my pussy. Just as I flex my hips, wanting to get closer, he pulls away and strokes the towel over my center a few more times before moving on to my legs.

Once every last drop of moisture has been wiped away, he spins me around until I'm facing the tub. The thick cotton slides from the top of my thighs, down my calves to my ankles and then back up again.

He is nothing if not thorough.

My skin is rosy and over-sensitized from his careful ministrations.

Just when I think he'll rise to his feet and make good on his earlier promise, he instructs, "Bend over and grab the edge of the tub."

I blink, thrown off by the request. "What?"

He swats my ass. "You heard me the first time. Don't make me repeat myself."

When I don't immediately comply, he smacks the other cheek harder, making it sting until I'm flooded with awareness.

"Now, Delilah."

My body trembles as need continues to build as I lean forward and wrap my fingers around the porcelain rim. Even though I'm staring at the picture window that overlooks the vastness of the lake, movement catches the corner of my eye and I turn my head until I'm able to view him in the mirror.

The way Austin squats behind me puts him eyelevel with my upturned backside. My face heats at the realization that he's staring at my ass, inspecting a taboo place no one ever has. I nearly jump out of my skin when he runs the plush fabric across the cleft that divides my cheeks. Back and forth he strokes, carefully dragging the material across my rosebud.

My teeth pin my lower lip in place. I never realized that something like this could be pleasurable. It's a shocking discovery. Air slowly leaks from my lungs when the towel finally disappears. I'm filled with a strange concoction of relief edged with disappointment. The emotions war with one another but there is no clear victor. Just as I'm about to straighten, his palms settle over my cheeks, massaging them. I can't help but shift, enjoying the touch but still self-conscious about his proximity to that secret part of me.

"Stop squirming," he warns, fingers sinking into the flesh.

If he's aware of my embarrassment, he brushes it aside and ignores it. Even though it feels amazing, nerves claw at me, looking for an escape. There's no way he doesn't see every single delicate inch of me.

What I don't understand is how something so wrong can feel so damn right.

It's become a common theme with Austin.

His touch feels so good but leaves me questioning whether or not it should. It would be easier if I could force the doubts from my mind and simply enjoy the way he plays with my body.

"Austin," I squeak, shame rushing through me.

It's not just his insistent caresses that make me feel this way but how much I secretly enjoy what he's doing. How he takes control and touches a place that's always been forbidden.

He releases one cheek long enough to give the flesh a resounding whack. It's not hard enough to cause pain or damage, just enough to have pleasure exploding inside me like a firework.

"This belongs to me. Be still and let me look at you."

My mind cartwheels as he pulls at my rounded flesh again, separating the globes. The cool air of the room rushes over me.

"Arch your back," he commands.

The deep cadence of his voice scampers along my spine.

It's not even a consideration to deny the instruction. I understand what will happen if I don't. In the end, he'll bend me to his will and take what he wants.

In the far recesses of my mind, I understand that if I truly wanted to put an end to this exploration, I could. That silent realization tells me everything I need to know about this situation. It forces me to mentally come to terms with my own secret wants and desires. Even if they make me uncomfortable and I'd prefer not to acknowledge them.

Instead of arguing, I bow my spine, raising my ass higher in the air.

"So fucking beautiful," he groans, sharp teeth scraping across the curve of my flesh.

A million little shivers slide through me before settling in my core as arousal drips down my bare thighs.

One hand tugs at my cheek as his other strokes over the tightly puckered muscle. A mixture of shock and arousal crashes over me like a tidal wave, and in that moment, it feels like I'm drowning all over again.

Only this time, there isn't anyone to rescue me.

I can't help but squirm against the insistent slide of his fingers.

Am I trying to get closer or away from him?

I release a breath when his finger disappears only to dip inside my pussy before returning and carefully probing the muscle, pressing an unrelenting finger against the tight ring. A gasp escapes as instinct kicks in and I clench.

He smacks my ass cheek. "Don't ever try to keep me out of a place that belongs to me. I'll touch every single part of you if that's what I want."

Deep down, I knew that would be his response.

With Austin, there will be no secrets.

No propriety or space.

My body will belong to him to use how he sees fit.

For his pleasure.

And mine.

Even if I'm filled with shame, he will force his way past my defenses and give me exactly what I need.

It's that knowledge that has me relaxing my muscles as my teeth sink painfully into my lower lip. My gaze stays pinned to the reflection in the mirror. The image of us—me standing with my back arched, holding onto the rim of the tub for dear life and him hunkered down behind me, inspecting and playing with the most intimate part of me is ridiculously sexy.

When the blunt tip of his finger presses into my body, I can't help the moan that falls from my lips. I wasn't prepared for the pressure or burn of the muscle stretching to accommodate the width of his digit. As uncomfortable as it is, there's something else simmering beneath the surface.

Something indescribable that feels all kinds of wicked.

As much as I want to hate it…

I don't.

"You're so damn tight," he growls. His voice is strained as if he'll lose it at any moment.

He pushes in half an inch or so before slowly withdrawing. Just when a sigh of relief is on the verge of escaping from me, his finger breaches the tight muscle for a second time and slides even further inside my body. His other hand continues to massage my cheek, pulling and stretching as he falls into a steady rhythm of pressing forward and gaining new ground before retreating and then repeating the movement.

"Your ass belongs to me, Delilah."

It's a statement of ownership.

One I'm unable to argue with.

Nor do I want to.

"I know."

That quiet acceptance is rewarded with a kiss to my cheek as he continues the steady motion. Pressure fills me each time he enters my body and slides inside. It's almost a shock when the burn begins to fade and pleasure sparks to life in the nerve endings before progressively building. It's like a newly ignited fire that needs to be carefully tended to in order to flourish.

And that's exactly what he does.

Stokes the flames burning inside my body.

"Good girl," he praises. "Know how I can tell that you like this?" Before I can respond, he continues. "Your pussy lips are glistening. I bet it wouldn't take much to make you come. All I'd have to do is rub your clit while stroking my finger in and out of your tight little asshole and you'd fall to pieces around me." His voice deepens, turning several shades darker. "You have no idea how tempting it is to do just that."

I suspect he's right. Even now, I feel the heat smoldering in my lower belly. My eyelids feather shut as pleasure takes hold. His finger slides deeper inside my body with each surge forward until he's able to flatten his wide palm against me.

"I wish you could see how perfect you look with my finger buried knuckle deep inside your ass. Fucking beautiful."

For a long, silent minute, neither of us moves a muscle. It's as if time stops and we're hanging in suspension. Me with my fingers wrapped around the porcelain, my ass tilted, breath coming fast and heavy. Him crouched behind my naked and vulnerable form, his thick digit lodged intimately inside me. I can almost feel my muscles adjusting to the intrusion.

Stretching to accommodate and accept this newly claimed

ownership.

Forcing my eyes open again, I stare at the mirror, mesmerized by the sight of us. When he leans closer, the heat of his breath drifts across my bare skin as he presses a kiss against my pussy.

He's right. I'm dripping with arousal and need. I didn't think it was possible to become turned on again so quickly, but I was wrong. If there's a way, Austin will find it and wring every last drop of pleasure from my body.

A whimper escapes from me as his tongue slides between my lips.

Any second, I'll shatter.

And there won't be a way to put me back together again.

"Delicious."

When I bow my spine, only wanting to give him further access to my delicate flesh, he draws away, peppering my backside with tiny, fleeting kisses that drive me to distraction. His finger never budges.

"Do you like this?" he whispers.

"Yes."

If you'd told me three months ago that I would enjoy a man playing with my ass, teasing the muscle and pressing deep inside my body until I was none too sure where he ended and I began, I would have called you crazy. It didn't seem possible that any pleasure could have been derived from this kind of play.

I was wrong.

So wrong.

"I like it too. I like touching you, making your body sing."

"I enjoy doing the same to you."

With a groan, he slips his finger from my ass. I gasp as a strange sensation of loss and emptiness fills me. It doesn't make sense that I would actually miss the feel of him buried deep within.

When I straighten, his hands settle on my hips and he swivels me around until we're once again facing one another. His hands drift to my backside before he drags me close enough for my legs to tangle around his waist so that my pussy is splayed across his rock-solid abdominals. The friction has me wanting to grind against him. With me locked around his midsection, Austin carries me to the bedroom before depositing me on the mattress where I land with a soft bounce.

"On your knees, sweet girl," he growls.

I scramble to do his bidding, only wanting more of these newly discovered feelings he's ignited within me.

"Mmm, that's right. Ass in the air."

Excitement spirals through me as his hand trails over my flank. He doesn't make me wait as he positions the blunt head of his cock against my entrance before sliding deep inside with one swift movement.

"Fuck, it's such a tight fit," he says with a raspy groan. "It's like your pussy is trying to strangle the life out of my dick."

Those gruff words send a tidal wave of sensation crashing over me.

I'm so wet that he's able to slide in and out with ease. It's nothing like the first time when he had to carefully inch his way inside me.

"As much as I want to make this last, there's no way that's going to happen."

His larger body presses against mine as his hips piston. The only sound that can be heard in the silence of the room is our harsh breaths mingled with the slapping of skin. He gathers up the thick strands of my hair and holds them tight until it becomes necessary to tilt my head. My scalp stings as pleasure sizzles through my veins before settling deep in my core. An orgasm builds like an impending storm. The possessiveness of his hold and the way he pins my smaller body to the mattress has me on the verge of coming. When he presses the tip of his finger against my rosebud, I come unhinged and splinter apart.

My eyes feather closed as I cry out. His movements become more frenzied as he finds his own release. The warmth of his orgasm paints my womb. Nothing has ever felt more amazing than when our bodies are in perfect synchronicity. My inner muscles clench, squeezing him, milking every last drop from his cock until there is nothing left to give. Until I've completely drained him and he's huffing out a breath, collapsing on top of me in a heap of well-honed muscle.

"Fuck," he mutters, sounding like he needs to catch his breath.

A tiny smile quirks the corners of my lips. I don't think I've ever felt more satiated in my life. And that has everything to do with the man still pulsing inside my body.

With his hand locked around my hair, he turns my head until the side of my neck is bared to him. His lips graze the delicate flesh, teeth scraping over me before sinking into the tender skin. Air clogs my throat as he pins me in place, marking me as his.

We stay fused together for a handful of minutes before he carefully slips from my exhausted body. A keen sense of loss suffuses me at his withdrawal. It's as if we're connected and whole when he's buried deep within me and severed into two broken pieces when we're not.

The cool air of the room drifts over my exposed skin as he disappears inside the bathroom. I squeeze my eyes tightly closed and attempt to regain my bearings on the emotions that are rampaging through me. My eyelids spring open in surprise when a warm cloth is pressed to my pussy. When I struggle, he places a hand against the small of my back to hold me in place.

"Let me clean you off."

"You don't have to. I can do it myself," I say, embarrassment flaming through me. After everything we just did, this shouldn't be a big deal and yet, it feels incredibly intimate.

"I want to." His voice softens. "So let me."

That's all it takes for the fight to drain from me as I allow him to wipe away our combined arousal. I have to admit that the heat pressed against my abraded flesh feels good. My muscles loosen as I sink into the mattress.

Once finished, he places a kiss against my swollen lips before padding back to the bathroom. I roll onto my side and curl up in a tight ball. A handful of seconds later, he returns and gathers me into his strong arms, pulling me against his chest so that his bigger body can cradle mine protectively.

It doesn't take long for my eyelids to grow heavy, drifting shut as exhaustion sucks me under and sleep claims me.

DELILAH

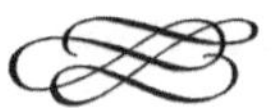

When I finally surface again, night has fallen, and darkness blankets the spacious room. Cast in shadows, nothing looks familiar. For just a moment, I'm confused and unsure where I am. As soon as the first burst of panic floods through me, everything that happened this afternoon crashes through my head.

The excursion on Lake Michigan.

Austin forcing me to sit at his feet.

Snapping photographs at the front of the boat.

Aubrey knocking into me and then falling into the water.

Wait a minute…

Dad's Nikon.

For the first time since Austin pulled me from the frigid depths of the lake, it hits me that I've lost my camera. It slipped from my hands and there was no way to save it.

A small sob rises within my throat as a fresh wave of grief crashes over me.

Tears well in my eyes before rolling down my cheeks.

I can't believe it's gone. Out of all my possessions, it's the one that has always meant the most. Only now in hindsight do I realize that it was stupid to bring it along this weekend. Especially on the boat. I should have left it at home where it would be safe.

It's only when I roll to the middle of the king-sized bed that I realize Austin's no longer here. Heat floods my face and a dull ache flares to life in my core as I think about all the ways he laid his hands on me.

I don't regret a single moment of what we did.

I refocus on the empty bed and wonder where he is before glancing at the bathroom. The door is open, and the space within is dark and quiet. There's a stillness to the air that makes me realize I'm alone in the room. It only takes a moment or two for the soft strains of music to meet my ears. It's muted enough for me to realize that it isn't coming from inside the house.

With a toss of the covers, I grab Austin's graphic T-shirt thrown haphazardly over an armchair in the corner of the room. As soon as I tug the soft cottony material over my head and down my body, I'm inundated with the fragrance of his woodsy cologne. Unable to resist, I lift the material and inhale a deep breath.

Who would have thought that someone's scent could be so comforting?

Or such a turn-on?

Moonlight slants through the window and from where I stand, it's easy to spot the flickering orange flames of the bonfire as they leap and twist toward the velvety star-littered sky. I gravitate to the glass and peer down at the scene taking place below. It's almost a surprise to find at least a hundred people or so drinking and dancing on the beach. It's debauchery at its finest.

I squint, searching the crowd for Austin, but I'm unable to make out any faces from this distance. There are too many writhing shapes.

Is Austin down there, partying it up?

I have zero interest in joining the fray.

But I'm curious as to where he is and why he left without waking me.

Before I fully realize my intentions, I swing away from the window and dig through my duffle until I find a pair of jeans and then throw on a thick sweatshirt. It was chilly this morning and into the afternoon. Now that the sun has fully set, it'll be even colder. Especially on the beach where it's always breezier.

I slip on an extra pair of tennis shoes I brought along before heading out the door. Once over the threshold, I glance down the long stretch of hallway, searching for signs of life. But there aren't any. No music or voices coming from inside. Silence presses in on me as I take the staircase to the first floor. Darkness fills every nook and cranny.

Everyone must be on the beach. From the swell of revelers outside, my guess is that classmates from other houses have stopped by. As I slip out the backdoor, the pulsing beat of music fills my ears. The closer I get to the bonfire, the more intense it becomes. The skunky scent of weed hangs heavy in the air. I've never tried it, but I recognize the distinctive aroma from past parties.

I hit the perimeter of the boisterous group and wind my way through couples dancing and kissing. Two girls are wrapped around one another. Their lips are fused as their hands explore beneath their sweatshirts. Three guys stand nearby, drinking their beer, eyes glued to the oblivious couple.

Even though there's a sharp bite to the breeze, clothing has been shed in the sand.

This isn't my scene, and I'm not interested in hanging out for long.

I scan each face as I slip through the throng, only wanting to find Austin and get the hell out of here. All are recognizable, but none are the one I'm searching for. It's a relief when my gaze settles on a friendly one and I pivot, beelining in that direction.

"Hi," I say with a forced smile before tucking a stray lock of hair behind my ear.

Duke gives me a chin lift in greeting before raising the brown bottle of beer to his lips and taking a swig. "Hey. I was wondering where you were."

"I crashed for a while and feel much better now."

Although it's doubtful that had anything to do with the nap and more with the way Austin controlled and manipulated my body, bringing me easily to several orgasms.

His gaze cruises over me as if to confirm that information for himself. "Good. I was worried about you. I'm glad nothing happened."

For a split second, my mind tumbles back to what it felt like to slip beneath the surface of the freezing waters and a chill scurries down my spine. I could have easily drowned had Austin not jumped in. It was his quick reaction that stopped me from ending up a statistic.

I shift from one foot to the other before glancing around. "Have you seen Austin?"

That question is all it takes for his easy-going expression to vanish. "Why are you bothering with him?"

My eyes widen.

When I remain silent, Duke steps closer, swallowing up some of the distance between us. "Look, I'm not trying to tell you what to do, just that you need to be careful. Especially after what he did this afternoon.

Heat floods my cheeks as I gnaw my lower lip. From the outside, I suppose that's exactly the way it looked. Like he's no better than Jasper. But that's not true, and I wish Duke could see that.

"There's a lot you don't know, and I can't explain it right now," I say carefully.

His eyes narrow as he cocks his head. It's obvious that he's frustrated by my response. "Why not? Every time I see him, he's got his hands on you, forcing you to do things you don't want."

The truth of the matter is that Austin hasn't forced me to do anything. Maybe I've pretended not to want it, but deep down, I crave his touch. If I'm unwilling to admit it to Duke, I'll at least acknowledge it privately to myself.

What he can't possibly understand is that I enjoy the hot rush of blood spiking through my veins and beneath my skin when Austin lays hands on me. Or stares at me. He makes me feel alive.

Seen.

And this afternoon, when he demanded that I crawl to him…

He was only calling me out on a promise I'd made. No one twisted my arm to go through with it.

I shake my head. "That's not true."

His brows skyrocket across his forehead and he gives me an *are you crazy* look.

Unsure what to say, I blow out a slow breath and glance away.

"So this is what Stockholm syndrome looks like, huh?"

A snort escapes from me. "Austin isn't forcing me to do anything. I'm in total control of my decisions. Okay?"

Even though he jerks his broad shoulders, a dubious expression settles across his face.

Instead of arguing, I redirect the conversation back to my original question. The one that forced me down to the beach in the first place. "Have you seen him or not?"

Duke's whiskey-colored eyes turn guarded. "Yeah. Just a little bit ago."

My muscles relax as the corners of my lips lift in relief.

Good.

I want to find him and get the hell out of here. It only takes one glance to realize that this is just the beginning of the craziness sure to ensue, and I don't want to be anywhere near it.

"Where?"

There's a moment of hesitation.

"With Aubrey."

My heart stutters a painful beat before pounding erratically against my ribcage.

He breaks eye contact and scans the crowd. "I saw them together earlier, but it's been a while."

Almost reluctantly, his gaze returns to mine. The look he gives me is chockful of pity. Even though he presses his lips together and doesn't say a word, I hear his thoughts loud and clear.

You're being played.

I straighten my shoulders and force a lightness to my voice. "Thanks."

Just because he was spotted with Aubrey doesn't necessarily mean anything. Although, I would be lying if I didn't admit that doubt is creeping in at the edges and some of the happiness I'd found in his arms earlier has evaporated. The questions that lurk in Duke's eyes continue to circle through my brain, and there's nothing I can do to stop it.

Aubrey might have spent the past couple months turning her nose up at Austin, but clearly, her thoughts on the matter have done a one eighty. She's been hanging all over him, vying for his attention.

The urge to find him and lay my concerns to rest rushes through me and I point toward a group of students. "I'm, ah, going to take off."

I don't get more than a few steps when he says, "Don't go. Just chill here for a while."

With a glance over my shoulder, I force a smile. "I'm fine. No worries."

By the concerned expression that flits across his handsome face, I can tell his mind has tumbled back to the party at Kingsley's.

"Are you sure? Want me to help find him?"

Hard pass. Having these two boys together is a recipe for disaster. "Seriously, I'm good."

I'm almost out of earshot when his raised voice meets my ears. "You can always bunk in my room with Everly, and I'll sleep on the couch. You don't have to stay there."

Duke is a good friend who only wants the best for me. I rush forward and throw my arms around his neck before whispering, "Thank you, but that won't be necessary."

I give him a quick peck on the cheek and hurry through the thick crowd. Now that I'm in the middle of it, the number of revelers has swelled and there are even more people packed onto the beach.

All I care about is finding Austin and clearing the air. The idea that he would hop from my bed to someone else's makes me sick to my stomach. How is it that the fragile peace we managed to find is already crumbling around our heads?

After twenty minutes of searching, there's still no sign of Austin. Either we keep missing each other or he's not here. That alone isn't enough to cause concern, except...Aubrey is MIA as well.

My mind tumbles back to all the ways I allowed him to play with my body. I was practically panting for him.

Begging him to use me.

Well…I'm done.

I have no idea if he's fucking with me or not, but I can't continue riding this emotional rollercoaster any longer.

It's over.

If it was ever really anything to begin with.

Which I'm starting to doubt.

Maybe the reason he thinks I'm playing games is because that's what he's doing.

It's a disconcerting thought.

And the one that echoes the loudest through my head as the soles of my shoes pound against the weathered wooden stairs to the back-door. It's a relief to find the house empty as I race through the first floor, up to the second and beeline straight to the bedroom we're sharing. Once there, I twist the lock and lean against the door before squeezing my eyelids tightly closed.

DELILAH

The way I'm ripped from sleep is jarring. One second, I'm submerged in a dream and the next, my eyelids are flying open and Austin is hovering over me, his solid weight pressed against my chest, pinning me to the mattress.

"Did you really think a flimsy lock was going to keep me out?"

That snapped out question is all it takes for a rush of memories to crash back into my consciousness, and I stiffen beneath him.

"Yes," I growl. As soon as I shift, attempting to buck him off, his fingers lock around my wrists before dragging them over my head.

His eyes narrow as his jaw locks. "What the hell has gotten into you?"

Even though I hate myself for the jealousy that whips through my body, it's there, eating me alive. I couldn't keep the words trapped inside if I tried.

"Good question. Maybe you should go find Aubrey."

When I jerk my knee, attempting to knock it into him, he flinches. His lips peel back into a snarl as he stretches out on top of me, making movement impossible. He holds himself up on his elbows so that I'm not completely crushed by his weight.

"Aubrey?"

Even in the darkness, I'm able to glimpse the confusion that swirls through his green depths.

"I woke up a couple of hours ago and you were gone. When I went outside, I couldn't find you." A beat of silence passes before I accuse, "Duke said he saw you with Aubrey."

There's a moment of silence and I feel every beat of my pulse as I wait for an explanation.

"Just because I was talking to another girl, that somehow means we had sex? Is that how it works now?"

I grit my teeth. "She's been hanging all over you since I slid into your SUV. Are you really going to deny it?"

His expression softens as he blinks. "Are you actually jealous?"

My eyes widen as I renew my struggles. "Of course not."

A slow smirk curves his lips. "Hmmm. I think you might be lying."

A dull heat creeps into my cheeks because he's right, and I hate it. "I don't care what you think." I gather all my strength, trying to twist and dislodge him. "Now get off me."

He doesn't budge an inch. My guess is that Austin outweighs me by a solid fifty pounds. The reality is that he isn't going anywhere unless he makes that decision.

And right now…

He's staying put.

"Nope. Not gonna happen." With a shake of his head, he lowers his face until I can feel the warmth of his breath drift across my lips. "I told you before that you belong to me, to do with whatever I choose. And what I want right now is to be inside that sweet little cunt of yours."

Just as I'm about to tell him to go to hell, his lips crash onto mine and his tongue plunges inside my mouth. There's a strange mix of coaxing and forcefulness in the caress. As if he wants me to capitulate but will take what he wants—needs—by any means necessary. His fingers tighten around my wrists, holding me captive until I'm completely at his mercy.

My resistance can only last so long against his relentless onslaught. He knows precisely how to touch me and what will make my walls crumble. Even though I try to keep a firm grasp on my anger, it's a losing battle. I'm swept away by the taste and feel of him.

It's only when I reluctantly give myself over to him, returning the kiss, that he draws away, leaving me to pant with the need he stoked to life. When my eyelids feather open, I find him staring with a sober expression. Gone is the smugness of minutes ago.

"If you want me to blindly believe what you tell me, then maybe you need to return the favor and have a little bit more faith. It goes both ways."

Air gets wedged in my lungs as his words plunge me into uncertainty. More than anything, I want to trust Austin. Trust that he won't hurt or betray me. But it's difficult. Nothing about our relationship has been easy. At every turn, there have been complications and roadblocks. We inch forward two steps only to get knocked back three or four and land on our asses. There are times when it seems like all we're destined to do is inflict damage.

Even when we're not the ones responsible for it.

If I were thinking clearly, I'd cut my losses and move on.

But how can I do that when there's this invisible string binding us, relentlessly tugging me in his direction?

It's not something I've ever felt before, and I have the sneaking suspicion I never will again.

The indisputable truth is that I can come up with a lengthy list as to why a relationship will never work. And yet, none of it matters when he's stretched out on top of me, pinning me to the mattress, his tongue licking at my mouth.

"I want to," I admit.

This time, when his lips settle over mine, there's a gentleness to the caress. Just like always, he knows what I need and gives it to me without question. That's all the prompting it takes to open and allow him in. What I want most is for him to wipe away the past few hours.

All the uncertainty, anger, and jealousy.

Our mouths stay fused as our tongues tangle before he peppers tender kisses along the curve of my jaw and chin. When he drifts along the column of my neck, I can't help but bare it, hungry for more of his attention.

A growl reverberates deep in his chest when he reaches the collar of the T-shirt I'm wearing. His fingers grip the hem before dragging it up my body and over my head in one swift motion. He sits up and stares at my chest as if committing every dip and curve to memory. When I shift, he reaches out and cups my breasts, pinching the nipples that ache with need. Lowering himself, he draws one stiff peak into the warmth of his mouth before sucking greedily. My back bows off the mattress as arousal shoots from the tip of my breast, straight to my core before throbbing to life.

It doesn't matter if he played with my body for hours earlier, teasing two orgasms from me—I'm starved for his attention. When it comes to Austin, I'm insatiable. It's not something I'm used to. In all honesty, I didn't think it was possible to feel this kind of intense arousal crash through my body.

Jasper inspired the opposite.

Just when it feels like I'm on the verge of self-combusting, he releases me with a soft pop before latching onto the other stiff bud and giving it the same fervent attention. My fingers tunnel through his short, thick hair, tugging at the strands.

Another growl rumbles up from his chest as he lifts his head to meet my gaze.

"I don't know how I'll ever get enough of you."

His words echo my own private thoughts.

The energy we generate is combustible. Any moment it'll explode, blowing us both to smithereens.

Not waiting for a response, he slides down my body and kisses my exposed flesh. Sensation ricochets throughout me before settling deep in my core. I shift restlessly as his fingertips slip beneath the elastic band of my panties, drawing them down my hips and thighs. Once the cotton has been removed, he presses a kiss against the top of my slit before burying his face against me and inhaling.

"I've never craved anyone the way I do you," he admits in a low voice that drips with need. "You're like a drug careening through my system. There's no way to get enough."

My teeth scrape across my lower lip as my gaze stays fastened on his. I couldn't look away even if I tried. The sight of his dark head nestled between my thighs is so damn sexy. It only intensifies the rabid hunger growing within me as if it has a life of its own.

His hand settles on the inside of my knee before drifting upward and pushing my legs farther apart. As he hovers above me, the warmth of his breath ghosts over my sensitive flesh.

"So fucking pretty." There's a pause as his gaze skewers mine in place. "This pussy belongs to me." When I remain silent, his voice deepens, sounding as if it's been roughed up. "Say it, Delilah. Tell me that your pussy is mine."

"It belongs to you," I groan. "*I* belong to you."

His fingers settle on me, pulling at my lips until my clit is bared to the cool air of the room. When his tongue darts out to lick over my sensitive flesh, arousal explodes through me.

I arch and he presses me down into the mattress before spreading my thighs even wider. "I want all your sweetness. Do you hear me? *All of it.*"

His tongue returns to dance around my clit, licking me from top to bottom and then back again before repeating the exquisite torture. Any second, I'll splinter apart, falling to pieces beneath his talented lips.

A whimper escapes from me as I writhe against him, seeking out more contact.

"Come for me, sweet girl," he urges.

Those five words are all it takes for me to tumble off the precipice and into oblivion. And then I'm shattering into a million broken pieces as he laps at my flesh. It's only when I float back to earth that he presses a kiss against my pussy and crawls up my body with heat filling his eyes. As soon as he's positioned himself at my entrance, he slides into me with one smooth stroke and buries himself to the hilt. The feeling of fullness that radiates from my core is like nothing I've ever experienced. What I realize in that moment of intense connection is that nothing and no one will ever complete me the way Austin does.

His gaze locks on mine as he flexes his hips and rocks into my body. There's a softness to our lovemaking that hasn't been there since the first time, and I can't help but relish it, knowing that as much as I enjoy his dominance, I like when his touch turns tender. Almost as if he's cherishing me with each and every caress.

His elbows cage me in as his palms settle on each side of my head as if to hold me in place. It's unnecessary. There's nowhere else I'd rather be than here with him filling my body.

"I want to be the one who gives you everything you need." The fierceness of his words and the force of his gaze arrows straight through my heart.

His movements are smooth and controlled with deep strokes that have need blooming to life within me. After orgasming only a handful of minutes ago, it seems crazy that my body could be ready to come all over again, but that's exactly what happens.

Our gazes cling as the connection between us continues to strengthen, binding me to him in ways I never realized were possible. Our breath mingles, becoming one until the outside world falls away and it's just the two of us. My legs lock around his waist, sending him deeper, fusing our bodies together in the most primal way possible. His jaw locks as his muscles grow taut as if it's a struggle to keep himself in check.

When his cock bottoms out, my inner muscles clench. Unlike the last time, when it felt like fireworks exploding behind my eyelids, this orgasm is more subtle. Instead of throwing his head back, Austin's attention stays riveted to mine. Our inhalations intensify as our bodies move in perfect rhythm.

That's the exact moment I realize that my heart will always belong to him.

And I can only hope that he'll hold it carefully in his hands.

DELILAH

The morning breeze slides over my cheeks as I stare out over the water. There's something so soothing to be found in the motion of the whitecapped waves as they roll toward the sandy shore-line, one right after the other. It's easy to understand how people sit and stare at the water for hours on end.

I'm tempted to settle in the sand and do the same.

Except…I'm impatient to return to the house and slide between the sheets with Austin before he wakes up. Unable to resist the lure of the sunrise, I slipped from our bed and quietly dressed before sneaking out the door. We're only here for one more morning, and I don't want to squander a single moment.

Who knows when I'll be back again?

Although, next time, there won't be any boat rides. I'll keep my feet firmly planted on the shore.

And the sunrise had been well worth it, the horizon painted in vivid shades of pink. For just a moment, I'd actually forgotten that I lost my camera and reached for it, confused when my fingers slid through air. Once the realization slammed into me, grief crashed over me like a tidal wave, threatening to suck me under.

I should be thankful that I have a backup at home. The new Nikon

Mom bought me is a nicer, sleeker version with all the bells and whistles, but still...

There's something about the old one. Knowing that once upon a time, Dad held it in his hands, stared through the viewfinder and pressed the shutter button when he found the perfect shot makes me feel connected to him. Never again will I slide my fingers over the smooth surface.

"Hey," a cheerful voice calls out, knocking me from the painful tangle of my thoughts.

I blink back to the present and find Everly standing a few feet away. She's wearing a T-shirt, shorts, and fancy running shoes. Her auburn hair is tied back in a thick ponytail and her cheeks are pinkened from physical exertion.

"Hi." I force a smile to my lips. "Looks like someone's out for an early morning jog."

She flashes a quick grin. "I forgot how much harder it is to run on the sand."

I nod as if I know exactly what she's talking about but don't. I've never been someone who enjoys exercise.

Her expression turns serious. "I didn't get a chance to check in with you yesterday." She steps closer, eyes roving over my face. "How are you doing? Are you all right?"

"I'm fine. Just a little waterlogged," I force myself to say lightly, embarrassed by the accident.

"That was pretty crazy. I'm so sorry about your camera. I remember you mentioning that it belonged to your father."

Her kind words have tears pricking the backs of my eyes and it takes effort to blink them away. I remind myself that it was just an object and I shouldn't attach so much sentimentality to it, but that doesn't make the loss any less painful.

"Thanks," I whisper.

Before I realize what's happening, Everly swallows up the distance between us and pulls me into her arms before squeezing tight. I've never been much of a hugger. Maybe that's because there haven't been many people in my life I felt comfortable or close to.

Instead of discomfort or awkwardness bubbling up inside me by the show of physical affection, it feels good. It takes a couple seconds before my muscles loosen and I sink into her warm embrace. It's almost a shock when a splash of wetness hits my cheek and my shoulders begin to shake. She rubs soothing circles across my back, all the while whispering words of comfort in my ear.

Once the tears dry up, embarrassment slams into me and I untangle myself before taking a giant step in retreat. "I'm sorry. I don't know where all that came from."

Then again, the past few weeks have been stressful. A never-ending rollercoaster of emotions. Just when I think it's coming to an end and I can finally take a breather, it rushes into high speed, roaring over the tracks. It won't take much for me to reach breaking point. The cracks in the façade are there, widening with each new development.

Her brows draw together as she gives me a sympathetic smile. "It's okay. Sometimes we just need to let it all out. Crying isn't a weakness. It's cathartic."

Feeling foolish for the emotional outburst, I swipe at a stray tear. "I appreciate your kindness, I really do."

She shifts and tilts her head. "It's not a problem. I like you, Delilah. And I know everything's been shit lately. I don't claim to understand what's going on, but I'm here if you ever want to talk."

Unlike when Sloane made a similar offer, I actually believe Everly is sincere. Even though she's friends with Summer, it's doubtful she would weaponize my secrets against me.

For just a moment, I waver. It's so tempting to blurt out the truth and purge it from my system once and for all. Even if she isn't able to do anything more than listen.

When I remain silent, indecision circling through my head, her hand drifts to my shoulder. "I'm serious. You can talk to me any time."

"Thank you." Instead of opening up, I say, "There are just some things I need to work out for myself."

"I get that. Your relationship with Austin seems...complicated. Honestly, I'm not sure what to make of it. And then there's Jasper."

The muscles in my belly contract at the mention of my ex's name. All I want is for him to leave me alone and move on with his life, but he refuses to do that.

"I think Austin and I are in a good place." After last night, I certainly hope so.

She nods toward the house. "Want to head back with me, or were you planning to stay out a little longer?"

My gaze gets drawn to the waves that roll toward the shoreline. Even though I had a near-death experience and lost Dad's camera, this trip hasn't been all bad. I finally feel like Austin and I are on the same page. The need to see him again floods through me, suffusing every cell.

"I'll walk with you," I say with a smile.

Her face brightens and I can't resist thinking that Everly is really beautiful with her bouncy auburn hair and bright, turquoise eyes. She's curvy with a killer body. Even though Duke acts like he can't stand her, I have the sneaking suspicion that there's more than meets the eye in regard to their relationship.

Whoever said the line between love and hate is thin was right.

Then again, sometimes it's just hate.

When we're about halfway to the house, Everly says, "You know, Summer really does like you."

Surprised by the comment, I huff out a disbelieving laugh. "That might have been true a couple weeks ago, but I doubt that's the case any longer."

She flicks a glance in my direction as the wind continues to whip over us. "She's protective of her twin and doesn't want to see him hurt."

"He's just as protective," I murmur.

"That's true. But don't worry, I'm trying to soften her up. We'll see how it goes."

"I won't hold my breath."

Once we reach the sprawling house, Everly stops. "I'm going to stretch for a couple of minutes but I'll catch you later, all right?"

I nod and flash a smile. "Thanks for the talk. It really helped."

"Any time."

With a wave, I jog up the wooden stairs and slip into the kitchen. I half wonder if I'll find Summer enjoying a cup of coffee like yesterday. Maybe we need to sit down and have an honest conversation about everything that's going on. The truth of the matter is that I have feelings for her brother and she's the last person I want to be at odds with.

Instead, I find the bright and sunny space empty. I glance at the clock on the microwave and realize that I must have lost track of time while walking the beach. It's much later than I assumed.

I have no idea if Austin will still be in bed.

Although, I hope so.

My heart picks up tempo just thinking about sliding between the sheets. Especially since he was gloriously naked when I snuck from the room earlier this morning. I don't think I've ever slept as well as I did curled up in his arms last night. After we made love, everything felt damn near perfect. My feet pick up the pace as need floods through me. As I walk past an antique credenza polished to a high shine in the family room, I spot a photo and my feet falter as my attention gets snagged.

It's an eight by ten of Kingsley and his parents. I recognize Keaton from the school functions I've attended over the past years. The resemblance between him and his son is uncanny. Both are tall with dark hair and eyes. Keaton has a bit of gray around his temples. My gaze shifts to the two females in the photograph. The older one is blonde and glamourous. I'm guessing that's his mother. My mind tumbles back through my memories.

What's strange is that I don't ever remember meeting her.

The fourth person in the picture is a young teenage girl. I step a bit closer, wanting to get a better look. She's gorgeous with long, wavy dark hair and matching eyes. Just like Kingsley and his father, it's easy to see the family resemblance between the three of them.

I'd always thought Kingsley was an only child. I had no idea that—

"That's Harlow," a deep voice says from beside me. "My sister."

A squeak escapes from my lips. I nearly jump a foot before

swinging around and taking a hasty step in retreat as my heartbeat explodes beneath my chest.

Our gazes stay locked. There's nothing about Kingsley's relaxed demeanor that should make me feel like I'm in peril and yet, I can't dispel the sensation creeping down my spine. It's as if I've spotted a dangerous predator who could spring at any moment. By the time I realize what's happening, it'll be much too late.

I gulp and swallow down the fear that claws at my insides. We've attended the same school since freshman year, and while he's never frightened me, I've always been cautious about giving him a wide berth and not getting too close.

He's just…*too much*.

Too good looking.

Too forceful and used to getting what he wants.

Even at eighteen years old, Kingsley exudes a power and confidence that most adults twenty years his senior don't possess. He might be a little more tamed now that he has a girlfriend, but still…

The last thing I want is to make an enemy of him. I've already been dancing on that thin line with his girlfriend.

"Oh. I, um—" My brain freezes, and every thought flies out of my head.

When I continue to stumble over my words, he takes pity on me by saying, "She attends a boarding school in England and hasn't lived here for years."

Even though it feels unwise, I rip my attention away and stare at the photograph. Now that my gaze is no longer trapped within his, it's easier to breathe. His eyes are so dark and piercing. It feels like he's somehow capable of sifting through my innermost thoughts.

"How old is she?" I congratulate myself on wrapping my lips around the words and forcing them out steadily as if I'm not shaking in my shoes.

"Seventeen."

"Why doesn't she attend Hawthorne Prep?"

A shadow flickers in his eyes and I swallow thickly, realizing it was the wrong question to ask.

"My father thought it would be an enriching experience for her to study abroad."

"I'm sure it has been," I agree.

When a heavy silence falls over us, I take a hasty step in retreat before pointing toward the foyer where the staircase to the second floor is located. "I'm going to head upstairs."

He scrutinizes me before finally nodding. "Sure. I'll catch you later."

"All right," I squeak.

And then I'm gone, scampering down the hallway. Much like Kingsley's mansion in Hawthorne, his beach house has a number of spacious rooms for entertaining. If I had to guess, I'd say that it was professionally decorated. Every piece of furniture and accessory looks as if it were handpicked to go specifically in this house. It resembles a spread in a glossy architecture magazine.

My hand wraps around the railing as I reach the staircase. Just as I step onto the first tread, whispered voices halt me in my tracks and my feet falter.

"Mmm, that feels so good."

Recognition slams into me.

Aubrey.

My ears perk, straining to pick up the slightest sound as a pit blooms at the bottom of my belly. Even though I should put some distance between myself and the couple making out in the study on the other side of the grand foyer, I swing around and sneak across the gleaming hardwood to the door that's cracked open no more than a few inches.

This time, when a whimper escapes, the sound is much closer.

My brain is screaming to leave well enough alone, but I can't do it. She could be in there with any number of guys.

But...

I need to know if it's Austin. All the suspicions I thought we'd laid to rest last night reignite within me before bursting into flame. My heart hammers a painful staccato against my ribcage as I slink closer. After everything yesterday—him jumping into the water to save me, holding me close, the bath, and then the way he touched me…

I had assumed the feelings between us were genuine. The realization that I could be wrong is like a dagger piercing my heart. My mind tumbles back to last night. Only now do I realize that he never denied being with Aubrey.

What he said is that I needed to trust him.

And rather stupidly, I did.

Careful not to make a sound, I inch closer to the study until I'm able to peek around the corner of the doorjamb into the brightly lit room. It doesn't take long for my gaze to land on the couple inside.

Air leaks from my lungs one painful molecule at a time until there's nothing left.

There's no mistaking the dark head, broad back, and muscular arms.

Austin.

He has her pinned up against the far wall. From this position, I have a clear view of the way he strokes his knuckles down Aubrey's cheek as she stares up at him with heavy-lidded eyes. He lowers his mouth to the side of her face before whispering something in her ear I'm unable to pick up.

After a handful of moments, she whines with a pout, "Why are you even with that girl? You can't actually like her."

His hand drifts from her face to her breast before giving it a squeeze. Another moan escapes from her as she shifts against him, thrusting out her chest in order to get closer.

"Don't be ridiculous. Of course we're not together. It's just fucking."

The admittance is almost enough to bring me to my knees. My hand flies to my mouth as a sob gathers in my throat and fights for release. Unable to stand the sight, I stumble back a step until the couple is no longer in view. Pain radiates throughout my entire being until it throbs in my fingertips and toes as I spin on my heel, racing blindly up the staircase.

A sheen of tears stings my eyes, blurring my vision, as I reach the second floor. It's a shock when I slam into a hard body and stumble back a step, teetering on the edge of the landing. With a gasp, my arms pinwheel as I attempt to regain my balance. Strong hands reach out and lock around my shoulders before yanking me forward until I crash against the steely strength of a hard chest.

"For fuck's sake, you almost fell down the stairs," a harsh voice snaps in my ear.

I push away just enough to meet Duke's gaze. His eyes narrow as he carefully searches mine. The anger filling his expression morphs into concern.

"What happened? Why are you upset?"

I wince, remembering how he tried to warn me last night and I refused to listen.

God, I'm so stupid.

"Can you take me home?" My tongue darts out to moisten my lips. *"Please?"*

He blinks, thrown off by the request. "You want to leave right now?"

"I need to get out of here."

There's a moment of silence as he scrutinizes me, searching for answers I'm unwilling to give. "Yeah, sure. I'll talk to Kingsley about borrowing one of his cars. Go pack your bags and we'll take off as soon as you're ready."

Relief rushes from my lungs and my muscles loosen. "Thank you."

With a tug of his fingers, he draws me to him before dropping a quick kiss against the top of my head. "It's not a problem, Delilah. Whatever you need. I'm here for you. Always will be no matter what."

Duke Carmichael is one of the few, if not only, people I can count on.

And at the moment, that feels like everything.

AUSTIN

I press Aubrey against the wood-paneled wall of the study as she stares up at me with heavy-lidded eyes. If I wanted to fuck her right here and now, there's not a doubt in my mind that she'd let me. She's been batting her thick, mascara-laden lashes at me ever since Coach started yanking Jasper out of the games and sending me in to turn them around.

Now that I'm no longer a pariah, everyone wants to be my friend. Guys are slapping me on the back and girls are coming out of the woodwork to flirt and offer up their...*services.*

It's fucking ridiculous and I want no part of it.

Aubrey has made it perfectly clear that she'd be happy to slide into my bed.

Or drop to her knees and open wide.

Whatever it is that I want.

Little does she know that what I'm after has nothing to do with sex. She let something slip last night by the bonfire that has been tickling the far recesses of my brain, and I haven't been able to let it go. I need to get to the bottom of it and figure out what it means.

One way or another.

She forces out her pink slicked lower lip in a pout. "Why are you even with that girl? You can't actually like her."

I wince inwardly before allowing my hand to drift to her breast and giving it a squeeze. I need to get her talking before this goes any further. There's no damn way I'm locking lips with this crazy chick.

A moan escapes from her as she shifts, arching into my palm. I pluck at the stiff little peak. "Don't be ridiculous. Of course we're not together. It's just fucking."

The lie leaves a bitter taste in my mouth.

"Good. I seriously can't figure out why Jasper is so obsessed with her. He's a total psycho. He'll do anything to get her back."

Here we go.

It's casually that I say, "Oh yeah? Like what?"

When I press my lips to the slender column of her throat, her eyelids feather closed, and she arches her neck, granting me greater access. "That feels so good."

"I'm curious about what he's done."

"Hmmm?"

"Jasper." It takes effort to keep my voice level and not snap with the impatience that vibrates through me like a live wire. "I want to know."

Her brows knit as her eyelids crack open. "Ugh. He's the last person I want to talk about."

When my teeth sink into the soft flesh of her neck, a whimper escapes from her. "You're the one who brought it up. I'm just curious about what you mean."

Her fingers curl into the soft cotton of my T-shirt in an attempt to drag me closer. "I don't understand what all the fuss is about. It's not like she's *that* pretty."

I suck her skin into my mouth. She tastes nothing like Delilah, and as much as I want to shove her away, I need to see it through. From the tidbit she dropped last night, she knows exactly what Jasper has been up to. All the games he's been playing at our expense.

I want answers.

And I want them now.

My fingers torment her stiff little bud as my voice grows rough, telling her what she wants to hear. "You're right. The guy is totally pussy whipped. I want to know all the ways he's been fucking with her." There's a pause before I add, "Like at the fundraiser."

A groan that has absolutely nothing to do with the way I'm playing with her slips free. "What he did that night was totally messed up."

All the rioting noise in my head goes quiet as my gaze sharpens. "You mean outing my dyslexia?" My lips flatten into a thin line so they won't curl into a snarl.

"Yeah. He snuck into the headmaster's office after football practice and dug through your records. I guess it was written in there somewhere."

Motherfucker.

It takes every ounce of willpower to tamp down the growl rising in my chest.

"About a month ago, he started to suspect that something was going on between you two."

"There wasn't."

"It doesn't matter, he wanted to destroy any tentative friendship so she'd have no other choice but to stay with him." A hard glint enters her eyes. "I told you already, he's obsessed. I don't understand it at all. What's so special about that girl?"

Everything.

Delilah is so fucking sweet. Nothing like the other girls who attend this school. What kills me is that I actually believed she purposefully led me on as some kind of a joke.

I should have known better.

I should have trusted my gut instead of allowing Jasper to fuck with my head.

So...if he orchestrated that, what else is he capable of doing in order to get her back?

I'm afraid to dig for the answers but I need to know the truth. I need to know how badly I screwed up. Accusing and punishing her for things she had no knowledge of.

I force out the response, even though nothing could be further from the truth.

"There's not a damn thing that special about her." I press against her body, ghosting my lips across hers as I graze my knuckles along her cheek. "You're the one everyone wants."

"Really?" Cautious hope flares to life in her eyes.

I almost feel bad about my deception until I remember that Aubrey knows exactly what Jasper has been up to and has eagerly gone along with all his plans. This girl deserves everything she gets. She's eaten up inside with jealousy. What she doesn't understand is just how ugly it makes her.

"He drugged her at that party, didn't he?" I whisper as my breath feathers over her parted lips.

The words might be arranged in the format of a question, but it's not one. Deep down, I already know the answer. The pieces of the puzzle were all there, waiting for me to move them into place and make a clear picture. And now that they do, I could kick myself for ever believing she was fucking with me.

Aubrey tilts her head as her eyelids lower and a whimper of need escapes.

When she remains silent, I repeat the question.

Only harsher this time.

"He drugged her, didn't he? That's why she doesn't remember anything that happened that night."

The arousal dancing in her eyes is snuffed out as a flicker of fear flashes in them.

That's all the confirmation I need.

Even though it's tempting to wrap my hands around her throat and choke the very life out of her for being a conniving bitch, I force my lips into an easy smile. "Come on, you can tell me the truth."

When she attempts to turn her head in order to avoid eye contact, my fingers settle beneath her chin before holding it captive so she has no other choice but to meet the steeliness of my gaze.

"I didn't want anything to do with it," she whines. "But he wanted her so bad and I..."

"Wanted me," I finish darkly.

"I know it looks bad, but I made sure that he didn't do anything more than take pictures," she says in a jumbled rush, color stinging her cheeks.

As if that makes the situation better or her any less culpable.

Then again…

Thank fuck she did. How could I ever forgive myself if Jasper raped Delilah while she'd been passed out?

The thought makes me gut sick.

When I remain silent, lost in a tangle of dark thoughts, she says, "It's not like anyone got hurt."

Didn't they?

It's becoming more and more difficult not to lash out. I flex the fingers of my other hand in an attempt to maintain control.

Fear riddles her voice. "You're not mad, are you?"

Fuck, yeah I am. But there's something else circling at the back of my brain, and I need to know. I nip her lower lip with sharp teeth, tugging on it before releasing the soft flesh.

"Delilah falling overboard yesterday wasn't an accident, was it?"

Wariness settles over her expression. "The boat rocked, and I accidentally knocked into her."

Lie.

My knuckles stroke along the curve of her jawline before trailing down her throat until the fingers can settle loosely around the slender column. Her gaze stays pinned to mine as her pulse flutters like the wings of a hummingbird beneath them.

"She doesn't know how to swim and could have drowned."

Her eyes flare. "I…didn't know. I just thought it would be a little dip in the lake. That's it."

"Not for her." My grip tightens, biting into her flesh. It would be all too easy to crush her fragile bones with one squeeze. "You almost killed her."

Her hands fly to my forearm as her eyes bulge from their sockets.

"Austin!" she rasps as I cut off her flow of oxygen.

I pop a brow. "What?"

"You're hurting me! Let go." Barely is she able to rasp out the words.

A slight smile lifts the corners of my lips. "No, I don't think I will. You purposefully put Delilah in danger and for what? Because you wanted a chance to get with me?" I shake my head. "No way. You're the last person I'd want anything to do with. Especially now that I know what you're capable of."

"But you said—"

"Yeah, I lied. Kind of like you."

Tears spring to her eyes. "I honestly didn't think anyone would get hurt."

"Well, someone did. What would have happened if he'd given her too much of the drug?"

"I only gave her half the dosage," she chokes out. "I was super careful."

Holy fuck. This girl is seriously out of her damn mind.

I scowl. "And that makes it better?"

When she attempts to shake her head, I squeeze tighter until all the color leaches from her face and her fingers curl, the nails biting into my flesh as she claws at me in panic.

"Do you realize that I could report both of you to the police?"

Wetness clings to her dark lashes before splashing onto her face. "I'm really sorry. Please don't. My parents will kill me if they find out about this."

Aubrey will be lucky if I don't strangle her first and save her parents the trouble.

"That's too fucking bad." It takes a concerted effort to loosen my hold from around her windpipe so that she doesn't pass out. "Want to know what you're going to do when we get back to Hawthorne?"

A potent concoction of suspicion and fear swirls through her wide eyes.

Good.

She should be afraid.

Terrified, actually. I know all of her secrets. And I plan to use every single one of them against her.

"You're going to tell Pembroke exactly what you've done."

Her eyes bulge for a second time as she tries to shake her head, but the grip I have on her throat makes movement impossible. "They'll expel me."

"I don't give a shit. Jasper's not the only one who can make someone's life hell, and trust me, I will." I drag her closer. "I'll make the rest of senior year a fucking living hell for you."

"Okay," she finally squeaks, tears rolling down her cheeks. "I'll tell him everything."

Unwilling to touch her any longer than necessary, I release my grip and step away, needing to put distance between us. More tears leak from the corners of her eyes as she sucks in a harsh breath, filling her deprived lungs with fresh air.

"I'm sorry," she whispers on a rising sob.

"Save it. Your apology means jack shit. The only thing you regret is that you got caught. You could have easily put an end to all this at any time, and you chose not to. You could have told Jasper to piss off and then given Delilah a heads up so she was aware of what he was up to. You did neither of those things. Don't ever doubt for a moment that you're a garbage human being."

Her mouth falls open as hot color scalds her cheeks. "It—"

I shake my head and take a menacing step forward before stabbing a finger at her. "Don't even say it or I swear to god, I'll happily choke the fucking life out of you."

She slams her lips together, refusing to utter another peep.

It's the smartest move she could make.

With that, I swing around and stalk from the study before taking the stairs two at a time. I need to find Delilah. When I woke up this morning, she'd been gone. I'd rolled out of bed before gravitating to the window, instinctively knowing that she would be on the beach. She might not know how to swim, but she's drawn to the water. I figured we could spend the day together.

Walking.

Talking.

Getting anything else that needed to be said out in the open.

I'd thrown on a T-shirt and jeans. Just as I'd stepped out of the bedroom, Aubrey had been there. Almost as if she'd been lying in wait.

She'd dogged my heels down the staircase. Once we made it to the foyer, she'd wrapped her hand around mine and dragged me to the study. Instead of shaking her off, I'd decided to ferret out whatever info I could.

Fuck.

My mind continues to cartwheel. Even though I'd suspected that Aubrey had been behind some of the shady BS, I'm blown away by the extent of it.

I need to find Delilah and tell her about everything I've uncovered. Then I need to drop to my knees and beg her forgiveness. I've treated her like shit. Just like I threatened Aubrey, I made Delilah's life hell. Not only did she tell me the truth, but she's been dealing with Jasper's psycho crap as well.

As I make it to the second floor, my sister walks out of the bedroom she's sharing with Kingsley.

"Hey, do you have a sec?" she asks. "I've been thinking about everything that's happened with Delilah."

My step never falters. I'm a man on a mission and won't be able to banish the unease sitting at the bottom of my gut until I speak with her.

"Can it wait? There's something I need to take care of first."

Her brows pinch together as her gaze sharpens. "What's wrong?"

I can almost see her antenna go up as she braces herself for more shit to get dumped on us. That's exactly what the past couple of months in Hawthorne have been like.

A fucking barrage of it.

"It's nothing like that." I pause before admitting, "I need to find Delilah. Have you seen her this morning?"

"No, I just got up."

"Okay." I huff out a breath. "Let me take care of this situation and then I'll find you."

Her teeth scrape over her lower lip. "All right."

She falls silent as I stride down the long stretch of hallway. My heart picks up its tempo when I twist the handle and shove open our bedroom door. Once inside the sun-flooded space, I glance around, hoping that she's returned from her walk. My gaze slides over the room only to find it empty.

Fuck.

I gravitate to the window and search the beach. There are a few people strolling the sandy shoreline, but none are Delilah. I would recognize her blonde head anywhere.

Maybe she's in the kitchen grabbing breakfast.

The longer it takes to find her, the more tension floods my muscles.

As I swing around, ready to stalk downstairs, my gaze lands on the place where her duffle had been shoved up against the far wall by the closet. My step stutters when I realize it's no longer there. That's all it takes for a trapdoor to spring open.

And then I'm in free fall.

Why the hell would she just take off?

Sure…she locked me out last night, but we worked through it. We had sex and afterward, she'd slept curled up in my arms.

Air gets trapped in my lungs as I head to the ginormous bathroom and peek inside the opulent space. Already I know that all the girly stuff strewn across the countertop will be gone. Every trace of Delilah has been wiped away, as if she'd never been there in the first place.

It's so tempting to punch my fist through the wall. Instead, I swing around and stalk from the bedroom into the hallway before meeting Summer's dark gaze. Kingsley stands behind her with his hands resting protectively on her shoulders.

They've become a solid unit in a short span of time. It's strange. Since we were born, it's always been the two of us against the world and sometimes, even our parents. We were a team. And now…that's how it is with him.

It'll take time to come to terms with this new dynamic.

I shake myself out of those strange thoughts as my gaze slices to Kingsley. "Have you seen Delilah?"

There's a heavy moment of silence as Summer tenses beneath his hands.

"She took off about ten minutes ago."

I blink, unable to process the words coming out of his mouth. They doesn't make sense.

There's no way she'd leave without talking to me first.

No.

Damn.

Way.

"Yeah." He shifts before dropping another bomb. "With Duke."

This time, when the urge rushes through my veins, I turn and slam my fist through the drywall as a string of curses falls from my lips.

AUSTIN

By the time I roll into Hawthorne, I'm clutching the steering wheel in a death grip and my head is spinning. Nothing about Delilah's behavior makes sense. I've tried more than a dozen times to call her, but it goes straight to voicemail.

Every text remains unanswered.

Her message is loud and clear.

She's cut off contact and wants nothing to do with me.

Instead of going home, I head to her house and park in the drive before slamming out of the G-wagon and stalking to the front door. I rap my knuckles against the thick wood and impatiently wait. When a handful of seconds tick by, I cup my hands around my temples and press my face to the small window. From what I can make out, it's dark and shadowy. There's not a flicker of movement from inside.

My brows draw together.

If Delilah didn't get dropped off at home, where the hell is she?

I push the bell for a second time and shove my hands into the pockets of my jeans. I might have driven home like a bat out of hell, but there's no way I beat them. I glance up and down the narrow, tree-lined street as if they'll turn the corner any moment and come into view.

Five minutes that feel more like an eternity slide by and there's still no sign of them.

Where the fuck would he have taken her?

Only one other place comes to mind.

His house.

My muscles tense as a wave of anger crashes over me.

I stalk back to the SUV before sliding behind the wheel and searching the online HP student directory. After plugging his address into my phone, I reverse from the drive and follow the turn-by-turn directions. I don't know much about Duke except that, like Delilah, he's at Hawthorne Prep on scholarship.

Two minutes later, I'm pulling into Hawthorne Estates, a rundown trailer park on the outskirts of town. I spot Kingsley's Mustang parked outside one of the trailers and cut the engine before slamming from the vehicle. Within seconds, I've yanked open the dilapidated screen door and am pounding my fist against the metal. It takes every ounce of self-control not to rip the damn thing from the hinges and force my way inside.

The guy doesn't make me wait long. Less than fifteen seconds pass before the door opens and Duke stands at the threshold.

He doesn't say one damn word, just glares. The way he peers at me with disgust, kind of like I'm a bug splattered across the windshield of his truck, makes me want to squirm.

Instead, I straighten my shoulders. "Where's Delilah?"

Part of me expects for him to give me the runaround and make this difficult.

That's not what happens.

"She's here."

When he doesn't say anything more, I grit my teeth, keeping a firm lock on my temper. "I want to talk with her."

"That's unfortunate. She doesn't have anything to say to you."

When I step onto the first tread of the front stoop, he slams out of the screen door and stalks down the concrete steps until we're nose to nose. I'll be damned if I back down.

His voice drips venom. "On the drive back to Hawthorne, she told me everything that's happened."

Even though it's tempting to look away as embarrassment simmers deep within, I keep my eyes trained on him. "I'm here to apologize."

Before I realize his intent, he knocks his hands into my chest. The force of it sends me stumbling back a few steps. "That's tough shit for you. I'm not gonna let you anywhere near that girl. You're done messing with her. Do you hear me? It's fucking over."

As tempting as it is to get into a fistfight with Duke, I refuse to do it. Especially when all he's done is defend Delilah the way I should have from the very beginning.

I drag a hand through my hair and search for the right words, something that will convey the depth of my feelings for her. I haven't always been good at expressing my emotions. I've spent a lot of time tamping them down and leading with my fists when shit got difficult.

But I care about Delilah. More than I've cared about any other girl. And I fucking hate that she doesn't realize it. I don't understand why she packed her bags and took off. Especially after how good everything was last night.

It takes a concerted effort on my part to gentle my voice and remain calm. "I just want to talk with her. That's it."

He shrugs. "Again, tough shit. She wants nothing to do with you, so get the hell out of here."

Fuck.

Fuck.

Fuck.

We glare for a solid sixty seconds. What becomes clear is that he isn't going to budge on his stance. He won't allow me within twenty feet of Delilah. The urge to throw a punch thrums through me, but I tamp down the knee jerk reaction.

If she needs time, I don't have much choice in the matter.

Although…that doesn't mean I'm giving up.

Not by a long shot.

DELILAH

I glance at Mom from the corner of my eye. She's humming along to the music that fills the car as we drive to school. When her gaze flickers to mine, she flashes a smile before her attention returns to the ribbon of road stretched out in front of us.

She's been on cloud nine since walking through the door late Sunday evening. Her bubble of happiness has only been reinforced by their little getaway. I don't even want to know what they were up to. If I think about it too hard, I'll likely vomit all over myself. After the rough patch we've been going through, I don't have the wherewithal to be at odds with her anymore.

I only hope that when this affair finally runs its course, she doesn't get hurt and no one in Hawthorne discovers what's been going on. I have no idea if Austin plans to carry out his earlier threats, but I hope not. I don't know why he would bother when he's obviously interested in Aubrey.

He can have her, if that's what he wants.

I no longer give a shit.

Mom has no idea what happened this weekend. The only thing I told her about is Dad's camera falling into the lake. Her response was that at least I still had the brand new one she purchased. Her unsympathetic attitude had me blinking back tears.

Although, why am I surprised?

She's wanted me to get rid of it for a while.

Guess she finally got her way.

After we returned to Hawthorne, I hid out at Duke's until Sunday afternoon before finally heading home. Last night, I forced myself to stay awake until the wee hours of the morning, afraid Austin would find a way into the house, and I'd wake with him on top of me.

It didn't happen.

Whatever we had—if anything—is over. Even though I realize it's for the best, heartache seeps into my chest before slowly spreading throughout the rest of my body.

Not only will I spend the remainder of senior year avoiding Jasper and his cronies, but Austin as well. I just need to keep my head down, focus on my schoolwork, and figure out where I'll go to college. Next fall, I'll be as far away from Hawthorne as I can get. It's the one thought that keeps me going.

By the time we drive through the iron gates of Hawthorne Prep and pull into the parking lot, flashes from last week are rolling unwantedly through my head. The last thing I need is for the photo scandal to get resurrected. With any luck, there'll be a lot of new juicy gossip making the rounds. There were plenty of people getting drunk and hooking up.

And not necessarily with the ones they should have been.

That can only work in my favor, right?

Once Mom kills the engine, I pick up my backpack and exit the vehicle. She does the same, chattering nonstop through the parking lot as we head to the main entrance. From beneath the fringe of my lashes, I glance at the small groups of students who are hanging out and talking before the first bell rings. Unlike last Monday, I haven't garnered any unwanted attention. I catch a few tidbits of gossip but nothing that pertains to me. My muscles incrementally loosen in relief as my shoulders lower from around my ears.

When I'm halfway across the lot, my gaze collides with gunmetal gray eyes. As our gazes lock, his lips slowly slide into a malicious smile and a shiver of dread scampers down my spine. It's tempting to rub my hands over my arms to banish the chill that has settled over me.

Ripping my attention away is almost impossible. I'm like a rabbit caught in a hunter's trap. How did I date this guy for six months and not see the evil lurking beneath the surface?

Was it willful ignorance on my part?

I don't know, but I'm certainly paying the price for it now.

"I hope you have a good day, sweetie," Mom says, breaking into those unsettling thoughts and drawing my focus back to her.

I force a smile. "Thanks, you too."

The woman is positively brimming with joy. It's not like I begrudge her happiness. I just know where it stems from and that there's no way it will last.

She pulls open the glass door and we walk into the spacious corridor already crowded with students. With a wave, she heads to the office while I beeline toward my locker. Just like in the parking lot, the buzz of conversation swirls around me. My ears stay pricked, listening for my name, but there's nothing.

Once I reach my locker, I spin the dial and yank open the metal before reaching inside to grab the books I'll need for my first few classes. Just as I'm about to slam the door closed, the fine hair at the nape of my neck prickles and I realize someone is watching me. I don't have to glance around to know exactly who I'll find.

It only takes a few seconds for my eyes to collide with green-flecked ones and my heartbeat stalls in my chest. No matter how much I want to remain unaffected by his presence, I'm not.

One look and my skin comes alive, humming with electricity. There's a magnetic pull that flares to life within me, and I have to mentally stop myself from taking a step in his direction. After every-thing that occurred, I don't understand why these feelings are still there, attempting to claw their way to the surface.

Austin leans against the locker across from mine in the middle of the congested hallway. His arms are folded over his broad chest as he silently stares. As casual as his demeanor appears, I feel the tension vibrating off him in thick waves from the distance that separates us. In that moment of intense connection, the world around us falls away and ceases to exist.

It's just the two of us in the hallway.

When he pushes away from the wall and takes a step in my direction, I snap out of the trance that has fallen over me and slam the thin metal door shut before scurrying to class, where I'll be safe from the likes of Austin Hawthorne.

A distant part of my brain wonders if that's even possible.

Maybe I've been given a slight reprieve, but deep down, there's no chance it will last.

It's almost a surprise when I make it to first hour in one piece. After I fled down the hallway, I half expected Austin's fingers to lock around my arm and for him to drag me off somewhere private. The sad truth is that once he lays his hands on me, I'll be lost in a turbulent sea of need. My brain is no match for my heart and body.

His conversation with Aubrey plays in my head on repeat.

"Why are you even with Delilah? You can't actually like her."

"Of course we're not together. It's just fucking.

I need to remember what it felt like to stand outside the study and hear those words trip so easily off his tongue. The pain that sliced through me was enough to bring me to my knees.

With a relieved huff, I slump onto my assigned desk and wait for first period to get underway. Students gradually filter in, chattering excitedly about the weekend and how much fun it was. Stories are shared before being passed along to their neighbor.

Again, there's nothing about me.

Not even my unexpected dip in the lake.

Thank god.

This has been an ugly chapter of my time at HP, and all I want to do is close it and move on with my life.

I open my pre-calc book and flip through the pages, looking for the place where we left off. I'm only half listening as Mrs. Baxter reads the morning announcements over the loudspeaker. With all the laughter and talking that hums around me, no one is really paying attention. It's only when her voice is abruptly cut off and loud grunting fills the air that the people around me fall silent and swivel in their seats. When a long, keening moan is broadcast to the school at large, laughter erupts.

Rough grunting and groans follow.

It almost sounds like…

Like…

Someone is having *sex*.

"Oh, Edmond," a soft voice whimpers. *"Yes, right there. Yes!"*

It doesn't take long for recognition to slam into me and my eyes widen with horror. Any moment, they're going to fall out of my head and roll around on the desk.

Mom.

My hand feels as if it weighs a thousand pounds as it rises to my gaping mouth.

More guttural noises follow before…

"Who's my dirty little whore?"

"Holy shit, that's Pembroke," the guy next to me shouts. "He's getting it on with someone!"

More raucous laughter fills the space until it echoes off the walls and rings hollowly in my ears.

"Go, Pembroke!" the girl next to me calls out before dissolving into a fit of giggles.

The stunned expression on Coach Baker's face would be hilarious if I didn't know my mother was having sex with our headmaster.

After a handful of seconds, our teacher makes his way to his feet and raises his arms. "All right, everyone. That's enough. Let's settle down and act like the mature individuals you're supposed to be. Obviously, there's a glitch in the system."

That embarrassed reprimand only makes people laugh harder.

"Oh, there's a glitch in the system all right," someone hollers back before chuckling.

"I love fucking you on my desk, Carrie," Pembroke growls right before the sound cuts out and silence fills the air.

"Did he say Carrie?" the guy next to me asks.

"Who the hell is Carrie?" another girl questions.

Speculation runs rampant as I rise to my feet on wooden legs and scoop up my books before walking out of the room in a daze. There is so much noise and chaos that Coach Baker doesn't realize that I've slipped away. I don't know what I'd tell him if he did ask.

All I know is that I need to escape from the confines of the room that feels like it's shrinking around me. My chest is tight, and it's becoming more difficult to breathe with every second that passes.

As soon as I stumble into the deserted hallway, I stagger to the bank of lockers before slapping a hand against the cool metal and folding over at the waist, trying to suck fresh air into my deprived lungs. I squeeze my eyes tightly shut for just a handful of seconds as my head spins like I'm on a Tilt-A-Whirl before straightening and forcing myself to move.

I can't believe this is happening.

I can't believe that someone—

I falter.

No.

Not *someone*.

I know *exactly* who did this.

My legs are so shaky that I'm afraid I'll stumble and fall to my knees. The thought of reaching my mom is what prods me into movement and keeps me going. As I turn a corner, a muscular figure looms in the middle of the hallway. I skid to a halt as our gazes fasten.

Fury crashes over me like a tidal wave, nearly sucking me under as I bare my teeth.

I can't believe he did this. He might have hung the threat over my head to coerce me into doing what he wanted, but I didn't actually believe he'd go through with it.

That he'd go to these lengths to lash out and hurt me.

As much as I'm loath to admit it, there's no way to deny the truth. When it comes down to it, Austin Hawthorne is no better than Jasper. Both boys are cut from the same cloth. That thought turns my stomach until it feels like I'll be sick.

"Delilah." Intensity swirls through his green depths as he takes a swift step toward me.

I do the only thing I can to ward him off and throw up a hand as my lips lift into a snarl. Shock flashes across his face as he grinds to a halt.

"How could you do this?" I growl.

Rage vibrates through every cell of my being.

Austin never gave me a reason to trust him, but I did. I believed he would never do anything to wound me. Obviously, that's my fault for being so gullible.

His eyes widen as he gives his head a violent shake. "No, I—"

"Just stop! I don't want to hear any more of your lies." My voice escalates with each syllable that shoots out of my mouth. "I know you did this. You're the only one who knew." There's a pause before I add, "Not only did you threaten to tell everyone about the affair, you blackmailed Pembroke with the information."

Emotion flickers in his eyes as he bursts into movement, eating up the distance between us with a handful of long-legged strides. Just as he reaches for me, I leap back, stumbling in my haste to avoid physical contact.

"Don't you dare touch me. You have *nothing* on me now. So, go fuck yourself!"

"Delilah, please..."

There is so much pent-up emotion in those two words. It claws at my insides, but I refuse to get suckered in by him again. Not only has he hurt me, but my mom as well.

Oh god.

Mom.

I shake my head, carefully darting past him. This time, he doesn't try to stop me. He allows me to flee from the scene.

Even though the copy room is less than eighty feet away, it's like time slows and it takes forever to finally reach the small space. I feel every beat of my pounding heart as I grip the edge of the doorjamb and crash over the threshold. My gaze flies around the cramped room before fastening on Mom. She's slumped in a chair with a look of shock etched across her face. A sick knot settles in the pit of my gut.

When she continues to stare off into space, not acknowledging my presence, I whisper, "Mom?"

There's no reaction.

It's like I'm not even here.

Fear slithers down my spine.

I raise my voice, hoping to knock her from the stupor that has cocooned its way around her. "Mom?"

With a blink, she gradually turns her head until her gaze can lock on mine. A vacant look fills her blue eyes.

"Are you all right?" I whisper before wincing.

It's a ridiculous question. Of course she isn't.

Tears fill her eyes and spike her lashes as she shakes her head. "How? How could something like this happen?"

Guilt crashes over me.

It's my fault.

At least, partially.

Even though I should confess and tell her who's responsible, I can't bring myself to say his name. At the end of the day, it won't change the situation.

Her affair with Pembroke has been thrust into the spotlight, and there's no way to drag it back into the darkness where it belongs.

DELILAH

$\mathcal{I}$ keep my head angled down and my shoulders hunched as I make my way through the crowded parking lot to the front entrance of the school. The past couple of days have been a veritable nightmare.

It didn't take long for everyone to figure out who Pembroke was screwing. As soon as the board caught wind of the incident, our headmaster was swiftly terminated. Within thirty minutes, he was escorted off the premises with a small cardboard box overflowing with his belongings. Mom was allowed to keep her job since she was a subordinate but is currently searching for a new one. The humiliation of having their affair publicly outed and gossiped about has been too much for her to endure.

Pembroke broke off their relationship through text and refuses to return any of Mom's calls. The man is a coward unworthy of her attention. It's so tempting to tell her *I told you so*, but how can I do that?

My heart breaks for her. This is the first man she's gotten involved with since Dad died, and it ended disastrously.

Even though Hawthorne Prep is the last place I want to show my face, there isn't much choice in the matter. I can't afford to miss my classes. Plus, what's the point in putting off the inevitable?

Unlike the other scandals, this one isn't going to blow over anytime soon. The aftermath will linger like a foul stench in the air for months to come.

Each new day feels like a summit that needs to be scaled.

It's exhausting.

Physically.

Mentally.

Emotionally.

"Hey, Delilah. Wait up," a voice calls out.

With a wince, I hasten my step. I'm tired of all the comments and questions. The smirks and jabs. The crude offers.

Should have known... Whore mother, whore daughter.

As much as I hate to admit it, I'm on the cusp of shattering into a million jagged pieces. Unlike Humpty Dumpty, I will never be put back together again. It's a disturbing thought that continues to rico-chet in my brain. Holding everything together is taking a herculean effort on my part. It'll be a miracle if I make it to three o'clock intact.

I cut quickly across the parking lot, only wanting to slip inside the stone building. The new plan is to hide out in the photography studio until the first hour bell rings. Mrs. Chambers has taken pity on me and doesn't ask any questions. Although, I'm sure she's heard all the rumors that are circulating.

It would be impossible not to.

I can all but feel eyes crawling over me as ugly snickers dog my every step.

When slim fingers lock around my bicep, halting my progress, I swing around, ready to bare my teeth. Everly's eyes widen as she drops her hand and takes a quick step in retreat, giving me some much-needed space.

"Sorry," she mumbles. "I didn't mean to startle you. I just wanted to check in and see how you're doing." Her voice dips as she quickly glances around. "It's been pretty brutal around here."

A choked laugh rises in my throat as hot tears prick my eyes. I've always known that most of the kids who attended Hawthorne Prep were assholes, but I couldn't have predicted just how cruel they could be.

"That's an understatement."

Her eyes flood with sympathy. "I know. I hate that all this is happening. It's so unfair and just plain mean."

Even though Everly and I aren't close, I appreciate that she's gone out of her way to be supportive. And trust me, our classmates have taken notice. The last thing I want to do is pull her down with me.

When I remain silent, she nods toward the school. "Should we head inside? There's about ten minutes before the first bell."

As tempting as it is to cling to the lifeline she's throwing, I step closer and drop my voice. "You don't have to do this."

Confusion flickers across her expression. "Do what?"

Heat stings my cheeks as I force myself to address the obvious. "Stand by my side. I don't want you getting hit by shrapnel and becoming collateral damage. You know what this place is like. It's not a matter of *if* they turn on you, it's a matter of *when*."

With a jerk of her shoulders, she straightens to her full height. "You're right, I know exactly what it's like. Which is why we're going to walk in together."

Her unexpected offer of solidarity has emotion welling up inside my throat. It takes effort to tamp it down. "I appreciate that."

More than she can possibly realize.

More than I'm able to put into words.

Especially right now.

I can't help but issue one last warning, needing her to understand what she's opening herself up to. I wouldn't wish this on my worst enemy.

"I just want you to be sure."

Unconcerned with the growing number of stares aimed in our direction, Everly slips her arm through mine. "Forget about these assholes." She sends a scathing look toward the groups of students standing around and gossiping. "In fact, you should feel sorry for them."

When I give her a questioning look, or, more accurately, one that says *are you crazy*, she continues. "Just think how pathetic it must be to peak in high school. Most probably don't even realize that it's all downhill from here."

That comment does the unexpected and lightens the mood.

It's amazing how one loyal friend willing to stand by your side is enough to boost your morale and make the bleakest of situations tolerable. Her offer of friendship isn't something I take lightly or for granted.

She gives me a determined nod before we start off again. After the first couple steps, I realize my chest no longer aches as if there is an elephant sitting in the middle of it. I draw a breath of fresh air into my lungs before slowly expelling it back into the atmosphere. The pit that has taken up residence at the bottom of my belly since Mom's affair came to light shrinks just a bit. It doesn't completely dissolve, but it no longer feels like I'm moments away from being sick.

It's only when the back of my neck prickles that I lift my head and scan the pockets of people. Just like always, my gaze is inexplicably drawn to his, as if I was aware of him standing there, watching me. His green eyes flare with dark emotion as if I'm the one who inflicted the damage. Even though I steel myself against the pain, it explodes in my chest like a gunshot wound. The combustible energy we always seem to generate tugs at the deepest part of me. I don't understand how I can feel so strongly about someone I should loathe.

No...

I *do* hate Austin. He's blown my world apart.

Unfortunately, my heart hasn't received the memo just yet, but it will.

With enough time.

It's like someone reached into my chest, wrapped their hand around my beating heart and wrenched it from my body while still dripping blood. I have to remind myself that he betrayed me in more ways than one. Not only did he hurt me, but my mother as well.

And there's no way to forgive that.

"Are you all right?" Everly whispers, breaking through the trance that has fallen over me.

I jerk my head into a stiff nod.

"Are you going to talk to him?" she asks tentatively.

"No. There's nothing for us to discuss. It's over. *We're* over."

"The stubborn expression on his face says otherwise."

That's too damn bad. Austin Hawthorne no longer calls the shots where I'm concerned. I force my gaze away from him and focus on the stone building looming in front of me. Thirty more steps and we'll be safely inside.

Ha!

As if there's any security to be found within the prestigious academy.

Just as I step onto the sidewalk, a voice rises above the din of the parking lot.

"Oh, Edmond. Yes, right there. Yes!"

Loud grunting follows my mother's impassioned voice.

"Who's my dirty little whore?"

I freeze as heat slams into my cheeks and the laughter surrounding me grows in volume, echoing in my ears. It's slowly that I force myself to turn until my gaze locks on Jasper. A smug smile curves his lips as he holds up a small Bluetooth speaker in one hand and his phone in the other.

The sound cuts out before repeating.

"Oh, Edmond. Yes, right there. Yes!"

Grunting.

"Who's my dirty little whore?"

That's all it takes for a trapdoor to open, and then I'm in free fall.

"You," I say in a choked voice. It's as if I'm being strangled from the inside out.

His expression turns into a full-on grin. He looks so fucking proud of himself, and it hits me like a punch to the gut that he's the one who did this. He's the one who played the audio over the loudspeaker for the entire school to hear.

"Why?" It's a stupid question. If I could snatch the word from the air and suck it back inside, I would.

A hard glint enters his eyes. "A better question would be—why not?"

His response makes me sick.

As we stare, it truly hits me that Jasper will never leave me alone. He'll always be there to torment me until there's nothing else left to do but curl up in a tight ball and wave the white flag. And then it'll get so much worse because he'll have free rein to do whatever he wants.

When I remain silent, he barks out a laugh. "Here's a little bit of advice—tell your mom not to fuck our headmaster where anyone can stumble upon them."

My hands clench uselessly at my sides as rage crashes over me, blinding me. I don't think I've ever felt more hatred in my life. It roars through my veins, igniting a firestorm in the pit of my belly. I don't realize I'm on the move, cutting a direct path to my ex until I'm a few feet away. His smile widens as he straightens to his full height. Even through the thick haze that consumes me, I realize he's loving this.

All but reveling in it.

The sick bastard craves the attention. It doesn't matter if it's positive or negative. He wants my eyes locked on him at all times.

But that realization isn't enough to stop me.

Once I'm within striking distance, I slam full force into his chest with both hands. He braces for the attack and only stumbles back a step or two. The smirk remains firmly intact. Frustration bubbles up inside me like a geyser. Any moment, I'll blow and spew all over the parking lot. I'm shaking with unspent fury.

"I hate you so fucking much," I growl, unable to stop the words from bursting free. It's like poison rushing through my blood, infecting every cell of my being.

A dark chuckle escapes from him and his eyes glitter with malice. "Bring it on, baby. My new mission in life is to make yours a living hell. If I can't have you, then I'll make damn sure no one else does either."

He's only reconfirming what I suspected all along. He's a sick son of a bitch, and I'm kicking myself for not realizing it sooner. For being snowed by his good looks and easy charm. For not running as fast as I could when the façade slowly started to slip and I caught glimpses of the monster lurking beneath.

The crowd surrounding us presses in, tightening the circle. People are pushing and shoving, jostling to get a better view of the altercation. Cell phones have been whipped out and are recording every juicy tidbit. Whatever transpires in the next couple of minutes will only ignite more gossip.

If I were thinking clearly, I'd retreat and ignore the asshole. Instead, I do something I never thought myself capable of. I ball my hand and draw back my arm.

A hush falls over the spectators.

The only thing I can focus on is the satisfaction I'll feel when my fist slams into his smug face. I don't care about getting suspended or expelled. In fact, I hope that's what happens. This place is a prison and I want out.

Just as I'm about to let it fly, a large hand wraps around my clenched fist, halting my movement. With a gasp, I spin around and find Austin. Our gazes lock as air gets clogged in my throat.

"Remember when you told me that Jasper wasn't worth it?" His voice is the epitome of calm, and it washes over me, taking the worst part of my anger with it. "You were right. He's not. All the ways he tried to fuck with us haven't worked. I'm still here, Delilah. And I'm not going anywhere."

The violence whipping through my body gradually dissipates, leaving behind a deep well of grief.

When I remain silent, unable to summon any words, his voice rises above the din of whispers that snake through the thick crowd as he turns to meet Jasper's eyes.

"Aubrey outed you. She told me exactly how you dug through my school records, looking for something to use against me." One side of Austin's mouth hitches with amusement. "You must have thought you hit the jackpot when you found out that I'm dyslexic. But it didn't work, did it?"

Austin's arm slips around my waist before he tugs me against his bigger body.

"You need to get it through your head that Delilah isn't yours. She will never be yours again, and there's nothing you can do to change that. You've done your worst and it wasn't enough. This girl is mine." His voice deepens, ringing out over the mass of students. "She belongs to me the same way I belong to her."

Jasper's face transforms, the smirk morphing into an enraged scowl. A growl rumbles up from deep within his chest as he launches himself at Austin. Before he's able to make contact, a tall, dark-haired woman pushes her way through the press of bodies and grabs him by the back of his blazer, holding him in place.

"Break it up," she barks in a commanding voice.

Jasper turns glaring eyes on her. "Who the hell are you?"

She doesn't release him as hers narrow. "Mrs. Brentwood." There's a pause. "The new headmistress of Hawthorne Prep."

Just as he lifts his lips into a snarl, she snaps, "I'd like to see you in my office immediately, Mr. Morgan. It appears some accusations have been levied against you for drugging another student at a party."

His eyes widen as a spark of fear ignites in his gray depths before he quickly smothers it. "I don't know what you're talking about."

"Nevertheless, the police are waiting in my office."

He stills, face turning ashen. "Police?"

"That's right." She inclines her head. "Several, in fact."

He jerks out of her hold before taking a menacing step toward the older woman. "Do you have any idea who my parents are?"

I didn't think it was possible for her blue eyes to become any more frigid. "Actually, they're both waiting in my office for your impending arrival."

His nostrils flare as he glowers at me. "You fucking bitch. See the trouble you've caused?"

My mouth falls open.

That's probably the closest thing I'll get to an apology.

"This isn't over by a longshot," he promises.

"On the contrary, Mr. Morgan, it is, indeed, over. Now get to my office immediately or I'll have the police physically drag you there. The choice is yours to make."

With one final snarl, Jasper spins on his heels and stalks away, pushing and shoving through the throng until disappearing from sight.

The older woman watches him leave before turning her attention to me. "Ms. Robinson?"

My eyes widen and I almost take a hasty step in retreat. Our new headmistress has proven in the past five minutes that she is a force to be reckoned with. Austin remains steadfast at my side.

Instead of shrinking away, I straighten my shoulders and hold my ground. "Yes."

"We'll need to see you in the office as well to give an account of what transpired at Kingsley Hawthorne's party."

"I don't remember much," I admit.

A flash of sympathy softens her eyes, making her seem more approachable. "That's quite all right. You just need to be honest with the police."

"Okay." I blow out a breath. "I can do that."

Her gaze sweeps over the students of HP and they silently scatter like rats from a burning building. With a nod, she says, "I'll see you inside."

Before I can respond, she strides away like a military general set on renewing order to the rank and file.

And then it's just the two of us. Austin shifts as his eyes stay pinned to mine. This is the first time in days we've spoken. It's painful to be this close and feel the intensity that vibrates through the air.

"Can we talk?" he murmurs, voice filled with hesitation. It's not a tone I'm used to hearing from him. He's always so self-assured and forceful.

Especially where I'm concerned.

Unable to maintain eye contact, I glance away and chew my lower lip with indecision. When I remain silent, he takes a tentative step in my direction before sliding gentle fingertips beneath my chin and turning it until I have no other choice but to meet his gaze head on. Until I can feel the warmth of his breath feathering across my lips.

It's nothing short of intoxicating. I have to battle myself to maintain control.

"Please?" he whispers.

Air escapes from my lungs like a slow leak as I gather my strength and shake my head. "I don't think that would be a good idea."

In fact, it's a terrible one. I know how he affects me, and I can't risk him ripping down the walls I've only managed to erect to keep him at bay.

"You really hurt me," I admit.

Pain flickers across his expression as his voice drops. "I know, and I'm so fucking sorry. You were never to blame for any of it, and I should have realized it from the start. Instead, I took my anger out on you."

"You used me. I was nothing more than an instrument for your revenge."

His eyes widen. "That's not true. My feelings…they were always there, simmering beneath the surface. Maybe they got a little twisted up, but they never changed."

I shake my head, unwilling to let his heartfelt words cloud my better judgment. I allowed that to happen before, and I'll be damned if I fall into the same neatly laid trap a second time. I conjure up a mental image of him and Aubrey together in the study and hold onto it for dear life.

"I saw you."

His brow furrows as I steer our convo in a different direction. "I don't understand. What did you see?"

I straighten to my full height and inch my chin higher. "The morning I left the beach house with Duke, I saw you and Aubrey together in the study." No matter how much I wish it were possible to turn off my feelings for this boy, I can't.

I still care about him.

He was my first.

For so many things.

Those memories aren't as easily evicted from my brain as he's been from my life.

Before I can blink, his fingers lock around my upper arms to hold me firmly in place.

His forehead furrows as his voice dips. "Wait a minute. You saw that?"

His lack of a denial steals my breath away as pain slices through my heart. The boy standing before me has so much power to wound me. I hate it but can't imagine a day when that's no longer true.

Understanding dawns across his expression. "That's why you left with Duke."

It's not a question.

"Yes."

He blows out a steady breath. "I don't give a shit about Aubrey."

A mirthless laugh falls from my lips as my eyes widen. "Is that supposed to make me feel better?"

He shakes his head as frustration flickers in his eyes. "That's not what I meant. Aubrey mentioned something on the beach the night before you left and I couldn't get it out of my head. I wanted to get her talking, so I pretended…"

"To be interested," I finish for him.

"Yeah," he admits with a sigh. "She told me everything Jasper did, from digging through my records to drugging you at the party and taking pictures." A hard glint sparks in his eyes. "I made damn sure she went to the police when we returned to Hawthorne. I don't give a shit that he outed me, but drugging you?" His jaw clenches and a muscle in his cheek tics a mad rhythm. "There was no way he was going to get away with it. I'm just sorry I didn't listen to you from the beginning. I should have trusted you."

I can only stare as I process everything that he's telling me. The shitty things that Jasper did have now been exposed.

Aubrey admitted to it all.

"It's why she shoved you on the boat," he adds as my brain continues to spin. "I guess you were asking too many questions."

My lips purse as I attempt to tease more memories of that night to the surface, but, for the most part, they remain elusive.

She probably didn't realize I couldn't swim, but still…

I could have died.

What a psycho bitch.

"Thank you. Without you getting to the bottom of the truth, we still wouldn't know what happened."

He takes a hesitant step. "Aubrey said that Jasper only took photographs. She was there the entire time."

The fact that I was passed out and don't remember if I was violated takes the situation to an entirely new level.

I don't understand how Aubrey could do that to me.

Or anyone.

How could she go along blindly with Jasper's plan?

It's so messed up.

"Delilah?"

I blink back to the present and the boy standing in front of me. "Yeah?"

Uncertainty flickers in his green depths. He's so close that it would be impossible to miss the various shades of green and gold that dance within his irises.

"Is there any way you can forgive me?"

The question rolls around in my head for a few silent moments. In the past, I've never been one to hold a grudge. I've always found it to be a waste of energy. What I want most is to move forward in peace and get through the remainder of senior year before leaving Hawthorne.

I give him a slight smile. "We were both victims in Jasper's machinations. I don't hold anything against you."

My ex is the one I can't forgive.

Hope flares in his eyes. "Do you think there's still a chance for us?"

My teeth scrape across my lower lip as I glance away, staring at the rolling green hills of Hawthorne Prep's campus. They're picture perfect with the autumn sun shining down on them. As much as I wish we could rewind time and start fresh, that's no longer a possibility.

I force myself to meet his stare and slowly shake my head. "I don't think so."

His eyes widen as his grip tightens on my arms. "You don't?"

"Too much has happened."

"Delilah."

The tortured way my name sounds as it escapes from his lips shatters my heart into a million jagged pieces. Whether he understands it or not, I'm doing what's best for myself. I need time and distance from the situation to process everything that transpired. There's no way I can do that with Austin at my side. He might not mean to, but he clouds my judgement.

Even as I stand in front of him, I feel myself wavering. The attraction is still there and just like he claimed, it hums beneath the surface, patiently waiting for a chance to break free.

When he doesn't drop his hands, I whisper, "You need to let me go."

He sucks in a harsh breath as his expression grows fierce, his fingers turning into manacles. "What you're asking is impossible. I can't do it. You gave yourself to me and nothing will ever change that."

His words bring a sting of tears to my eyes.

It's true.

That's exactly what I did.

And…I wouldn't go back and change it.

The last thing I want is to fight with him. I can't do it when there is so much emotion churning inside me. So much that needs to be sorted out.

"But if you want me to back off, that's what I'll do, because it's what you need to heal."

Instead of releasing me, he drags me closer and wraps his arms around my body until I'm cocooned in his comforting strength as he presses a tender kiss against the crown of my head.

"I love you," he whispers in my ear. "And nothing will ever change that."

A sob gathers in my chest, making it impossible to breathe as I shove my way out of his arms. Once I've retreated, I inhale a lungful of fresh air and pray that it helps to clear my head.

Our gazes cling as I take a careful step away. His muscles tense and I get the feeling that he's fighting himself not to leap forward. If he does, I don't know if I'll be able to survive the onslaught of emotion without falling to pieces.

My head and heart have never been at war.

But they are now.

All I know is that I can't allow my heart to win this battle.

When I take another tentative step, his eyes flare and his hands tighten into fists until the knuckles turn bone white. When he remains perfectly still, I draw in a shaky breath before swinging away and running toward the stone building as swiftly as possible.

I expect his fingers to lock around me, dragging me back to him.

But it doesn't happen.

It's only when I reach the glass doors and yank them open that I throw a hasty look over my shoulder to find that Austin has disappeared from sight.

And my life.

DELILAH

With my lunch tray in hand, I stop and survey the cafeteria, looking around for a place to sit. It's been two weeks since everything exploded in the parking lot. Only now does it feel as if everything is slowly returning to normal.

Well…a new kind of normal.

A better kind of normal.

Mom quietly turned in her resignation and found a new job at Hawthorne Public.

Trust me, the irony isn't lost on me.

Or her.

She no longer refers to the kids as low-life animals and seems to enjoy working in the office.

The Morgans quietly pulled Jasper out of school after the meeting with the police. Last I heard, he was attending a pricey reform school in England. With him gone, I no longer hesitate around every corner and wonder if he's lurking in the shadows, waiting to pounce. Or if he'll come up with a new twisted way to punish me.

Aubrey was suspended for the remainder of senior year. She'll still be allowed to graduate from HP but can't attend in-person classes.

She sent a letter apologizing for her part in drugging me. I appreciate the sentiment but suspect her parents forced her to write it as part of her punishment.

Without my ex stirring up trouble, things have grown quiet. No one wants to bring up what Jasper did for fear of being attached to the scandal and facing stiff consequences from our new headmistress. Even the mean girl squad is taking a break from being their bitchy selves. The atmosphere is more what I always imagined Hawthorne Prep would be like before I actually stepped foot inside the building.

After a handful of moments, I spot an empty table near no man's land and beeline in that direction. No longer is there the sensation of eyes crawling over me as I walk by. Once I've reached my destination, I set my tray down and settle in the middle of the table.

I don't have a problem sitting by myself. Strangely enough, throughout everything that's happened, I feel like I've grown stronger. I can handle myself and whatever comes my way. Nothing could be worse than dealing with Jasper.

I unscrew the cap from my water bottle before lifting it to my lips and taking a swig.

As I pick up my fork, ready to dig into my seared scallops and baby spinach with spiced pomegranate glaze, a deep voice says, "Hey. Mind if I join you?"

Recognition sets in as I glance up and find Duke standing across from me with his bagged lunch in hand.

"Sure." I wave toward the long stretch of empty table. "That is, if you can find a spot."

With a snort, his lips curl into a smile. "I'll do my best to squeeze in right here. We'll just have to find a way to make it work."

Once settled, he opens his paper bag and takes out two sandwiches along with a Gatorade.

After he wolfs down one of them, he asks, "Are you doing all right?"

I nibble on my PB&J as the question circles around in my brain. It's almost a surprise to realize that I am. I've made it through to the other side and lived to tell the tale. How many people can say that?

"I'm good."

"Glad to hear it." He picks up the other half and takes a big bite.

"Is it okay if we sit with you?" Everly asks.

Summer and Kingsley stand beside her.

My gaze darts to the auburn-haired girl before reluctantly sliding to her friend. Summer Hawthorne stares at me from eyes that are deep green with gold flecks that dance within them. Unlike weeks ago, they're no longer filled with hostility and scorn.

A deep ache fills my heart before gradually spreading throughout my chest. As much as I've tried to relegate Austin to the past, it's proven to be an impossible task. He continues to fill all of my waking thoughts.

And most of my dreams at night.

I shoot a quick glance at Duke from beneath the thick fringe of my lashes. His jaw has tightened and a muscle tics in his cheek. Everly doesn't bother giving him the time of day. I'm not sure if her easy dismissal inflames his temper or not.

Even though she's friends with Summer, Everly has stuck by my side and over the past two weeks, we've grown closer. Not only is she nice, she has a great sense of humor. If Duke would just give her a chance, he'd probably change his mind. Although, one look at the hostility blazing from his narrowed stare is enough to tell me that a reversal of his opinion isn't going to happen anytime soon or without a fight.

"Of course."

Summer settles beside Duke with Kingsley on the other side. Everly sits next to me and opposite her friend. As we dig into our lunches, discussions regarding our new headmistress pop up. What has become apparent is that she doesn't care about appeasing the wealthy parents who send their kids to the elite prep school, and she's unwilling to look the other way when students behave badly.

Which they do quite often.

My guess is that's the reason the atmosphere around here has undergone such a drastic improvement. Whatever the explanation, it's a welcome change and a breath of fresh air. I no longer dread walking into this place each morning.

"I heard Brentwood has a kid starting here soon," Everly says.

"Hmm. That should be interesting, considering how welcoming most of these assholes are," Summer interjects with a snort.

"If that's true, no one will mess with her kid. Not after the way she ran Jasper out of town," Kingsley adds.

We all nod in agreement.

The woman is formidable.

And a little bit scary.

A few more people join our table, filling up the spaces. Halfway through lunch, I glance around, surprised to find myself surrounded by my classmates. There's so much laughter and chatter. The loneliness that's always plagued me is conspicuously absent. Even though I was never really alone and always surrounded by people, I never felt like I belonged. I was still an outsider with my nose pressed against the glass, wishing things could be different.

That's no longer the case.

If it still feels like something, or more accurately, *someone* is missing, I shove that thought away before it can take root inside my brain and focus on the conversations taking place around me.

When Summer clears her throat, my gaze flickers toward her.

"I, um, wanted to say that I'm sorry for how I treated you. You didn't deserve my anger. I was stupid and bought into the lies Jasper was spewing." Her normally strong shoulders slump under the weight of her apology. "Honestly, I should have known better."

The conversations taking place around us grind to a halt as people turn and listen.

I blink, surprised that she's making such a public apology. Kingsley throws his arm around her shoulder and tugs her close before whispering something in her ear.

Summer and Austin have been so protective of each other. Neither wants to see the other get hurt. And the students of Hawthorne Prep haven't exactly been welcoming to them since their arrival.

So…I get it.

And I can forgive.

Her behavior was never malicious.

"It's all right."

Her eyes soften as she shakes her head. "It's not." There's a pause. "After what happened with Jasper at the beginning of the school year, I assumed you were playing games."

"I would never deliberately hurt him," I whisper.

I want the best for Austin and care more than I'm willing to admit. Even privately to myself. I can only hope that with enough time, my feelings will eventually fade into nothingness.

"I know. It's why I was so angry. I couldn't understand how I could have been so wrong about you."

Air leaks slowly from my lungs. After more than a month of tension, it feels like Summer and I have finally come to a place of understanding. Maybe now, we'll be able to bury the past and start fresh.

Just when I assume she'll drop the topic, she says in a low voice, "I know Austin made a lot of mistakes, but he really does care about you."

Even though I try to stomp out the sadness before it can wreak further havoc, I'm not quick enough. It rushes through my veins, suffusing every cell.

My teeth rake across my lower lip as I contemplate a response. What I won't do is give her false hope where there is none to be found. As painful as this separation is, it's been good for me. I'm standing on my own two feet and finding my own way in the world. I've become my own person.

One who isn't afraid to branch out and take a few risks.

What I'm not doing is lurking in the shadows, hiding behind either of these boys.

Unable to hold her searching gaze, I glance away. My attention is immediately ensnared by dark green eyes, and my heart stutters to a standstill before thundering in my chest.

No matter how much time slips by, my reaction to Austin Hawthorne is always the same and just as visceral. It's as if he became an integral part of me and I have no idea how to purge him from my system.

What scares me most is that the longing I feel deep in my soul will never fade. It'll always be a part of me.

With my arms folded behind my head, I stare at the ceiling as my mind tumbles over the past month. All the ways I fucked up and hurt Delilah.

The distance that now separates us is as wide as an ocean and impossible to cross.

In hindsight, I can't blame her for insisting on it. I was an asshole and should have placed more trust in her.

Even though every instinct is prodding me to pursue her with a single-mindedness, I've done as she requested and kept my distance.

It's fucking torture.

She's like the sun, and all I want to do is revolve around her brilliance.

You need to let me go.

Those six words cut me to the core and make me feel like I'll bleed out.

Deep down, I know if I'd laid my hands on her, I could have changed her mind. But how could I do that after the hell I put her through?

The answer is that I couldn't.

I wasn't lying when I told her that I loved her. I've never said that to anyone else other than family.

But I do.

I love Delilah.

It's for that reason I need to make my peace with her decision. If she honestly doesn't believe I'm what's best, then I need to move on. Although it doesn't feel like I'll ever get over her. She'll forever lurk in the back of my brain and in my heart as the one who got away.

The one I allowed to slip through my fingers.

And that sucks.

The knock on the closed bedroom door jerks me from those depressing thoughts. Before I can tell whoever it is to go away, Summer pokes her head inside the room.

"Hey." Her voice is tentative as if I'm minutes away from leaping off the nearest skyscraper.

I grunt out a response. It's the best I can muster under the circumstances.

What's funny is that I've never had a problem shaking off past relationships and moving on in the blink of an eye. I'd go so far as to say it's always been a relief when they ended.

This is anything but.

This feels like someone plunged their hand into my chest and ripped out my beating heart before holding it up for everyone to inspect.

When I remain silent, she slips further inside the room before leaning against the door frame.

"Want to talk?"

I snort.

Hell, no.

"Austin…" Her voice trails off as if she's unsure how to voice her concerns.

She should really know better by now. I know what she's thinking without her having to verbalize it.

Call it a twin thing.

Taking pity on her, I mutter, "You know that I'm not really in the mood for company, right?"

"Yeah, but I really hate seeing you like this."

I don't like it any better than she does, but there's nothing I can do except move through it the best I can.

What's the alternative?

Exactly. There aren't any.

"You're just so…*sad.*" Her concern is palpable.

I jerk my gaze away to stare at the ceiling. As close as Summer and I are, this isn't a topic I want to discuss with her. In the end, it won't do a damn bit of good.

I fucked up.

And there's no way to fix it.

My twin is nothing if not tenacious. Usually, it's one of her finer qualities. Not in this situation, though. What she needs to do is leave me alone to lick my wounds in private.

Is that really too much to ask?

From the corner of my eye, I watch her hover in the doorway.

Apparently so.

"Have you tried talking to her again?"

"Nope." I force myself to state the truth. "She doesn't want anything to do with me."

That acknowledgment is like shoving my heart through a meat-grinder.

Over and over again.

I just want the pain to stop.

Even if it's just for one fucking minute.

"I don't think that's true. I saw the way Delilah looked at you the other day in the cafeteria. She still cares, Austin. If you really have feelings, then maybe you need to fight for her."

Have feelings?

That's not even a question.

What I'm trying to do is abide by her wishes and give her the space she needs to heal.

Summer has no idea what happened with Delilah, and I'm sure as hell not going to tell her. It's impossible to think about all the things I did without shame rushing in to fill me. Not only did she have Jasper tormenting her, but then I blackmailed her into doing what I wanted.

"She asked me to let her go, and that's exactly what I did."

Exasperation shimmers from Summer in heavy waves as she shakes her head and rolls her eyes. "Guys are such blockheads."

My lips twitch. Can't argue with that. Her assessment of the situation is spot on.

"Look, you've given her enough time for the dust to settle. Now you need to have a conversation and see if she still feels the same way. For all you know, she's missing you just as much as you are her."

Doubtful.

Plus…

I see her around school and watch her when she's not aware of it.

Am I venturing into stalker territory?

Possibly.

What I can't deny is that she's flourishing and finally coming into her own. She's making more friends and putting herself out there. She's no longer hiding behind her camera the way she used to.

It's fucking amazing to see, and I'm happy for her.

It's exactly what she deserves.

Only the best.

And obviously, that's not me.

When Summer continues to stare, I huff out a breath. "If I tell you that I'll think about it, will you go away and leave me in peace?"

Her eyes narrow and her lips thin as she gives the question serious consideration. "Yes."

"Then I'll think about it."

Bleakness fills her expression as her shoulders slump.

That's all it takes for guilt to prick me.

When I say nothing more, she pushes away from the doorjamb. "I really hope you do. I'd hate for you to lose something amazing because you're being a stubborn jackass."

I can't help the snort that escapes from me.

With that, she slips from the room and closes the door quietly behind her.

As the heavy silence settles around me, I can't stop Summer's words from circling through my brain. The longer I think about it, the more I wonder if she might be right.

Am I just fucking things up even more?

It's a question without an answer.

DELILAH

I'm not sure what wakes me from a sound sleep. All I know is that one minute, I'm dreaming and the next, my eyes are flying open and I'm staring into the velvety darkness that surrounds me, searching for…*something*.

My skin prickles with awareness, but there's nothing.

Nothing is out of place.

The air is still.

Undisturbed.

With an aggravated huff, I roll onto my side, only wanting to get sucked back under into slumber and the dreams swirling around in my head. Even though school has improved under the new headmistress' guidance, there's still a sadness within me that is impossible to shake.

And I know exactly who is at the root of my melancholy.

It's frustrating. I want to return to the point when Austin Hawthorne didn't exist in my world. When he didn't consume all of my waking thoughts. When I wasn't bombarded with constant memories that make me long for something that's no longer possible.

I squeeze my eyes tightly closed before releasing a steady breath. When they crack open again, I realize there's a black object no more than a foot from where my head rests. For a long moment, I stare in confusion, searching my brain for a rational explanation, but I know that whatever it is wasn't there earlier.

Awareness floods through me as I straighten to a seated position and reach over, flicking the switch so that the room is illuminated with soft light. Movement from the pink fuzzy papasan chair shoved in the corner catches my eye, and my hand flies to my mouth to stifle the scream that rises in my throat.

My heartbeat thrashes painfully beneath my breast. Any moment, it'll break loose and flop around on the carpeted floor. "What are you doing here?"

He leans forward until his elbows can settle on his spread thighs. "I needed to see you."

My mouth turns cottony as I eat him up with my eyes. When was the last time Austin was this close?

Weeks ago.

The sad truth is that I've missed him. It takes every bit of self-control not to launch myself at his muscular body.

Instead, I strengthen my resolve. "There's nothing left to say."

He rises to his feet before swallowing up the distance that separates us in the blink of an eye. It becomes necessary to lift my chin in order to steadily hold his gaze.

"Then I guess you can sit and listen while I talk."

When he's no more than a foot away, he grinds to a halt. Our gazes stay locked in the silent war as a shiver scurries down my spine and electricity hums in the charged air that surrounds us. That's when I realize we will always generate this kind of irrepressible energy when we're near one another.

It's not something that will fade.

No matter how many years pass.

Unable to hold his penetrating stare as that knowledge sinks in, I glance away. Once again, my attention falls to the object beside me. I suck in a sharp breath and blink, wondering if my eyes are playing tricks on me.

It's a camera.

And not just any camera, either. It's the very same Nikon that fell to the bottom of the lake. I rip my gaze away long enough to throw a questioning look at Austin.

"How?" The word comes out sounding more like an unrecognizable croak.

He settles cautiously on the bed before slipping his fingers around mine. "It's not the one you lost. I wish it were."

"I don't understand. How did you know what model it was?"

"Your mom gave me the information."

I blink in surprise, thrown off by the response. "Really?"

I...can't believe she did that and never said a word.

"Yeah."

I glance at our entwined fingers as my brain continues to somersault.

Why does his hand wrapped around mine feel so right?

It would be so much easier to leave him in the past and move on with my life if that wasn't the case.

When I remain silent, lost in the chaotic whirl of my thoughts, he adds, "I told her how much you missed your father and that the camera was a connection to him that meant a lot. She seemed to understand and got me the information I needed."

As much as I want to hold back the flood of tears, they prick my eyes.

He waves his other hand toward the camera. "I know it won't replace the one that belonged to him, but I wanted you to have it."

My gaze returns to the black object. It looks just like Dad's. Carefully, I reach out and pick it up. The weight is the same. If I closed my eyes, I wouldn't know the difference by the shape or texture. I turn it over in my hands. There are a few nicks and scuffs that mine didn't have, but otherwise it's identical.

I...can't believe Austin did this.

And just like that, the walls I've been struggling to hold in place come tumbling down. I glance at him and our gazes fasten. Looking away feels impossible. It always has been but now, even more so.

"Thank you. This means...everything to me."

And it does.

It's not Dad's camera. I can't click the shutter button or stare through the view finder and know that a decade ago, he once did the same.

But...

Austin went through a lot of trouble to replace something meaningful. This camera will be special for entirely different reasons. I'll never be able to look at it or use it without thinking not only of my father, but him as well.

How will I ever untangle myself from him?

"I understand you might not be able to forgive me for everything that happened, but I need you to know that no matter what, I love you, and what I want more than anything is the best for you. Even if it's not me."

I blink as a lone tear slides down my cheek. His expression softens as he reaches out and thumbs away the wetness before bringing it to his mouth and sucking the digit.

If my walls hadn't been demolished by the unexpected gift, his admittance finishes off the job.

I couldn't shove him away even if I tried.

When I remain silent, he continues in a tangle of words as emotion floods them. "I never want to do anything that makes you unhappy. You deserve the very best of what life has to offer. I mean that from the bottom of my heart. I refuse to be like Jasper and make your life miserable because you no longer want to be with me. Instead, I'll stand beside you as a friend and cheer you on as all your dreams come true." His shoulders straighten as he forces out the rest. "Even if that means they don't include me."

My heart clenches before twisting painfully in my chest.

As I scrutinize his solemn expression, I realize he means it. He's not just blowing smoke up my ass. He's already proven that he'll let me go if that's what is in my best interest.

Reaching out, he slides a hand across my cheek before his fingers slip into my hair, cradling the side of my head. "I love you, and that will never change. No matter how much time passes."

The distance disappears between us before he strokes his mouth gently across mine. For just a heartbeat, his movements stall, and we remain fused together. His breath becomes mine and vice versa. The world shrinks until it only encompasses the two of us.

Everything outside this bedroom ceases to exist.

When his tongue peeks out to lick at the seam of my lips, I open until his warm, minty breath can feather against my flesh. Everything about Austin Hawthorne intoxicates me. It always has. From the very beginning. I want to suck in a big breath of him and hold it captive in my lungs.

My lips part just enough for his tongue to slip inside my mouth and mingle with my own. There have been so many times when he was forceful and overwhelmed my senses, taking what he wanted. This caress is the exact opposite. It's tender and shatters my heart into a million broken fragments that will never be pieced back together again.

Just as I sink into the kiss, he draws away. His eyes search mine before filling with a mixture of resolve and sadness.

"I should go."

Everything within me seizes.

No.

No.

No.

The thought of us not being together tears at my insides.

When he straightens to his full height and takes a step toward the window, I come alive and pop to my feet.

"Austin."

As he swings around, I do what I've been dying to since I found him in the chair. I launch myself at him. He catches me with a soft grunt before crushing me against the steely strength of his body.

"Don't make this any more difficult than it has to be," he whispers brokenly. "I'm trying to do the right thing here and let you go."

"Please don't. It's not what I want. Or need."

Not anymore.

He stills, voice dipping low. "But I thought…"

I shake my head, realizing the truth. "Maybe that's what I needed in the beginning, to find my own way, but I have." I draw away enough to search his eyes. "I love you and want you in my life."

No...I *need* him in my life.

He's silent for so long that I wonder if he'll deny what I now crave most.

Him.

"Are you sure, Delilah? Because if you tell me that you're mine, there's no going back. You'll belong to me. Forever and always. I won't let you go." His hands rise to cup the sides of my skull until it's impossible to look away. "Not again."

My lips curve into a smile.

In the blink of an eye, my world has shifted. My heart soars, feeling so much lighter than it has these previous weeks when we were separated, and that has everything to do with Austin. The boy I fell for the moment our gazes collided in the office on the first day of school. The one who stood a little too close, crowding my personal space and invading my thoughts.

It was hard to admit while I'd been dating someone else, but I've wanted him ever since then.

And now...

He's mine.

And I'm his.

I wouldn't have it any other way. The road we had to travel to get to this moment was necessary to grow and become the couple we now are.

"I won't let you go either," I tell him fiercely, meaning every word.

He smirks. "Is that a promise or a threat?"

A grin spreads across my face. "A little bit of both, I suppose."

"You're a girl after my own heart, Delilah Robinson."

"As long as I'm the only one. That's all that matters."

"You are, sweet girl. Forever and always."

DELILAH

"Better hurry up," Mom calls from the kitchen. "Austin will be here any second, and you don't want to keep him waiting."

For a moment or two, those familiar words echo throughout my head. There used to be a time when it was a different boy she referred to. My belly would pinch, and nausea would take up residence inside the pit of my gut.

But it's not my ex picking me up this morning.

It's Austin.

Instead of anxiety, excitement explodes in my belly.

The last thing I want to do is keep him waiting. I take one last look at my reflection to make sure everything is perfect. This is our first official date as a newly minted couple. It's so tempting to jump up and down and scream, all the while doing a little happy dance.

Not in a million years did I think we would ever get to this place, but I'm so ecstatic we have. All the pain of the past has been worth it.

Unable to sleep, I bounced out of bed a couple hours ago and took a shower before blow drying my hair. I left it all long and wavy around my shoulders. Exactly the way Austin likes it. Then I added a bit of lip gloss and mascara to darken my lashes. I've never been one to wear a ton of makeup, but this gives my lips a pretty shine and makes my blue eyes pop with vibrant color.

Since the temperatures have continued to drop and it's chilly, I'm wearing a pale pink sweater that is soft to the touch and a short denim skirt with thick tights. Tall black boots showcase my legs and give me just a bit of added height.

I release a steady breath and press my palm to my lower belly, hoping it will settle the pterodactyl-sized butterflies that have winged their way to life in my abdomen.

It doesn't.

This is ridiculous.

Why am I so nervous?

We've been together for a few weeks.

He sneaks through my window and crawls into my bed on a nightly basis. A few hours before dawn, he'll slip back out and will pick me up for school in the morning. We hold hands in the hallway when he walks me to class, and we eat lunch together every day. He drives me home after football practice and we make out in his G-wagon when it's parked in my drive as we say goodbye.

So...this shouldn't be a big deal.

But that doesn't change the fact that it is.

Maybe this outing just solidifies our status and makes it official.

Or maybe it's because he refuses to tell me where we're going or what we're doing.

"Delilah?" Mom calls again before peeking her head inside my room. I catch her gaze in the mirror.

A smile spreads across her face. "You look beautiful." It turns just a bit wistful around the edges. "I wish Dad could see what a gorgeous young woman you've grown into. He would be so proud of all your accomplishments."

"Thank you." Her words mean everything to me.

If I needed time to work everything out in my head, so did Mom. Edmund really did a number on her self-esteem. He made promises he had no intention of keeping. She's thrown herself into her new job and has been working with a counselor. We've discussed the idea of setting up a joint appointment to tackle some of our communication issues. We only have each other, and it's important we have a good relationship.

I blink away the moisture that tries to gather in my eyes before swiping my small black purse from the dresser and following Mom into the living room.

"I think you're really going to enjoy today," she says.

My eyes widen as I stutter to a stop. "Wait a minute. You know where we're going?"

She throws a glance over her shoulder. Any hint of nostalgia disappears as she flashes a devilish grin. "Yup." She pops the P at the end.

My hands settle at my hips. "Austin told *you* where he's taking *me* for our date but refused to even give me a hint?"

Her blue eyes sparkle with excitement. "That's right."

Mom has done a complete one-eighty where Austin is concerned. After we worked everything out, he showed up at the door the next day with a bouquet of brightly colored wildflowers for her.

Over the past two weeks, she's gradually thawed, dropping her preconceived notions about both Austin and the Hawthorne family. Mrs. Hawthorne even invited Mom over for dinner so they could get to know each other. As terrible as it is to have the loss of their husbands in common, it solidified their friendship and gave them something to talk about before discovering they had a lot of other similarities. They've become fast friends. Mrs. Hawthorne is down to earth and not like a lot of these Hawthorne Prep moms.

Before I can bombard her with more questions, there's a knock at the front door. Mom bursts into movement, rushing toward the tiny entranceway. I think she might be more excited about this date than I am.

Although, that would be difficult.

As soon as I catch sight of him, air stalls in my lungs, making it impossible to breathe.

Or maybe I just forget how.

If I took my time getting ready this morning and making sure every hair was in place and my outfit was perfect, so did he.

Have I ever seen him look more handsome?

Nope. I don't think so.

He's wearing a gray Henley beneath a black leather jacket and dark wash jeans that hug his muscular thighs. Tan Timberlands complete the outfit. His hair is freshly washed and looks as shiny as a raven's wing.

Our gazes collide and awareness sizzles through my body, electrifying the tips of my fingers and toes. Once I'm ensnared within his green depths, it's impossible to look away.

"Hi." My voice comes out sounding ridiculously breathy.

Even from across the room, I feel the heat of his gaze as it licks over every inch of me.

"You look gorgeous," he says.

"Thanks. You're looking pretty handsome yourself."

When a slow smile spreads across his face, my belly hollows out and my knees weaken. Any moment, I'm going to dissolve into a puddle. It takes effort to rip my attention away from Austin to meet my mother's gaze.

Another smile blooms across her face. "You two enjoy yourselves."

"Thanks, Mrs. Robinson. Are you sure you don't want to come with us?"

Her eyes soften as she shakes her head. "Nope, this date is just for the two of you. I've got plenty to keep me busy around here."

"Okay. If you're sure."

With a nod, she waves us toward the door. "I am."

We step outside and I glance up at the cornflower blue sky. Even though it's sunny, there's a definite snap to the chilled air. As soon as we reach the cement walkway that cuts through the small patch of front lawn, Austin stops and tugs me into the warm circle of his arms. It's my favorite place to be.

"You really do look gorgeous," he whispers against my lips before swooping in for a kiss.

Once we come up for air, I say breathlessly, "Thank you."

My heart flutters madly in my chest.

Even though it's only nine o'clock in the morning and I spent the night curled up against him, arousal sparks to life in his eyes before he delves in for a second time. As soon as his tongue sweeps across my lips, I open, losing myself in the caress. After a handful of minutes, he reluctantly draws away. The hungry expression makes me wish it were possible to drag Austin inside the house and have my wicked way with him.

"I guess we should get moving," he says.

I'm still in a daze as he tows me to his shiny black G-wagon before opening the door and assisting me inside.

Once my head clears, the question trips off my tongue. "You told Mom where we're going?"

The heat snapping in his eyes fades and his lips lift into a knowing smile as a chuckle slips free. "I wanted to make sure everything was perfectly planned."

I thrust my lower lip out in a pout. "And you're not going to tell me?"

His gaze drops to my mouth as a growl rumbles up from deep in his chest. Before I can pepper him with more questions, he presses another searing kiss against my lips before stretching the seatbelt across my chest and fastening it in place.

"You'll just have to be a good girl and wait."

He gives my nipple a little tweak. A potent concoction of pleasure-infused pain explodes inside me. When I gasp, he steps away with a sly smile and closes the door before jogging around the front of the SUV and sliding onto the seat beside me. A few seconds later, the engine roars to life and we pull away from the curb. As we drive down the tree-lined street, his fingers slip around mine, giving them a gentle squeeze.

I settle against the plush leather and realize that I couldn't be happier or more content than I am in this moment. After all the hurt that had been inflicted, I didn't think it was possible for us to find our way back to one another.

Somehow, that's exactly what we've managed to do.

Love won out.

As we reach the main road, I expect him to turn toward town.

Even though I haven't the faintest clue where we're going, everything is located to the north of where I live. Instead, he swings in the opposite direction, leaving Hawthorne behind in the rearview mirror.

My brows draw together as I peer at him, waiting for an explanation. When he remains silent, a smile trembling around his lips as if he can hear the thoughts running rampant through my head, I realize he isn't going to shed any light on the situation.

With that one turn, all of my suspicions have been blown to smithereens. The theater, restaurants, school, and library are all to the north. I genuinely have no clue where we're going. Instead of bombarding him with questions and trying to drag the information out of him, I settle against the plush seat and enjoy the ride.

At the end of the day, it doesn't matter what we do.

Or where we go.

As long as it's together.

I don't realize that I've fallen asleep until Austin's hand gently sweeps across my cheek, his thumb drifting over my parted lips. It takes a moment for my eyelashes to flutter as I blink to awareness, attempting to regain my bearings.

"Hey, sleepyhead. You've been out for a couple of hours."

My eyes widen as his comment tumbles through my head. "Hours?"

How's that possible?

How can we be so far from Hawthorne?

"Yup." He grins. "Guess someone must be keeping you up at night if you were so tuckered out."

"Maybe if a certain person would stop sneaking into my room, then I could get a solid eight hours of sleep."

His expression turns fierce. "I think we both know that's not gonna happen. *Ever.*"

I release a pent-up breath and admit softly, "I wouldn't what it to."

"Better not," he growls, slipping his hand around the back of my neck and dragging me forward until his lips can collide with mine.

As soon as our tongues tangle, all the thoughts buzzing through my head go silent. The only thing that matters is Austin and the way he touches me, bringing me to life.

By the time he pulls away, my lips are swollen and my core is throbbing an insistent beat. It doesn't matter if he made love to me before slipping from my room early this morning. The only thing I can focus on is what it'll feel like the next time he slides deep inside my body.

We fit together so perfectly.

Almost as if we were made especially for one another.

"As much as I enjoy sitting here and plundering that sweet mouth of yours, we need to get moving."

"Moving?" I echo in confusion before everything crashes back into my brain.

Austin planned a surprise.

It takes effort to pull my gaze from his heated one and stare around us with interest. My breath catches at the blueness of the lake and the massive white structure next to it. I would recognize the building anywhere from the photographs I've spent years pouring over.

The Calatrava.

The art museum in Milwaukee.

It's even more stunning in person.

My mind empties.

I...have no words.

When I remain silent, uncertainty flickers across his expression. "They have a photography exhibit I thought you might be interested in checking out."

"They do?" I whisper in stunned amazement. I'm having a difficult time wrapping my mind around the fact that he brought me here for our date.

Our first real date.

Somehow, Austin realized how much it would mean to me and made it happen.

Unable to articulate my feelings, I throw myself into his arms and squeeze tight as hot tears burn the backs of my eyes.

"Thank you. No one has ever done anything like this for me."

He presses me close before kissing the side of my face. "Hope you realize there's nothing I wouldn't do for you, sweet girl."

We remain locked together before he pulls away enough to say, "Come on, we've got a lot to see this afternoon."

Excitement fills me at the prospect.

Not only to explore the art museum, but to experience all the amazing things life has in store for us.

EPILOGUE

AUSTIN

*wo years later...*

AS I WALK OUT of the stadium after a grueling three-hour practice, I catch sight of Delilah waiting for me on a park bench with her head bent as she taps away on her computer. The long mass of her blonde hair is piled on top of her head in a messy bun.

Studious is one way to describe her.

Mine is another.

We both ended up at the University of Wisconsin-Madison freshman year of college. I was awarded a full athletic ride and Delilah was able to cobble together a mixture of scholarships, grants, and financial aid so her mother pays the bear minimum. After conquering all of our obstacles, there was no way I was going to let her out of my sight for the next four years.

We both agreed that no matter where we ended up, it would be together.

I'm playing football and studying kinesiology. Madison has a Division I program and I'm hoping that if I continue to do well, I'll have a shot at turning pro. That's always been my dream, and now it seems like it might actually be within reach.

Delilah has just been accepted to the teaching program. Her passion is elementary education with a focus on reading disorders. She's also minoring in photography. Sometimes she jokes and says that when she's hired as an elementary educator, she'll start a photography club so she can nurture artistic passion in others. Having a creative outlet to focus her energies on helped her through a lot of tough times, and she wants to give other kids the same opportunity.

Whatever Delilah does, she'll be amazing, because that's the kind of person she is.

Passionate.

Driven.

Caring.

I'm so damn lucky that she's mine.

Her love isn't something I'll ever take for granted. It doesn't escape me just how close I came to losing her. To missing out on the incredible life we're living.

For just a second or two, I stop and stare as bright sunlight pours over her blonde head. She's so fucking beautiful.

We've been together for two years. It's almost impossible to remember what life was like without her filling it. Kind of like I was living in black and white. With her, it's all bright Technicolor.

We currently live in the dorms, but junior year, we're taking that next step and getting an apartment together. It's come to the point where we need our own space. Delilah's roommate is tired of me bunking with her every night, but I refuse to spend it alone. I like the feel of her wrapped up in my arms. And there's no way in hell she's sleeping in my suite with another dude there.

Just as I'm about to take a step in her direction, she glances up and meets my gaze. A quick smile springs to her lips and my heart spasms in my chest.

It's like this every damn time.

As soon as she lifts her hand in a wave, I snap out of the daze that's fallen over me and eat up the distance between us with a dozen long-legged strides. When I'm close enough, I snatch the computer from her hands and set it carefully on the bench before hauling her into my arms and smacking my lips against hers. It doesn't take long for the kiss to deepen.

I'm so damn greedy for her.

"Get a room, Hawthorne," one of my teammates hollers.

My mouth stays fused to hers as I lift a hand and give him a one-fingered salute.

Asshole.

There's a lot of snickering as the group strolls past.

These teammates are so different from the ones I had in Hawthorne. These guys are turning out to be more like brothers. It's a kinship I missed. Unlike the Hawks, we really are one big family who looks out for and takes care of each other. It's not just lip service before they knock you to the ground and kick you in the nuts.

There's not much I wouldn't do for these guys.

When Delilah and I finally break apart, we're both breathing hard. I might have spent all my energy on the field, but the only thing I can focus on is getting this girl home and making her mine again.

Just like I did this morning.

There's no better feeling in the world than sinking into the warmth of her body.

For me, she's home.

She always will be.

"Missed you, sweet girl," I whisper.

"Missed you, too."

"Ready to get out of here?"

She nods before nipping at my lower lip. A growl rumbles up from deep within my chest. It takes every ounce of willpower not to take her mouth all over again.

But that would only delay us.

And I'm not about to do that.

Here's hoping her roommate pulls a vanishing act for the next few hours.

"Better knock that shit off right now, or you'll find yourself flat on your back with an audience while I take you."

She snorts, used to my comments by now. "Like you'd allow anyone to watch me come."

I narrow my eyes.

She's right about that.

"Getting kind of sassy, aren't you?"

A grin curves her lips. "Maybe."

Without breaking eye contact, I rest my forehead against hers. "Sounds like someone needs to have her ass spanked."

"Don't make promises you have no intention of keeping," she whispers.

That comment shoves me right over the edge. My chest vibrates with another growl as I crouch and scoop her up into my arms.

I get two steps before she blurts with a laugh, "I need my books!"

An exasperated huff escapes from me as I set her down. On wobbly legs, she scrambles to pack up her belongings before rejoining me. As soon as she's within striking distance, I toss her backpack over one shoulder and lift her into my arms. One of her hands drifts to my face before cupping my shadowed cheek.

"Do you have any idea how much I love you?"

I press into her delicate palm as I continue walking. People turn and stare before smiling. A few girls giggle, their eyes going dreamy. As far as I'm concerned, every woman should be swept up into her man's arms and carried off to the bedroom.

"It can't be as much as I love you," I shoot back, hoping she never doubts my feelings.

Her lips lift into a soft smile. "You're wrong about that. I'm pretty sure I fell head over heels in love the first time I caught sight of you in the office. And I never stopped. Not even when I needed distance to clear my head. You were always there, tangled up in my thoughts and lurking in my dreams as if you were already a part of me. Our love story was never going to end any other way than this."

Her sweet words wrap around my beating heart like a tight fist, squeezing until breath becomes impossible.

"You're right about that, sweet girl. We were meant to be."

In answer, her hand slips around the back of my head before she pulls my mouth to hers.

"Now take me back to my dorm and make love to me."

She doesn't have to ask twice.

I hasten my step and do exactly that.

* * *

Want to read the free bonus epilogue and get a glimpse of Delilah and Austin in the future?
Download it here -) https://bookhip.com/NLNLTMA

Want to pre-order my next release?
Do it here -) https://books2read.com/westernwildcats
You can meet my newest hero, Ryder McAdams, in Campus Flirt.
Download it for free -)
https://bookhip.com/BMXXLBA

HEARTLESS

SKYE

"**Y**ay! The bitches are back together again, and tonight we ride!" Lanie wraps her arms around me and squeezes tight. "It's been too long, girl! *Way too long!*"

A reluctant smile curves my lips. "I know. It's good to be back." The circumstances surrounding my return are less than ideal, but I'm happy to see Lanie again. She's been my best friend since middle school, and I've missed her. FaceTime and texting are nice, but it's not the same as talking in person. She links her arm through mine as we walk across the open field.

I glance at the cute cowboy boots that adorn her feet. When she told me that we were going to a field in the middle of nowhere, I didn't believe her.

That was my first mistake.

Second mistake?

Not going with sturdier footwear.

Instead, I'm wearing a pair of flimsy sandals. They're cute as hell, but that's not going to do me a whole lot of good across this terrain.

Lanie insisted we celebrate my return by dragging me to a bonfire in a farmer's field. Already, the place is crawling with drunk-off-their-asses, barely legal adults. Shouting and raucous laughter fill the balmy night air.

Even though I know it won't do me any good, my gaze coasts anxiously over the ever-swelling crowd. Nerves dance across my spine as I silently pray Hunter will be absent from the revelry. Or, if he is here, we'll somehow be able to avoid one another.

If I know Lanie—and I do—she'll be up my ass to cut loose and have fun. How can I do that when Hunter and I now attend the same college? At any given moment, I could turn a corner and smack right into him.

The thought of that happening makes me nauseous.

As much as I want to play it cool and act like my ex-boyfriend doesn't matter, the words slip from my mouth before I can stop them. "You don't think he'll be here, do you?" I shoot her a look that's rife with concern.

Lanie doesn't bother to ask who I'm referring to. She doesn't have to. She's all too aware of my past. She had a front row seat to our relationship and its demise.

"I don't know." She pauses and pops her shoulders into a careless shrug. "Maybe."

"What?" My feet grind to a halt as my mouth dries, turning cottony. I'm barely aware of the blades of straw poking my feet through the leather sandals. "But you said—"

Her expression hardens, transforming into one of impatience. "Even if he *is* here, the chances of you running into him are slim." She waves an arm toward the massive group of students who have gathered to mourn the end of summer by drinking themselves into a stupor. "Look around. Half the university is here. There's no way you're going to see him, Skye, so stop worrying about it and live a little."

My teeth sink into my lower lip before I suck the fullness into my mouth. No matter what Lanie says, I'm going to worry.

When I remain silent, my best friend plants her hands on her hips and glares. Here comes Lanie's version of tough love.

"Would you rather sit home by yourself on a Saturday night

because you're too chickenshit to show your face? Afraid that you *might* run into Hunter Price?"

I'm sorry, is that really a question?

From the annoyed expression that flickers across Lanie's face, I decide to keep those thoughts to myself.

"Skye Elizabeth Sinclair!"

I wince as my full name cracks through the air. It brings an unpleasant image of my mother to mind. This is what I get for living with someone who isn't afraid to call me out on my bullshit. Maybe I should have taken Dad up on the offer to live with him.

I decide to go with something close to the truth. "I was hoping to avoid him for a while," I mutter. "That's all."

And when I say a while, *what I really mean is forever.*

Is that really too much to ask?

Lanie sighs as her expression softens. Marginally. "I know, but you're going to run into him on campus or at a party eventually. It's inevitable. Accept it and move on."

I snort.

Easy for her to say. Lanie doesn't have any ghosts from her past that are ready to jump out and scare her.

I have a carefully constructed plan in place for the year. It involves lying low and flying under the radar, so Hunter doesn't even know I'm here. "Yeah, I guess…"

Unwilling to let me backslide, Lanie loops her arm through mine and pulls me toward the growing group of partiers. "It'll be fine. I promise."

Unfortunately, my bestie isn't in a position to guarantee me anything, and we both know it.

The closer we get to the party, the more my anxiety ratchets up. At least night has fallen. The only light emanates from the bonfire that flickers in the distance and the stars that twinkle across the dark velvety sky.

For the time being, I'll remain vigilant. There's really nothing more I can do.

I inhale a deep breath before carefully blowing it out.

Maybe Lanie's right, and I'm making a big deal out of nothing. It's been three years since we've seen each other, and a lot has happened since then. We've both moved on with our lives. I'm sure he's forgotten all about me. As those thoughts circle through my head, my shoulders loosen from around my ears, and my heart stops thumping a painful beat.

The moment we reach the outer ring of people, Lanie is swept off her booted feet and spun around in a tight circle like a rag doll. Her short floral dress flies around her thighs. Laughter rings throughout the air as her arms slip around her boyfriend's neck.

Jaxon Conway has a typical football player's physique. He's a mountain of a man—tall, broad in the shoulders, and muscular. He looks like he could easily bench press Lanie's VW Bug. I would be intimidated by him, but he's quick to laugh and has warm brown eyes. He's like a teddy bear—big and gruff on the outside but tender and mushy on the inside.

"Missed you, babe," he growls.

"It's only been a couple of hours since we saw each other!"

"Doesn't matter," Jax complains. "I still missed the hell out of you."

"Aww." Lanie's voice softens, becoming dreamy. "I love you so much."

"I love you more," he responds with enough heat to melt the panties off Lanie's body.

Ugh.

Make it stop.

These two are so sickeningly sweet that I get a toothache every time I'm around them. Although, if anyone deserves a good guy, it's Lanie. Like most girls in their early twenties, she's dated her fair share of assholes. Jaxon is almost too good to be true. Kind of like a mythical unicorn that sprang to life. He's an athlete who isn't interested in screwing as many girls as he can get his hands on.

Ever since I rolled into town a few days ago, Jaxon and Lanie have been glued together at the hip. I get the feeling he'll be our unofficial third roommate for the year.

Know what's been getting a lot of use?

My noise-canceling headphones.

Most nights, those two sound like they're auditioning for a porno. Let's hope it calms down soon.

Jaxon and Lanie coo at each other before their mouths fuse, and they start going at it like a pair of cats in heat. I clear my throat and glance everywhere but at them. If we were hanging out at the townhouse, this would be my cue to exit stage left. But we're not at home; we're in the middle of a field a few miles from town. There's nowhere for me to go, and no one for me to talk to.

Awkwardness descends as I flick a piece of straw from my shirt.

Maybe I should take this opportunity to grab a beer. There must be a keg around here somewhere. You can't have this many college kids congregating in one spot and not have alcohol. That would be considered sacrilegious, right?

With any luck, by the time I return, Jaxon and Lanie will have stopped mauling each other long enough for us to move on with our evening. It's not like he's being shipped off to war tomorrow and they'll never see each other again.

Sheesh.

My gaze meanders to them in hopes that they've gotten their fill of each other.

Nope. The face sucking has become even more intense. Any moment, clothing is going to spontaneously combust from their bodies.

I don't really want to be around when that happens.

So...a beer it is.

Not that either of them is paying me the least bit of attention, but I point toward the mass of bodies that have multiplied in the fifteen minutes since we've arrived. "I'm going to grab a drink." When my words are met with kissy noises, I say, "Try not to miss me too much while I'm gone."

Lanie waves a hand absently in my direction as they continue to get it on.

"Okay then," I mumble before reluctantly taking off on my own.

The number of people gathered here is a little overwhelming.

Lanie's right; half the university must have shown up. Everyone is talking, laughing, and drinking. In other words, they're having a great time.

Me, not so much.

It takes a good ten minutes to find the keg. Or maybe I should say *kegs* since there are six of them next to the back end of a midnight black pickup truck blasting music from massive speakers. I can barely hear myself think over the thumping bass. Then again, maybe that's for the best. It's a relief to get out of my head, even for a few minutes.

I locate the line for the beer and take my place at the end of it. I'm not much of a drinker, but I need something to smooth out all of the rough edges so I can relax and enjoy myself.

My flesh prickles with awareness, and I run my hands over my arms to banish the disconcerting sensation. I glance around, scouring the crowd for one face in particular but don't see him anywhere. That alone should alleviate my anxiety, but it doesn't.

My parting with Hunter wasn't what one would call amicable. I don't blame him for being hurt and angry. Whether Hunter understands it or not, I did what needed to be done. As painful as it was, I'd do it all over again. I loved Hunter more than life itself.

A part of me still does.

Probably always will.

If everything I've read online is true, then my sacrifices have been well worth it. Hunter will get snapped up in the NFL draft before graduating this spring. Ever since I can remember, that's been his goal. If one person deserves for all his dreams to come true, it's Hunter Price. Unwilling to dwell on my ex, I shove him from my mind and take in the scene before me.

People are gathered together in groups, greeting one another as if they're long-lost friends who haven't seen each other in decades. It's surreal to be surrounded by so many people yet feel so removed from it all. As if I'm more of an observer than a participant. Other than Lanie and Jaxon, I don't know anyone else. I'm sure people from high school attend CU, but I lost touch with most of them after I moved away.

By the time I make it to the front of the line, I'm antsy and ready to head back to my friends. Even if they're still going at it. Which is really saying something. I'd much rather stand around as a third wheel than be an island onto myself. I dig through my front pocket and hand over a couple of bucks in exchange for a blue plastic cup before it's filled to the rim with golden liquid.

The cute guy manning the keg flashes me an easy grin as his eyes drift over my body. When he's finished with his perusal, his gaze once again settles on my face. Kudos to this guy for not gawking at my boobs like he's never seen a pair of D cups before.

"Here you go, beautiful," he says, handing over the cup with a gallant flourish.

This little bit of silliness lightens my mood. "Thanks."

Our fingers brush as I take the Solo cup from him.

"Next time, cut to the front of the line." He gives me a flirty wink. "I got you covered."

I flash him a grateful smile. Maybe tonight won't be so bad after all.

With my drink in hand, I'm ready to make my way back to Jaxon and Lanie. Only now does it occur to me that they could have moved from the spot where I'd left them.

Who's to say I'll even be able to find my way back?

A knot of unease settles at the bottom of my belly. My fingers go to the purse slung across my chest. It's big enough to hold my phone, but that's about it. I could always shoot Lanie a text, but who knows if she'd hear it. And I have no idea how to navigate my way back to our apartment. The unsettled feeling that had taken up residence in my gut turns into full-on nausea.

Only now do I realize that walking away was a bad idea. I should have stuck to Lanie and Jax like glue. But standing around and watching them make out felt pervy.

And not in a good way.

With those thoughts swirling through my brain, I spin around and slam into a wall of impenetrable muscle. The impact knocks me off-balance, and I stumble back a step. Before I can fall, strong hands reach out and grab my shoulders, yanking me forward. My breath catches, and my heart pounds at the narrowly avoided tumble.

I shake my head to clear it as beer sloshes over the rim of my plastic cup and spills onto the ground at my feet. I'm lucky it didn't end up down the front of my top or the shirt of the unsuspecting person I plowed into.

How humiliating would that have been?

Ugh…I don't even want to think about it.

"I'm so—"

My voice falls off as I glance up, my gaze colliding with narrowed blue eyes. Hunter quickly sets me free as if his fingers have been burned. Neither of us breaks eye contact. All of the raucous noise of the bonfire dies away until it's just the two of us standing alone in the middle of a dark field.

This is the moment I've been dreading.

My eyes roam over his face, cataloging the myriad of changes that time has wrought. When I walked away, Hunter had still been a boy, his lean muscles beginning to thicken. Now the transformation has been complete, and he's a full-grown man. Hunter has always had size on his side, but somehow, he's managed to grow both taller and broader. He must be somewhere in the vicinity of six three or four. I have to crane my neck to hold his gaze. The graphic T-shirt he's wearing stretches tautly across the wide expanse of his chest and hugs the chiseled strength of his biceps. It's enough to make my mouth dry and my knees soft.

If I have one weakness, it's for thickly corded arms. All that tightly harnessed power waiting to break free…

A shiver of desire scampers down my spine before I stomp it out.

Unaware of the effect he's having on me, Hunter's deep voice cuts through my thoughts.

"What are you doing here, Skye?"

It's the harshness of his tone that has my gaze snapping back to his as heat floods my cheeks. I can't stop myself from staring. The little bit of cyberstalking I've done over the years has in no way prepared me for coming face-to-face with my ex-boyfriend. He's grown into his dark looks, becoming even more of a heartbreaker than he was in high school.

My tongue darts out to smudge my parched lips as nerves dance along my skin. I search Hunter's eyes, looking for any hint of softening, but there's none to be found. His gaze is as frigid and detached as I imagined it would be. The tiny kernel of hope that our time apart would be enough to heal our past wounds shrivels and dies inside me.

There is no forgiveness in his heart.

But then again, did I really expect there would be?

Maybe. It would have made coexisting on campus for the next year so much easier.

It's obvious from his terse behavior that Hunter would prefer to pretend I never existed in the first place. As much as I would love to give him that, I can't. Unforeseen circumstances have forced me home.

I straighten my shoulders and attempt to keep my voice level. I don't want him to hear the slight tremble that is working its way through my body. "I transferred to Claremont for my senior year."

His shadowed jaw ticks as he clenches his teeth. *"Why?"*

The way he bites out that one word leaves me wincing.

I take a quick step back and lift my chin, not wanting him to see how much power he still holds over me. Time has done nothing to diminish it. "That's none of your business."

Whether Hunter realizes it or not, he still owns a piece of my heart. It's better for both of us if he never suspects the depth of my feelings.

His hands tighten into fists as he closes the little bit of distance that I've managed to put between us. Instead of scrambling back the way every instinct is clamoring for me to do, I hold my ground until we're standing toe-to-toe. My heart pounds a painful staccato against my breast as his harsh breath feathers across my parted lips.

There was a time when I couldn't get close enough to Hunter.

Now I can't get far enough away.

Sorrow floods through every fiber of my body that it has to be this way between us. Next to Lanie, Hunter was my best friend. He was my first everything.

Date.

Kiss.

Love.

Heartbreak.

Everything we once shared has been blown to pieces, and we're nothing more than strangers. Actually, what we are is much worse. His animosity is palpable. It radiates from him in suffocating waves that threaten to choke the life out of me.

"You shouldn't have come back," he growls. "You don't belong here anymore."

That may be true, but there's nothing I can do about it. I'm here. And I'm not going anywhere.

I shift my weight and force myself to say, "Claremont is big enough for the two of us."

"No, it's not. Stay the fuck out of my way, Skye." His eyes flash with barely suppressed hostility. "You won't like the consequences if you don't."

Before I can summon up a retort, he stalks away. Rooted in place, I track his movements until he fades into the crowd. Not once does he turn around and acknowledge my presence. I've been dismissed. Relegated to the black hole that is our past.

Once he disappears from sight, my knees weaken as the pent-up breath rushes from my aching lungs.

I haven't been on campus for a full seventy-two hours, and in Hunter's eyes, I'm public enemy number one.

Want to read more of Hunter and Summer's story?
You can download the free prequel here -)
Get your FREE copy of Heartless Summer (bookfunnel.com)
And you can check out Heartless here -)
https://books2read.com/u/m2Moq7

CAMPUS PLAYER

DEMI

"*M*orning, Demi!" Gary, one of the stadium custodians, calls out with an easy smile and wave as he saunters toward me. "Up and at 'em bright and early this morning, I see."

My heart jackhammers beneath my ribcage from the twenty-minute run as I flash him a grin. "Always!"

"You have a good one! I'll see you tomorrow!"

Since I've already moved past him, I holler over my shoulder, "Same place, same time!"

Even with *The Killers* pumping through my earbuds, I almost hear the deep chuckle that slides from his lips. Our morning greetings are a ritual three years in the making. I've been running through the wide corridor that leads to the stadium football field since I stepped foot on campus freshman year. This will be something I miss when I graduate in the spring. Five days a week, I'm up at six, logging in a four-mile run before returning home, jumping in the shower, and heading off to class.

At this time of the day, the stadium is still relatively quiet, with only a few people wandering the hallways. There's something both serene and eerie about it. I've been here on game days when there are thirty thousand fans packed shoulder to shoulder, rooting on the

Western Wildcats football team. Three-fourths of the stadium filled with black and orange is an amazing sight to behold. Football is a religion at Western. Unfortunately, the same can't be said for the women's soccer team. We're lucky if there are a couple of hundred spectators in the stands.

I've come to terms with it.

Sort of.

I keep my gaze trained on the light at the end of the tunnel and push myself faster. As soon as I burst out of the darkness, bright sunlight pours down on me, stroking over the bare skin of my arms and shoulders. It's late August, and summer is still in full swing. A whistle cuts through the silence of the stadium, and my gaze slices to the field. Nick Richards has been head coach of the Wildcats for the last decade. He also happens to be my father.

Two days a week, the guys are up at six in the morning for yoga. Dad is a big believer in flexibility. Even though I'm winded, a smirk lifts the corners of my lips. Watching two-hundred-and-eighty-pound linebackers contort their bodies into Downward-Facing Dog, the Warrior II Pose, and the Cobra is enough to bring a chuckle to my lips. Some of the guys actually like it, but most grumble when they think Dad isn't paying attention. Little do they know that he sees and hears everything.

My father catches sight of me and flashes a quick smile along with a wave in my direction. He has a black ball cap pulled low and aviators covering his eyes. There's a clipboard in one hand as he paces behind the instructor.

When I point to the field, he shakes his head. He might make the guys do yoga, but he refuses to participate. Something about old dogs and new tricks. Every once in a while, I'll tell him that he needs to get out there and set a good example for the team. He usually shoots me a glare in return.

Every Wednesday night, Dad and I get together. Our weekly dinners became a thing when I moved out of the house and into the dorms freshman year. He's busy coaching football, and my schedule is packed tight with school and soccer. Getting together once a week is the best way for us to stay connected. It doesn't matter if we're in the middle of our seasons; we always make time for each other. Especially since Mom lives in sunny California. After eighteen years of marriage, she got fed up with being a distant second to the Western University football program. She packed up her bags and walked out. I hate to say it, but Dad didn't notice her absence for a couple of days. Which only proved her point. Now she's remarried, learning to surf, and is a vegan. I visit for a couple of weeks during the summer before soccer training camp starts up at the end of June.

Even though it's only the two of us, our weekly dinners are set for three people.

I tell myself to stare straight ahead and not glance in his direction.

Don't do it!

Don't you dare do it!

Damn.

My gaze reluctantly zeros in on him like a heat-seeking missile. Long blond hair, bright blue eyes, sun-kissed skin, and muscles for miles. And he's tall, somewhere around six foot three.

I'm describing none other than Rowan Michaels.

Otherwise known as the bane of my existence.

My dad discovered the talented quarterback the summer before we entered high school and took him under his wing. Which has been...aggravating. In the seven years since, Rowan has become an irritatingly permanent fixture in my life. He's the brother I never wanted or asked for. He's the gift I wish I could give back. He's the son my father never had but secretly longed for.

On a campus with over thirty thousand students, one would think that avoidance would be easy to accomplish. That hasn't turned out to be the case. Somehow, we ended up in the same major—Exercise Science. I get stuck in at least one class with the guy each semester. This time it's statistics, which is a requirement. Three times a week, I'm forced to see him. And then there are the weekly dinners at Dad's house.

Every Wednesday, Rowan shows up without fail.

It's so annoying.

No, *he's* annoying!

Our gazes collide, and electricity sizzles through my veins before I immediately snuff it out and pretend it never happened.

I am not attracted to Rowan Michaels.

I am not attracted to Rowan Michaels.

I am not attracted to Rowan Michaels.

Maybe if I repeat the mantra enough times, it'll be true. That's the hope I cling to. I've made it through the last seven years trying to convince myself of this. I only have to get through our final year together, and then we'll go our separate ways—me to graduate school or maybe to the Women's National Soccer League, and Rowan to the NFL. He's one of the most talented quarterbacks in the conference. Hell, probably the country. There is little doubt in my mind that he'll be a first-round draft pick come next spring.

Trust me when I say that Rowan Michaels fever is alive and well at Western University. His fanbase is legendary. The guy is a major player.

Both on and off the field.

Girls fall all over themselves to be with him. They fill the stands at football practice, show up at parties he's rumored to be at, and basically stalk him around campus.

It's a little nauseating. Don't these girls have any self-respect when it comes to a hot guy?

I wince at that unchecked thought.

Fine...I'll begrudgingly admit it; he's good-looking.

I shake my head as if that will banish the insidious thoughts currently invading my brain. Enough about Rowan. It's time to focus on the reason I'm at the stadium at this ungodly hour. I rip my gaze from him as I hit the cement staircase. After half a flight, all thoughts of the blond quarterback vanish from my mind. How could they not when my quads, glutes, and calves are on fire, screaming for mercy as I force myself to the nosebleed section. By the time I finish, my legs are Jell-O, and I still have a two-mile run back to the apartment I share with my best friend off-campus.

I give Dad a half-hearted wave before leaving. It's the most I can muster. His lips quirk at the corners as he shakes his head. He thinks I'm crazy. At the moment, I can't argue with his assessment of the situation. Although, it's the extra training I put in that helps me run circles around the other team in the second half of the game.

The jog home feels like it will last forever. By the time I unlock the apartment door, I'm ready to collapse. I beeline for the shower and jump in before it's fully warm. My skin prickles with goose flesh, but it feels so damn good. Twenty minutes later, I'm dressed and ready to take on the day. My hair has been thrown up in a messy bun, and I'm making a protein smoothie that will fuel me for my morning classes.

Just before taking off, I poke my head into Sydney's room. I know exactly how I'll find her, and that's buried beneath a small mountain of blankets. She doesn't disappoint. We met the summer before freshman year in training camp and have been besties ever since. She's the yin to my yang. The peanut butter to my jelly. The Thelma to my Louise. Where I'm more introverted and cautious, she's loud and boisterous. She's been known to leap without necessarily looking at what she's jumping into. Every so often, it gets us into trouble. Sydney and I have lived together since sophomore year. I gave up trying to cajole her ass out of bed for a six o'clock run after the first week of us cohabitating when she nearly took my head off with an alarm clock.

"It's that time again," I sing-song obnoxiously, "rise and shine."

There's a grunt and then some shifting from under the blankets that tells me she's alive.

When I chant her name repeatedly, each time escalating in volume, she growls, "Get the fuck out!"

"Awww," I mock, "that's so sweet. I love you, too."

Sydney snorts before a hand snakes out from beneath the blankets to give me a one-fingered salute. Then she grabs a pillow and tosses it in my general vicinity. It falls about five feet short of its mark.

I stare at the dismal attempt. "If you're trying to cause bodily harm, you'll have to do better than that."

"Piss off."

"All right then." I shrug. "See you after class." With that, I close the door behind me.

My farewell is met with another indecipherable mouthful. If this weren't something we went through on the daily, I'd worry she was in the midst of a stroke. Sydney is definitely not a morning person. She's more of an early afternoon person. Another thing I've learned over the years? The action of waking up to a brand-new day is a gradual process. She's like a bear rousing prematurely from hibernation. It's not a pretty sight. She's lucky I don't take her insults personally.

I grab my backpack from the small table crammed into the breakfast nook area along with a coffee before heading out the door. The apartment I share with Sydney is located three blocks from campus, which is highly sought out real estate. We're fortunate Dad is friends with the guy who manages the building. It's probably one of the only perks of having a father who is a head coach of a college football team.

You'd think there would be more, but you'd be wrong. Honestly, being Nick Richard's daughter is more of a hindrance than anything else. People assume you receive special treatment on campus, from professors, or that you have an in with all the football players.

Or worse...

Much worse.

After a bunch of ugly—not to mention untrue—rumors circulated freshman year, I've done my best to distance myself from the Wildcats football team. They're a great bunch of guys, but I don't need all the ugly gossip and speculation that comes along with being friends with them.

As I reach Corbin Hall, the mathematics building for my stats class, my gaze is drawn to a clump of students standing around outside the three-story, red-brick building. In the center of that crowd is Rowan. I don't have to see him physically to know that he's close. The muscles in my belly contract with awareness. It's like a sixth sense. One I wish would go away. He's the last person I want to be cognizant of.

As I jog up the wide stone stairs to the entrance, my gaze fastens on him. A smirk twists the edges of his lips, and my eyes narrow before I drag them away and yank open the door to the building.

Relief rushes through me as I step inside the air conditioning and disappear from sight.

"Hey, Demi, wait up!"

I turn at the sound of my name before slowing my step. The dark-haired guy jogging to catch up smiles before falling in line with me.

Justin Fischer.

He's a baseball player and teammates with Sydney's boyfriend, Ethan. We've been seeing each other for about a month. It's still casual at this point. With school and soccer, I don't have a ton of time to invest in a relationship. He seems to understand that and isn't pushing to be more serious.

When he leans in for a kiss, I angle my head. At the last moment, he tilts in the opposite direction, and we end up bumping teeth instead of locking lips. With a grunt, I pull away and chuckle. My fingers fly to my mouth to make sure I haven't chipped a tooth.

Maybe I've been reluctant to admit it to myself, but that kiss sums up our relationship perfectly.

Awkward and a step out of sync with each other.

"Sorry," he murmurs with a slight smile. I search his face and wait for any telltale sign of sexual chemistry to ping inside me. Unfortunately, my insides remain completely unfazed, which is disappointing but not altogether unexpected. I had a sneaking suspicion when we first got together that it might turn out this way.

"No problem," I say, hoisting my smile and brushing aside those thoughts.

"I haven't seen you for a couple of days," he remarks as we turn a corner and continue walking.

"It's been busy." Which isn't a lie. School might have recently started, but the academics at Western are rigorous. And being a Division I athlete is more like a job. If you're not ready to put in the work, don't bother showing up. There's no half-assing it around this place.

"When's your next game?" he asks.

"Tomorrow at six." My gaze flickers in his direction. Not that I expect him to come, but...

Fine, so maybe I do. If he wants to be my boyfriend, then he needs to show a little support.

His dark brows draw together. "That sucks. I've got a mandatory study hour I have to attend."

I shrug off the disappointment. It's another nail in the coffin of this relationship as far as I'm concerned. "That's cool. It's not a big deal."

"But I'll see you tonight?"

Oh. Right.

Tonight.

Well, damn. In a moment of weakness, I threw out an invitation to join our Wednesday evening dinner. It's one I now regret. If only there were a gracious way to rescind the offer.

"If you're busy, I totally understand—"

"Are you kidding? No way." With a grin, he shakes his head. "I wouldn't miss it for the world. I'm looking forward to meeting Coach Richards."

Great. So this is more about my father than me? Exactly what every girl wants to hear.

I force a brittle smile. "Awesome. He's excited, too."

That might be something of an overstatement.

Justin nods toward the end of the corridor. "I better get moving. Professor Andrews is a real stickler for punctuality."

"Yup. See you later."

This time, when he leans in, our lips align perfectly. The kiss is nothing more than a fleeting caress. There and gone before I can sink into it.

And I'm left feeling...absolutely nothing.

I bury the disappointment where I can't inspect it too closely before giving him a wave as he takes off. For a moment, I stand rooted in the hallway and watch as he disappears through the crowd. There's nothing to distinguish Justin from the thousands of guys who look exactly like him on campus. He's of average height and build with dark hair and espresso-colored eyes. He's nice enough. Although, if I'm completely honest, he's a little self-absorbed. He talks about baseball all the time. If Ethan hadn't introduced us, he's not someone I would have looked twice at. We don't have a ton in common.

As much as I hate to admit it, this relationship has probably reached its expiration date.

Now it's a matter of pulling the plug.

Ugh. I hate breakups. Although, it's doubtful this will end up destroying him. I'll have to make it through tonight and figure out the rest.

With a sigh of resignation, I head to the classroom and find a seat tucked away in the far corner of the small lecture hall. A lanky guy I recognize from a few of my other classes settles beside me. He flashes a dimpled smile as we empty our backpacks.

The tiny hair at the nape of my neck rises seconds before Rowan enters the room. It's like my body knows when he's within a thirty-foot radius. I glance at him from beneath the thick fringe of my lashes before shifting away. Air becomes wedged in my lungs as I wait for him to take a seat. And it won't be next to me because I'm—

"Hey man, would you mind moving?"

Surrounded on both sides.

Damnit. I'm hoping the cutie next to me will tell Rowan to go take a flying leap.

What? It could happen. Not everyone at this university is enamored of the football-playing god. Although I realize the odds aren't stacked in my favor. Rowan is the most recognized athlete on campus. People fall all over themselves to accommodate him.

It's a little sickening.

Okay, maybe more than a little.

"Sure, no problem, Michaels." The guy next to me hastily packs up his books before vacating the desk. Unable to ignore him any longer, I glare as Rowan slides onto the seat next to me.

"Did you really think you could evade me that easily?" Laughter brims in his deep voice. A voice, I might add, that does funny things to my insides.

"One can always hope, right?"

"Oh, answering a question with a question." He leans closer, eating up some of the much-needed distance between us. "I like it."

I roll my eyes as his lips stretch into a satisfied grin. Irritation bubbles up inside me when sexual tension blooms at the bottom of my belly. Or maybe that tension has settled a little lower.

It's definitely lower.

I'm tempted to swear like a sailor. How is it possible that I feel nothing for the guy I'm actually dating, and yet my pulse skitters out of control for someone I don't even like? It's so freaking ironic. It's been this way since we met, and nothing I do stomps it out. I can try to fool myself into believing it's not there, but that doesn't make it any less true.

It's a relief when Professor Peters takes his place at the podium and clears his throat. Once he's captured everyone's attention, he delves headfirst into the probability of dependent and independent events.

Grateful for the excuse to ignore Rowan for the next fifty minutes, I open my textbook and concentrate on the lesson. Just as the blond boy fades into the background, his bare knee bumps into mine. Electricity ricochets through my entire being. I glance at him to see if he's noticed the strange energy we always seem to generate and find his ocean-colored gaze fastened to mine.

My guess is that he does.

Damnation.

Want to read more of Demi & Rowan's story?
Check it out here -) https://books2read.com/u/mYAxqV
Want to read Campus Flirt for free?
Download it here -) https://bookhip.com/BMXXLBA

ABOUT THE AUTHOR

Jennifer is a USA Today bestselling author who has published twenty-five new adult novels. Her work has been translated into German, Dutch, and Italian. Jen has a bachelor's degree in history and a master's in educational psychology. She started out her career as a high school counselor before relocating with her family out of state and focusing on her passion for writing. When she's not tapping away at the keyboard and dreaming up swoonworthy heroes to fall in love with, you can find her bike riding or planning her next trip to the beach. She lives in Michigan with her husband and four kids.

If you would like to receive regular updates regarding new releases, please subscribe to her newsletter here-
Jennifer Sucevic Newsletter (subscribepage.com)

Or contact Jen through email, at her website, or on Facebook.
sucevicjennifer@gmail.com

Want to join her reader group? Do it here -)
J Sucevic's Book Boyfriends | Facebook

Social media links-
https://www.tiktok.com/@jennifersucevicauthor
www.jennifersucevic.com
https://www.instagram.com/jennifersucevicauthor
https://www.facebook.com/jennifer.sucevic

Amazon.com: Jennifer Sucevic: Books, Biography, Blog, Audiobooks,
Kindle
Jennifer Sucevic Books - BookBub